I0659096

Formula Seven and Genesis of the New World Order

BY
MICHAEL MARCH

Edited by Gerald Shaw

First Edition Design Publishing
Sarasota, Florida USA

United States   Canada   United Kingdom

FORMULA SEVEN and Genesis of the New World Order
Copyright ©2018 Michael March

ISBN 978-1506-907-65-9 Amazon
ISBN 978-1506-907-11-6 PRINT
ISBN 978-1506-907-12-3 EBOOK

LCCN 2018958084

September 2018

Published and Distributed by
First Edition Design Publishing, Inc.
P.O. Box 20217, Sarasota, FL 34276-3217
www.firsteditiondesignpublishing.com
In conjunction with Whispering Bridge Publishing

ALL RIGHTS RESERVED. No part of this book publication may be reproduced, stored in a retrieval system, or transmitted in any form or by any means — electronic, mechanical, photo-copy, recording, or any other — except brief quotation in reviews, without the prior permission of the author or publisher.

Acknowledgements

I would like to thank the following people:

My parents for teaching me the sanctity of human life.

My children, Scott, Alan, and Lisa for putting up with me.

My partner, Rose Marie, for her inspiration, understanding, and love.

Unity North Church in Marietta and especially Reverend Richard Burdick. God bless you for the love and knowledge you've shared.

Scott, my older son deserves a special heads-up. He created the original concept for Formula Seven and allowed me to make the story my own.

The members of The Writers' Circle, and a shout-out to our leader, Gelia Dolcimascolo. Your shining lights have opened my eyes and helped me to understand the beauty of the written word. Each of you has helped me piece together my puzzle.

The Atlanta Writers Club, thank you for existing. I've met many fine and talented people within the ranks of the organization.

I can't forget my greatest supporter, Ms. Harriet Louden, a lady of charm and distinction.

CHAPTER ONE

The View from the Evidence Room

Los Angeles, California, June 12, 1989

The bark of the two-way radio shattered the agent's concentration. "Bravo One to Central, over."

Sonny, sitting behind the wheel of his Chevy Caprice, lowered his night-vision field glasses and gripped the radio handset. "Roger, Bravo One. This is Central. Go ahead, over."

The husky voice barked through the wireless again. "Package is secure, Central. We'll be going off grid and heading to Point Charlie in five mikes. Over."

"Roger, Bravo One. See you at the rally point. Central, out."

Sonny couldn't have been happier with Bravo's achievement.

For the last two weeks, his people had pulled uninterrupted surveillance on this red brick building. His Alpha team had gotten the go-ahead at sixteen-hundred hours. With the lab's schedule and shift changes down to a precise science, all went off according to plan.

They'd completed emptying the contents of the eighty-five hundred-square-foot facility on Figueroa and were way ahead of schedule. As the trucks rumbled away from the loading dock, Sonny checked the luminous dial on his watch again. He marked the time on his notepad: twenty-one forty-two.

Like taking candy from babies. Sonny chuckled as he visualized pulling red Twizzlers out of the mouth of toddlers and sliding the sticky licorice into evidence bags.

A ten-year man with the FBI, he'd recently received a promotion and assigned to lead this Special Activities team. He didn't know why his people would be kidnapping monkeys and

1

appropriating scientific equipment and files, and he didn't much care. He only knew the name of the target, Cyrus Markum, and the need to eliminate any record of his research for the good of the nation. The specifics of the mission remained classified and above his pay grade. Without the need to know or the inclination to press for details, Sonny followed orders and stuck with the program.

Several miles away, his Bravo team had already removed their latex gloves and foot booties and stashed them inside their sedans. On the move and following the prearranged routes to the designated drop-off point, they'd be meeting with Sonny in about thirty minutes. The two Alpha team trucks had a ten-minute head start. He and his trailing car would catch up and reach their destination almost simultaneously.

*   *   *

The two trucks had already maneuvered through the garage doors and sat idling inside the huge warehouse by the time Sonny arrived. The Bravo team members killed time, waiting in their cars. They'd already delivered the package to the detachment supervisor, who waited for him in the second-floor office.

Slamming his car door, Sonny walked through the entrance of the immense white building. Looking up as he passed underneath the large lettered sign, he read the words: Amalgamated Packaging and Distribution Corp.

He had no idea where the two fifty-five footers would be heading next. That didn't affect him. He'd accomplished his part of the mission. The Proliferation team would be taking it from here.

The old wood creaked as he climbed the stairway. He found his boss sitting behind a metal desk in the corner of a large room. A smelly victory cigar dangled from between his fingers. A cloud of lung-searing smoke hung in the air, stinging Sonny's eyes.

"Great job, Pastore, went off like clockwork." Charlie Rogers handed his subordinate a large manila envelope. "Here's your next assignment. The details are in there."

Sonny reached for the packet but didn't open it. His boss took another pull on his stogie and exhaling, injected another ring of dense blue smoke into the stagnant air. Sonny held his breath and stepped away from the oblong circle of carcinogens.

"You'll love this job, Sonny. It's surveillance on a group of religious fanatics out of Berkeley. They have three churches, two in Colorado. We'll be adding a few more people to your crew. I'm sure you'll handle it. Let me know if you need anything. Take care."

Sonny tested the heft of the package and tucked it under his arm. "Sure thing, boss. Should be a piece of cake."

Charlie took another pull on his cigar and blew a ring of bluish smoke. Sonny held his breath again.

As he came down the stairs, he puffed-out his chest, feeling smug and self-satisfied. Why not? He'd added another notch to his belt and his team had their new orders. After relaxing for a few days, he'd be heading back to continue his important work. He loved keeping America safe from their enemies, both foreign and domestic.

*   *   *

Why the unusual government interest in this Cyrus fellow? We'll need to strap ourselves into the trusty Eisenstadt Micro cesium time machine and journey back almost four and a half decades to find out. So, hang on. You should find the ride interesting.

Room 401, Cincinnati Children's Hospital, April 18, 1945, Ten A.M.

The attending physician scowled and stepped away from his pint-sized patient. The young boy standing at the foot of his brother's bed shrieked in agony. "No, no, no. This can't be. Why did God let this happen?"

Two torrents of tears streaked his face. "Mommy, please, tell me? How could this happen to Leonard? He's only five-years-old. Why would God do this?"

Flanked by his parents, Cyrus' chest pushed against the rail. The metal dug into his skin, but he ignored the pain. His younger brother lay unmoving on the mattress, his face ashen.

His mother tried to remain strong, groping for the words that might comfort her surviving child. "Leonard isn't suffering

3

anymore, honey. He's at peace with God and the angels in heaven."

"Your mother's right," his father added. "We should never question the Lord. We must accept his judgments."

The eight-year-old lifted his hands and grabbed the bed's metal bar. "I can't accept that. There has to be more to life than that."

Too devastated to argue, his father turned from his son and watched the nurse pull the sheet over the face of his younger son. "I understand, but Leonard wouldn't want for you to be unhappy."

Sobbing heavily, Cyrus addressed his parents in a way they couldn't have expected. Placing his left hand over his heart, he raised the right and bared his palm. "Mom and Dad, I promise you that I'm going to study really hard and dedicate my life to science. I want to wipe out disease and prevent this tragedy from happening to other families."

Center for Disease Control, Atlanta, Georgia, April 1975

Dr. Cyrus Markum wouldn't be deterred from his quest. A practitioner of biotic engineering, he'd devoted his life to the discipline of epidemiology. For the last five years, the Center for Disease Control served as his home away from home. Finding the meticulous daily regimen far from mundane, he supervised a small group of clinical researchers. His quartet operated under the auspices of the World Health Organization and specialized in infectious disease and humoral immunology exploration.

Decked out in bio-hazard paraphernalia, the scientists labored relentlessly, intent on eradicating the remnants of the variola virus. The disease no longer presented a problem in civilized society, but still remained a highly communicable disease in the underdeveloped nations of the world.

The biologists spent their time monitoring the daily activities of their chimpanzee test subjects, meticulously recorded the medical reaction to the life-threatening antigens. Intending to boost the immune system of the primates in the initial grouping, these subjects received daily inoculations of the newly developed vaccine. The chimps in the control group, similarly exposed to the virulent strain of variola major, received none of the antitoxin.

The primates intermingled freely in the laboratory habitat. Unfortunately, the populace of the menagerie fluctuated, a sad but inevitable result of the experimentation. A third of the non-immunized subjects would ultimately expire, their demise primarily instigated by bronchopneumonia. That statistic remained an unavoidable consequence and already factored into the comprehensive equation.

Every fourth Monday of the month, the white van pulled up to the back door of the facility and lab technicians unloaded the new shipment of hairy West African chatterboxes. Though Cyrus abhorred subjecting these miniature replicas of homo sapiens to abuse, he rationalized that mankind certainly took precedence over the well-being of the jabbering chimps. How unlucky for them that their species possessed duplicate blood cells and ninety-five percent of the genetic material of their hominid counterparts. But, after all, their sacrifice would benefit mankind.

*   *   *

Cyrus descended from the patriot, Chester Walcott, who served under George Washington during the American Revolution. In 1776, Chester and the Continental Army paddled across the Delaware, and the day after Christmas, the army of rag-tag militiamen trounced the Hessians in Trenton. A week later, the patriot took part in defeating General Cornwallis' forces in Princeton. Chester, his dad's fourth great-grandfather on his mother's side took a volley of grapeshot from a piece of field artillery at Monmouth, but remaining undaunted, fought on until freedom reigned in the colonies.

The Stars and Stripes hung over the fireplace in the Markum living room. A large lithograph of the Declaration of Independence and another of the Bill of Rights adorned one of the walls in the dining room. Extremely proud of his heritage, his father, Riley, believed passionately in the principles of freedom and the safeguarding of civil liberty.

"Cyrus, we live in the greatest country in the world." He imparted this piece of wisdom to his son one evening over dinner. "We must do whatever we can to defend it from its enemies."

As a ten-year-old, this child had a better understanding of freedom than most kids his age but fumbled over such hypothetical concepts. "Poppa, there's little I can do. I'm only one person."

His father put a hand on his son's shoulder. "Individuals built America. One man begets one vote. Don't ever forget that united we stand, and it's only when we stay divided that we fall. Always remember, my son, you must follow the teachings of God. The Lord takes precedence over country."

His parents belonged to the Protestant Episcopal Church and were devout Anglican Christians. His father worked as a planner for the city transit system while his mom tended to the home.

Fulfilling the promise to his brother's memory became Cyrus' goal in life. He'd spend endless hours at the library, poring over every science book and medical journal he could drag to the table. Completing his studies at Walnut Hills High School with a ninety-nine-percent grade average, he graduated as the top student in his class of two hundred and sixty-eight. When the teacher handed back his Scholastic Aptitude Test results, Cyrus glared at her, outraged that he'd gotten a question or two incorrect.

"Mrs. Larkin, I need to speak with you," he petitioned his homeroom teacher. "I think someone in the office made a clerical error grading my paper."

Mrs. Larkin placed her hands on her hips. "Mr. Markum, you're in the highest percentiles in both the math and English SAT tests. Nothing would be gained questioning the results."

"It's the principle, Mrs. Larkin. I don't believe I answered any questions incorrectly. I deserve an explanation."

No clarification would be forthcoming.

With an IQ test score of 168, Cyrus played the part of a mushrooming prodigy. The recipient of the prestigious Ohio State Science Achievement Award and awarded not one, but two scholastic subsidies, he cruised through college and graduate studies. He attained a BSC in biological engineering, an MS in biotechnology, and a Ph.D. in molecular biology at Johns Hopkins University. Following his doctorate, he accepted a government fellowship with the American Scientific Research Group in Berkeley, California.

His post-doctorate work commenced in the summer of 1961. But, his big break came in January 1966, when the Atomic Energy Commission asked him to head up a team studying the effects of radiation and radioisotopes on the human body. Proffered a four-year contract as supervisor of the biosciences and biotechnology division of the Lawrence Radiation Laboratory at Livermore, the scientist thought the offer a great opportunity.

Within three weeks' time, he and Matthias packed up their belongings. Attaching a U-Haul to the back of their red Chevy Impala convertible, the couple, along with their twin teacup Yorkshire terriers, Angus and Jillian, headed forty miles southeast from El Cerrito to their new home in Livermore Valley.

Thrilled almost beyond words, his partner abounded with energy. "Oh, Cy, this is only the beginning. I know remarkable things are in store for us. Just wait and see."

Cyrus laughed, filled with joy at his lover's reaction to the move to the wine country.

Matthias, taking enormous pride in his reputation, both as a connoisseur of wines and as a gourmet chef, believed the grape region called to him A contributing editor for the upscale magazine, *Hors Devourers, and Aperitifs,* he'd also authored two volumes dedicated to the preparation of epicurean delights.

After successfully operating *Café Claire,* a brasserie in the Richmond District of San Francisco for several years, his life suddenly changed dramatically. He never contemplated selling his restaurant, but one Tuesday this past February, several executives from a huge corporation showed up just after the lunch crowd. The bigwigs offered an extremely lucrative buyout. The contract called for a two-month transition period and the deal would assure Matthias that if he didn't subscribe to fiscal recklessness, he could live quite comfortably for the remainder of his life.

In the eight months since that day, he and Cyrus spent their off-days venturing an hour northward, exploring the wineries of Sonoma and the Napa Valley. With new vineyards rising from the fertile soil throughout the area, the wine enthusiasts found the adventures inspiring.

Today, Matthias kept up a stream of banter. "Can you imagine, Cy, the wineries of Livermore Valley will be only scant minutes from our door? We'll have so many places to explore."

He leaned over the center console and kissed his partner on the cheek. "You've made me so happy. This is a dream come true. You know that!"

Cyrus focused on the road ahead. Matthias checked on the pair of tiny canines wiggling around on the plaid blanket in the back seat. Picking up one of the tiny passengers in each hand, he gave each a smooch, before placing them back on their soft cotton nest. They yapped a bit. Their teensy tails wagging, as their paws found balance on the high denier thread count fabric.

He wriggled in his seat and cuddled Cyrus' arm. "You know my goal, babe. One day, I'd like to own my own winery."

His partner giggled at his exuberance.

"Don't you laugh, Cy. You never can tell what the future holds."

"I'm sorry. You're absolutely right. One never knows what's in store."

A pragmatist, Cyrus' worldview consisted of varying shades of gray, black, and white. When it came to their relationship, he believed in its full potential. His partner played the eternal optimist, and a big reason their relationship worked.

He'd never dabbled with romantic connections before. Women did nothing for him. Besides, he'd rationalized, his scientific research took precedence over such triflings.

His thoughts voyaged back to that Saturday, that fateful morning high in the Berkeley Hills. The day Matthias walked into his life.

After a visit with his mom in Ohio, Cyrus had the weekend before needing to report to the lab. Enthralled with the peacefulness of the Botanic Gardens in Tilden Regional Park, he used the opportunity to stroll through the stunning gardens and surrounding woodlands. He hiked up to Inspiration Point and stood gazing out at Mount Tamalpais, its peak shrouded by clouds of white fluff.

A velvety voice startled him. "The view is magnificent. You can almost see the summit stretching toward the heavens. It's absolutely breathtaking."

Cyrus turned toward the sound. He beheld a sight as spectacular as any of the seven wonders of the world. Clad in a sleeveless teal tee-shirt and navy-blue shorts, a bronzed Adonis stared back at him. His chiseled good looks, accentuated by curly black hair, created a magnetism that tugged at his soul and pulled him closer.

Cupid's golden shaft burrowed deeply into the center of both their hearts. A waterfall of understanding flowed over each of them. True love had saturated each of their souls.

Cyrus found his voice. "Are you thirsty? Would you like to go get a drink?"

"That would be perfect. I know a nice wine and cheese shop nearby. By the way, I'm Matthias."

Their whirlwind romance took off. Within three weeks, they'd moved in together. Their individual lives merged into a unified existence. A picture-perfect relationship developed. They became partners on both the physical and spiritual planes.

It all led up to today. Now, they had Livermore in their sights. Butterflies churned in both their bellies. Cyrus planned to take advantage of his opportunity and further develop his skills and enhance his reputation. His partner supported him and possessed high hopes of his own. The talented chef without a kitchen craved a new challenge.

Matthias recently outlined chapters for a third book. He earned a lucrative income from his writing but considered putting words to paper more of a hobby than a life's work. The sale of his eatery had filled his bank account nicely. With exceptional credit, the budding impresario sought an opportunity to grow.

Born to Jacques and Marie Desjardins, in April 1935, he came from a long line of French Canadians. At the insistence of his Aunt Claire, his father packed up the family's belongings and moved from Montreal to New Orleans just after Matthias turned two.

Claire, a sturdy beauty with long flowing locks of red hair and a sugary smile, had a game plan. Her husband, a member of a wealthy Acadian family, owned a small fleet of fishing boats. It seemed only natural to utilize her culinary skills and allocate a small portion of the abundant fresh catch to nurture her own business.

The blackboard menu on the wall of her quaint twelve-table establishment included spicy Cajun cooking inspired by her mother-in-law. She expanded her fare with the addition of traditional French recipes passed down by her side of the family.

The lunch crowd especially loved her deep-fried soft-shelled crab, which she served on grilled sourdough brioche. Claire augmented the creation with buttermilk hushpuppies and added a side of honied coleslaw to complement the plate decoration. The wonderful tangy flavor of her slow cooked "swamp-style" jambalaya proved a delicacy at the Louisiana State Fair, where her creation rose above the competition and the recipe garnered the prestigious "Top Pot" ribbon.

Along with her expanding menu, her celebrity grew. Customers waited up to an hour for a seat at one of her tables. Claire's mouth-watering seafood gumbo, along with her duck cassoulet and specialty quiches, allowed her little cafe on Decatur Street to develop into a fixture in the French Quarter. Her fresh-baked crème brulee cheesecake, served with a liberal helping of fresh strawberries, also triggered quite a stir. The savory dessert decorated the March cover of *Sweet Confections* magazine.

When Matthias turned twelve, he began busing tables at the family's new restaurant on Bourbon Street. By the age of sixteen, he'd matured into an accomplished chef. At twenty-three, he petitioned his father to stake him in a move westward.

"*Pere*, may I speak with you?" Matthias asked his father nervously one Friday at closing time.

"*Oui, mon fils*," his dad replied, as he placed the container of heavy cream on a shelf in the refrigerator. "What's on your mind?"

The junior Desjardins reached beneath his apron and pulled out a large sheet of paper. Spreading the map of California on an empty table, he pointed to the San Francisco Bay area. "This is where I want to move, Father. I'm ready to open my own restaurant."

His parents discussed the almost two-thousand-mile move and decided the time had come for their son to spread his wings and soar on his own. They could well afford to invest in the future of their sole offspring. Before a year passed, Matthias rented a one-bedroom apartment only a stone's throw from Golden Gate Park. The charming North Beach neighborhood, filled with an eclectic blend of beatniks, tourists, and a snowballing gay scene, fit with his new lifestyle. Within three months, he'd discovered a prime piece of property.

As the eatery flourished, so did his reputation for innovative gourmet cooking. His family took pride in his success. Matthias repaid the loan within three years. His Aunt Claire, already a luminary in local cooking circles, found greater fame with her nephew's triumph. He sang her praises in his magazine articles and throughout the pages of his first book on Cajun recipes. He helped the Louisiana Lady and her recipes to go national.

He turned up the radio and sat back. He had plans of his own.

CHAPTER TWO

Back from The 'Nam

New York City, July 18, 1968

The subway's lights flashed twice. The car went dark. After a few seconds, the lights returned. They flickered once more, then stabilized. Daniel stared at his reflection in the glass. Reaching inside his jacket pocket, he tapped his discharge papers. *Yes, this it's real.* He knew he should be happy. He'd survived his year in the jungles of Southeast Asia.

Stashed inside his sweaty right sock sat the ninety-two dollars severance pay, doled out by the Fort Dix paymaster less than two hours ago. He didn't expect trouble on the ride home, but, at times, New York City could be a dangerous place.

The subway hadn't changed at all, still noisy, sweaty, and torturously slow. Each time the doors opened inside a station, the stench of decaying garbage invaded the subway car. The laboring air conditioner spewed out lukewarm air. At each stop, the oppressive heat rushed in as the doors opened. The waves of torrid air reminded him of the unrelenting climate he'd left behind.

He looked up as the intercom crackled. A male voice blared from the overhead speakers. "Ladies and gentlemen, our next stop will be Atlantic Avenue. Change here for the IRT number two, four, and five trains, also, the B, the D, the..."

The screech of the train's grinding brakes drowned out the conductor's voice. The ding-dong of the warning bell sounded as the doors slid open. A woman clutching her baby, and a smelly homeless guy lugging a black garbage bag fought to exit through the stampede of people rushing in. Chaos reigned. Passengers dashed, dove, bumped, and pushed, intent on laying claim to an available piece of a plastic bench. Dan snickered. Yep, just like he remembered.

The doors closed. The train jerked forward, then inched along, making one stop, then another. Dan couldn't wait to get home. As the number two train emerged from the underground tunnel and entered the Newkirk Avenue station, his heartbeat increased. The doors closed again. The train rolled forward.

The conductor's voice resonated through the subway car: "Ladies and gentlemen, we're entering the Flatbush Avenue station, the final stop on your southbound number two train. Please take all your personal belongings and watch your step as you exit. Thank you for riding the New York City Subway System. Have yourselves a wonderful day."

The train shuddered slightly before coming to a complete stop. The chimes sounded as the doors opened. The six or seven people still aboard, headed out the doors before the hissing noise of compressed air escaping from the brakes echoed throughout the station.

Dan bounded up the steps and into the sunshine of his Brooklyn neighborhood, the junction of Flatbush and Nostrand Avenues. He inspected the familiar Jentz Ice Cream Parlor sign. Two stores down, the cakes and cookies sat artfully arranged in the glass display case of Ebinger's Bakery. One of them had his name on it.

Tears came to his eyes as he gobbled down the last two bites of the oversized black-and-white cookie. As he walked the three blocks to his apartment building, his mind sprinted. How would he wash away the last year of his life?

Two of his closest pals paid the ultimate price for America's freedom. Cliff should be here with him right now. They arrived the same day in "Nam and slated to come home together. They'd made plans to visit Brooklyn; then, after a week, out to Los Angeles. A Viet Cong with an RPG rocket had an alternate plan.

Another of his close friends had also become just another statistic, his body blown apart by a mortar round. Dan felt the guilt flush through him. Why had they died, when he came through with nary a scratch? He didn't have the answer?

He looked up at the twenty-story apartment building. An ostentatious testament to the material success of its residents, the four-year-old brick and mortar monolith stood majestically, watching over Flatbush Avenue. A twenty-four-hour doorman and a full-time security guard tended the main entrance.

Dan's heart thumped out a rhythm of happiness and anticipation. He couldn't wait to get upstairs and hug his mom and brother and plant his feet on the terrace and stare at the Manhattan skyline. On a cloudless day, you could see the Empire State Building.

The elevator door opened. He double-timed it down the hallway to his family's apartment. Dan kissed his mom softly on the lips and hugged her tenderly. "I love you, Mom. I'm so happy to be home."

She whimpered and hugged him tightly. "Your father and I have been worried sick about you. I've prayed for you every night."

"I can only imagine what you've gone through, Mom. It had to be rough. But I'm home now."

The bathroom door flew open. His brother came rushing into the living room.

"Hey, Dan, it's great to see you."

The two threw their arms around each other.

Gene examined his older brother. "Wow, look how skinny you got. That Army food must have sucked. How much you weigh?"

"Don't worry about me. I'm fine. I thought about you over there. I missed you, asshole." Dan poked his brother in the shoulder. "It's great to be back home."

Gene pushed his brother toward the bathroom. "Come on. Get in there. Let's check this out."

The electronic scale told the story. "One hundred and twenty-six pounds," Gene announced. "Wow, you're a skinny Minnie. We've got to fatten you up. Dad's coming home early from work. We have a six o'clock reservation at Lundy's."

Dan licked his lips. "That sounds delicious. I can't wait."

July 24th, Dubrows Cafeteria

Dan ordered a coffee at the Kings Highway restaurant's counter. The prospect of meeting with one of the guys from the old crowd excited him, though he'd been caught a bit off guard when Ben Tepper called him this morning. Before Dan left for the

Army, the two had hung out together but had not been what you would call the best of friends. He considered Ben a bit shady and at times, unpredictable.

Talk about a Freudian paradox, Ben fit the profile perfectly. The narcissistic tendencies counterbalanced his superior intelligence quotient. He misused his brainpower. Instead, Ben perfected the fine art of escaping punishment for his objectionable and illegal actions. His record of nefarious escapades extended far beyond the ordinary. His sophomore year of high school, he assisted dozens of fellow students in improving their grade averages. He appropriated a stack of blank report cards from the records office and sold them to whoever had the cash. That bit of deception lasted two semesters. The house of cards came crashing down when an irate mother got wise to the scheme and reported him. School expulsion and an immediate transfer from Madison to Midwood High School followed, but the underclassman avoided any criminal prosecution.

Busted for sale and distribution of marijuana a few months later, Ben's face graced the cover of the *New York Mirror* and the *Herald Tribune*. His dad, a wealthy business owner, paid a high-priced attorney, who shrieked entrapment so loudly, that all charges miraculously dissolved.

His arrest for selling illegal fireworks came next. The police held him in lockup overnight, but once again his father used his money and connections successfully. A small fine served as the penalty for his son's indiscretion.

Dan knew to be watchful of his possible antics, as he gave Ben and his California traveling companion the once over as they pulled up chairs and sat across from him at the table.

"Hey, Ben. How's it going? I haven't seen you for what, like two years? You staying out of trouble?" He reached out his hand.

"Definitely. All that crap's ancient history." He pointed to his pal. "My buddy, Bill."

"Good to meet you."

The two exchanged nods.

Bill took a swig of Coke. "What's up. I heard good things about you."

Dan winked. "Yeah, I can just imagine."

He got off on Bill's aura. The dude looked to be the spitting image of the Indian brave on the Buffalo nickel. With shimmering shoulder length black locks and watery brown eyes, his high cheekbones, thin lips, and oversized proboscis accented his classic look.

He turned his focus to Ben. "I'm glad you called me. It's good to see a guy from the old clique. I waded through a world of shit this last year. The military sucks a big one."

"Yeah, you got that right," Ben quipped, scooping up a large forkful of apple pie. "Like I told you on the phone, you should come back with us to Berkeley. That's where it's happening." He attacked the fork and swallowed the gob of gooey pastry.

Dan took a taste of the bitter coffee while examining Ben's fresh look. His kinky brown hair had grown out and fashioned into a funky "Jewfro." A neatly trimmed brown mustache and small goatee ornamented his upper lip and chin. The styling worked, setting off the deep blue of his eyes.

Ben leaned his elbows on the table. "You know, Bill's a Cheyenne Indian. He's the great-grandson of one of the warriors who kicked Custer's ass at the Battle of Little Big Horn."

"Hmm!" Dan had his doubts about that tidbit of Americana. "Get the fuck outta here. For real?"

Bill stayed quiet, busy watching a girl at one of the other tables.

The Cheyenne culture interested Dan. He tapped Bill on his arm. "I read that Indians smoke Peyote. Is that true?"

Bill's attention shifted with the mention of drugs. "Oh, yeah, man. Peyote buttons are a trip. You ever try any?"

"Never have," Dan admitted. "What's it like?"

"It's far out, man. You swallow a couple, and twenty minutes later, you think you're sitting on the moon looking around at the stars. They make Mescaline out of it, but you got to try LSD. That stuff's way more intense."

Dan leaned back in his chair. "No shit?"

Ben threw his fork down. "Will you two stop talking this bullshit? Later! We came here to talk about Berkeley."

Ben's idea made sense. Dan longed to become a part of the counterculture. What better place to visit than Berkeley, the hotbed of the social revolution? That's where his generation worked to build a better society, one free from racism and religious intolerance? Flying out to California sounded like the right move.

"You know what, Ben? I think that's a hip idea."

Bill's long mane bounced around on his shoulders as he threw his head back. Dan felt envy. He couldn't wait for his own hair to grow out. He intended on letting his own freak flag fly. He knew his parents wouldn't be too keen on his travel plans, but that's another story.

His dad didn't care for his attitude and confronted him yesterday. "You're not the same person since you came home," he claimed. "I'm sorry, son, but if you don't change your ways, you'll have to move out. You're a bad influence on your brother."

That made crazy sense. His dad didn't know it, but Gene sold pot and hashish to the locals and supplied Dan.

Ben's call had come at the perfect time.

Dan took another hit of coffee. "Berkeley sounds good, guys. I'll let you know for sure tomorrow. I'm gonna go party with my brother tonight."

*   *   *

What better place to be than the Electric Circus on St. Mark's Place, on a Friday night? Cat Mother and the All-Night Newsboys would be opening the show. The Chambers Brothers, the headlining the show, had a smash hit, "Time Has Come Today." The tick-tock of a drumstick smacking the side of a cowbell came over radios and record players throughout the city. Dan planned to get stoned and enjoy himself.

Gene worked with the Zig Zag rolling papers while Dan drove. The brothers Dundee passed the joint as they crossed over the Williamsburg Bridge and entered the Lower East Side of Manhattan. The boys floated in their own world, cruising above the stratosphere.

As Dan waited on line, he gawked at the people swarming around him. Colorfully dressed young adults lined both sides of the street. The smell of marijuana smoke filled the air. Dan took in the scene of city life as he pulled out his five bucks and slapped it on the counter.

"Pay the lady," his brother joked as they grabbed their tickets and hustled through the door.

Gene hadn't exaggerated the party scene one iota. On stage, a fire-breathing juggler dazzled the crowd. Once he left the stage, a male and female trapeze artist took his place. Swinging and somersaulting above the crowd, the acrobats caused quite a commotion.

"Holy shit! Look at them," a girl standing behind Dan yelled.

"Ooh," moaned her friend. "I bet I could do that if I practiced." She applauded and stamped her feet.

Gene turned around and laughed. "You got to have a pair of huge *cojones* to swing around up there."

The girl stuck out her tongue. She and her friend walked away.

Dan didn't say a word. He continued to gape.

Several white-faced mimes circulated on the dance floor, adding their antics to the extravaganza. People danced, grooving to the psychedelic music that pumped from the half-dozen large speakers mounted on the walls.

The East Village ballroom carved out from old turn-of-the-century brownstones, pulsated with energy. Strobe lights flashed, intermittently tossing intense bolts of blue illumination around the dimly lit dance floor. At the rear of the stage, abstract video clips flooded the diaphanous fabric hanging from the ceiling. Dan's body tingled. Oh, yeah! The Army could suck his dick.

A little later in the evening, while the roadies sound-checked the Chambers Brothers' equipment, the house speakers blasted out rock and roll. Dan grooved across the dimly-lit ballroom, weaving his way toward the concession stand. Stepping aside to avoid several whirling dancers, he failed to notice the young woman coming his way. Their hips collided.

A cup flew from her hand. Liquid splashed on the floor. Dan managed to slow his momentum and avoided a full-bore collision. Unable to maintain full bodily control, he fell backward, making a four-point landing on the wooden dance floor.

"Oh, crap," he muttered. Embarrassed, he scrambled to his feet. "Miss, I'm so sorry. It's totally my fault. Are you okay?"

The young lady gave him a sideways glance. "I'm fine. You know you should be more careful." She straightened out her blouse. "Are you okay?"

"I'm good, thanks. With so much going on and with the people moving around, I didn't see you." He noticed the empty plastic cup. "I spilled your drink. Can I get you a new one?"

"Yes, that would be very nice. Cherry Coke, please. You don't have to worry. I'm not hurt. I know you didn't do it on purpose."

Dan felt a rush of excitement. He tried to stay cool and not to stare, but this girl blew his mind.

"My name is Joanne." Her big brown eyes opened wide. "What's yours?"

He hadn't felt this alive in a long time. The intoxicating scent of her Shalimar fragrance overpowered his senses. This girl ignited a fire in his heart as well as his libido. With her long dark hair and a Playboy Playmate's physical proportions, she looked to have it all.

He felt the need to make an amusing remark. "My name is Daniel Dundee. I come from a long line of pirates."

She didn't seem amused. Had he miscalculated? It took a second, but she broke into enthusiastic laughter. "You're crazy. I mean that in a good way."

Relieved, he pointed to the concession area. "Why don't we head to the lobby? I'll get you a drink."

Dan suddenly found himself hurtling through a space-time continuum. Could this sensation of gravity loss and timelessness be the result of this girl? The soda cup felt weightless as he lifted it from the counter and handed it to Joanne.

"Thank you. Let's find my friend, Cookie." She pointed to the end of the stands.

They found her friend relaxing on one of the cushy maroon sofas that lined the outside of the concession area. Cookie bounced up. "Who's the cute guy?"

"Dan. He's a pirate."

"Hi, I'm Cookie." Her friend looked confused. "What does Joanne mean, you're a pirate?"

Dan felt comfortable. "If I tell you, I'll have to make you walk the plank."

Cookie laughed it off. "I'm not that kind of girl. Why don't we go into the lounge? It's much more comfortable in there."

Joanne agreed.

"Sure, that's great," Dan answered. "I just need to touch base with my brother. He must be wondering where I went off to."

Joanne pointed to a glass door next to the ladies room. "We'll be right in the lounge." She grabbed his hand. "Make sure you come back and bring your brother."

"Oh, don't worry. You can bet I will."

*   *   *

Dan and Joanne's first date proved interesting. The Jets and Sharks mixed it up in a film that examined the socioeconomic enmity of the fifties. An original Broadway musical, the story pitted a gang of working-class whites protecting their turf, against a group of Puerto Rican teenagers. Joanne had seen *West Side Story* twice before and enjoyed the chance to describe the social symbolism to Dan.

"It's based on Shakespeare's *Romeo and Juliet*," she explained energetically. "But, it's set in modern times and takes place on the Upper Westside of Manhattan."

Even in the darkened movie theater, he sensed her face lighting up.

Joanne wiggled in her chair. "I think Natalie Wood is gorgeous."

Dan snuggled closer. "I think you're better looking."

That night, in the third row of the balcony, their mutual infatuation took root.

"Why don't we take a drive to Plum Beach and check out the submarine races," Dan suggested as they left the Flatlands Avenue movie theater.

What better way to finish off a date than to park in a desolate area, flip on the radio, and make out. If a guy played his cards correctly, he might even get a base hit and make the turn toward second base.

Joanne gripped Dan's arm with both her hands. "That's funny," she giggled. "I know your game." She looked at her watch. "Sure. Why not? Let's go, it's still early."

*   *   *

The lights on the Marine Parkway Bridge glimmered in the distance.

"Daniel," Joanne whispered, nestling closer. "I like you. You're so much different than any of the other guys I've dated."

"I hope that's a good thing."

She reached for his hand. "Much better than good."

He stretched his arm around her shoulders. "I think you're terrific. I've never felt this way before."

Joanne pushed herself up onto his lap.

A bit rusty with the nuances of the dating ritual, he hesitated momentarily. "Uh, excuse me, but what would you prefer, tongue or regular?"

As the words left his lips, he wanted to pull them back into his mouth and swallow them. *How could he have asked such an idiotic question?*

Joanne laughed. "I see you've been out of circulation for a while."

She took hold of his right hand and pressed it against her breast. Gently placing her palm behind his head, she proceeded to answer his ill-conceived query. Her serpentine appendage darted between his parted lips.

Oh boy! Dan had made solid contact and blasted a line drive into the gap. It looked like it would roll to the wall. He might have a chance for an inside-the-parker. As he rounded the bases and slid safely into home plate, he knew this girl could turn into monumental trouble. Confused from his year at war and wary of the wicked world around him, a new variable had thrust itself into the equation.

*   *   *

At about eleven the next morning, Dan parked the Cougar and headed upstairs. His breakfast meeting at IHOP went off well. He'd firmed up plans with his traveling buddies and booked their flights to Berkeley.

As he walked into the apartment, his mom looked up from the kitchen table. "Danny, how was breakfast?"

"Great, Mom. We went to IHOP."

"Randy called about half an hour ago. He wants you to call him back."

"Thanks, Mom. I'll call him in a little while. I gotta use the toilet first. I drank three cups of coffee." He closed the bathroom door behind him.

So, his friend Randy McBride called. The two had been tight before Vietnam. Dan soaped up his hands. *That crazy dude, Randy.* The poor guy could never catch a break when it came to the ladies. He could give lessons on getting dumped. How about the time Margie Strickland stuck it to him? *Messed up, man.*

That night, Randy had dragged him to Luigi's, a mob joint on Flatbush Avenue. His broken-hearted friend lined up five Singapore Slings and downed them, one after another.

"Women suck," Randy drunkenly philosophized, a few minutes afterward, his words slurred and barely intelligible. "They love to break your heart. You better listen to me. I know what I'm talking about."

Belching loudly, he pushed himself up from his stool, grabbing the bar rail for support. "Dan, I gotta go drain the lizard. You need to give me a hand."

"What? You want me to hold it for you? Randy, you're such a schmuck. You never learn. You always do this."

"Gimme a break, will ya? You're my best friend. Just give me a little support. I think I'm gonna be sick."

"Oh, shit." Dan grabbed hold of his friend's arm and dragged him along. "Let's move it!"

He maneuvered his none-too-responsive pal through the narrow hallway. As soon as their feet hit the bathroom tiles, his fiendishly blitzed friend delivered up forty ounces of pinkish colored liquid, garnished with small pieces of maraschino cherries and half-chewed up chunks of pineapple.

Bam! Bam! Bam! Three loud raps on the bathroom door, followed by the roar of a deep voice gave Dan something else to think about.

"Hey! Open up. It's the manager. What's going on in there? Let's go, morons. Open the fucking door."

"Open it up, right fucking now, or I'll kick your ass," an even louder, and scarier sounding voice screamed at them.

"We're coming out. Hold on," Dan answered, unlocking the door. He maneuvered Rusty out the door and into the hall.

One of the huge guys stood with his big fists balled up. He glared at them. "You idiots are lucky I'm in a good mood tonight. Get the hell out of my place!"

Randy balanced on rubbery legs. He leaned on Dan. The bouncer jostled them toward the back of the restaurant. Forced through the small kitchen, he and his drunken pal found themselves pushed forcefully out the back door. Dan found himself surrounded by a dozen dirt-encrusted garbage cans and a dumpster that smelled indescribably wretched.

Randy tripped over one of the cans. It toppled, spilling rotting fruits, veggies, and who knows what else. His drunk friend hit the ground.

"Nobody loves me," he complained. "I'm a good guy. Why can't I find a girl?"

Dan helped him up. "Don't worry about that now. We gotta get out of here."

They crept along, their faces pressing against a brick wall, with the back of their heads scraping against rigid hedges. Finally, they stumbled out onto the sidewalk, battered, but breathing.

The stink of the putrid refuse still lived in Dan's memory, but probably not so much in Randy's. An excess of alcohol in the system would've dulled his ability to recall such an inspirational experience.

CHAPTER THREE

Beginning of The Sorrow

Livermore, California, July 1968

By any stretch of the imagination, Friday evening's dinner party turned out to be a phenomenal triumph. Charles Jones, the owner of Precious Pattie's Fine Wine and Grapery, couldn't have been more impressed with Matthias.

"Jonesy," as people addressed him, now, in his early fifties, and with more money than he'd ever need, wanted to relax, and enjoy the rest of his life.

"Pattie's my grandmama," Jonesy explained. "After my mama died from the Spanish flu, she raised me."

He crossed his heart. "I never knew my daddy. I'm not proud of it, but I don't think my mama knew who knocked her up. When I opened the winery, it seemed only natural to name it after Pattie."

He winked at his hosts. With his black handlebar mustache and multi-colored feather protruding from the band of his English derby, he looked like he'd be more comfortable living in the Gay Nineties, pedaling his unicycle down the road, whistling "Little Brown Jug."

"Pattie's still going strong at ninety-two," the winery owner added.

Matthias poured more red wine into his guest's glass and handed it to him. "That's wonderful."

Jonesy took a long drink. "You're probably curious about the precious part of the name. Well, Pattie, for sure, is precious to me, but I'm gonna tell you the real hoopty-doo."

He took another swallow. "The company name comes from precious metal... gold, to be precise! Pattie's granddad, Walter, lived in Oregon in eighteen and forty-eight. That's when the California gold rush began. Later that year, Walter traveled down to Sutter's Mill and sold tools and supplies to the miners."

Jonesy sniggered. "Yep! The dude made himself a small fortune. After a year or so, he opened a bank in Hangtown. That's about thirty miles north of where James Marshall originally found the golden flakes. After I came home from the Second World War, I took some of the family money and built Precious Pattie's."

Luck and a local wine tasting event brought Matthias and the eccentric viticulturist together. Jonesy felt an immediate connection with the younger man. Having no heirs and bored with the day-to-day business routine, he'd been looking to find the right person to take over his business. Once Jonesy investigated his possible candidate's finances and family history, he suggested this pow-wow.

Jonesy laid his glass on the table. "Please, both of you. I need your attention. I've come to a decision."

Matthias stood up and lowered the sound on the record player. "You're talking about the purchase of Precious Pattie's?"

Jonesy rapped his knuckles against the tabletop. "No. I'd like your recipe for the delicious chicken we just ate. Of course, I'm speaking about the winery. I want you to become my partner. If you're free on Monday, we should meet at my lawyer's office."

Matthias couldn't believe his luck. The contract called for the initial transfer of 30 percent of the stock. Provisions in the purchase agreement set up a schedule where Jonesy would eventually divest himself of his shares entirely. Thrilled with the reasonable terms, Matthias planned to approach his Aunt Claire for the additional funds needed. He had no doubt, that after reviewing the financial reports with her banker, she'd give the go-ahead.

In the meantime, Cyrus labored at the laboratory twelve hours each weekday and worked half-a-day most Saturdays. The schedule afforded little opportunity for the couple to maintain a productive and satisfying relationship. That didn't seem critical at the time. His lover had enough to think about, as he embarked on his new venture.

A crash course to convert Matthias into a skilled winery owner commenced the day following the contract signing. Learning about the planting and harvesting of the select grape clusters, along with the prescribed methods of wine production, gave him only a taste of the business. The fine art of fermentation followed and included training in the bottling process for both the still assortments and the more popular sparkling wine variations. Sales analysis and the explanation of their distribution network followed. Celebrating his new passion, he grasped the rudiments and advanced techniques rather easily.

Cyrus offered whatever encouragement and emotional support he could, yet unaware that their relationship had already hurtled off the rails.

*   *   *

On an overcast Monday evening in October 1969, reality plunged its sharpened blade through Cyrus' heart. After visiting his mom who'd been convalescing from a bout with pneumonia, he'd arrived at the San Francisco airport on a United Airlines flight from Cincinnati.

Downing the last swig of his coffee, Cyrus pressed the push-buttons on the pay phone and waited. After four rings the Ansafone engaged. He heard Matthias' voice on the recorded announcement.

"Hmm, that's strange," he commented aloud, scratching his head. Why wouldn't his partner be at home? Perhaps he had to use the bathroom. Cyrus hung up. Grabbing his luggage, he shrugged and walked toward the line of taxis that waited outside the terminal.

Even before thrusting the key into the Schlage front door lock, he sensed trouble. The spot in the driveway where Matthias parked his green Austin Martin sat empty. It should've been sitting there, right next to the beautiful assortment of Calla Lilies and California Asters their landscapers had arranged for them last month. At that hour he should be home, especially since he knew the flight arrangements.

What about the sound of the yapping teacups? The adverse possibilities confounded him. What if Matthias and the Yorkies had gone for a drive and suffered a road mishap? Could one of the dogs be sick or have hurt himself?

Dropping his bag, Cyrus walked to the stand in the foyer. He noticed a folded sheet of paper sticking out from under the base of the phone. He picked it up and unfolded it. His earlier concern transformed into shock and confusion. The rage came next.

Backing up a step, he kicked at one of the legs of the antique walnut side table. The valuable piece of furniture crashed to the floor. The telephone skidded across the floor. Its receiver separated from the base. The buzz of the dial tone added to his irritation. He looked down at the New Testament that had spilled from the table's solitary drawer and flipped open.

He picked up the Bible and the paper lying beside it.

Dear Cyrus, the note began. *What has once been a wonderful relationship has deteriorated beyond the point of any return.*

The explanation pointed to the doctor's extreme work schedule as the main culprit. Matthias felt that the man of science could no longer contribute enough emotionally. He'd be staying with a friend temporarily. *Please, don't try and find me*, the note cautioned.

Cyrus crumpled up the paper. Why hadn't he recognized the warning signs? Damn! He'd been too preoccupied with his test tubes and beakers. How could he have been so oblivious to his lover's emotional needs?

The idea of his partner with another sickened him. He shuddered at the visual imagery. Could there be a new someone? Or might this be only a bump in the road, a cry for attention? His scientific training trained him never to form a hypothesis without accessing the factors and dynamics of an equation. For the moment, though, the integers had fallen out of alignment. Where could his partner be?

He had an idea. He'd pay a visit to the winery in the morning.

* * *

He turned the knob on the office door at precisely nine a.m. Paintings of neatly labeled varieties of grapes bedecked the brown walls. A small circlet of gray corks hung to the right of each. At the center of the room sat a small table, filled with a spherical display of bottled wines. Hanging from the ceiling, dual silver chains supported a white sign, offering a sip to whoever might be so inclined.

Maggie sat behind her desk. She tapped away on a typewriter. On the cluttered desk, a beige coffee mug, steam escaping, sat next to a stack of magazines. The receptionist and "girl Friday," always pleasant in the past, withheld her customary smile. Instead, her fingers reached into the top drawer of her desk.

"Hello, Doctor Markum. I know it's awkward, but Matthias isn't here. He asked me to give this to you." She handed him a small packet.

Though enraged, he controlled any outward expression of hostility. "Too bad that he gave you the dirty work, Maggie." He forced a smile.

Running a hand through his wavy brown hair, he slipped the package into his jacket. He removed his black horned-rim spectacles and wiped them. The glasses didn't need cleaning, but it gave him a moment to gather his thoughts.

"Did he leave a number for me?"

She looked down into her cup. "No. I'm sorry. He didn't give me any specific message, just told me to give you the package."

How unlike the Matthias he knew, but belaboring the point with Maggie would be a useless effort. She'd worked for the winery for several years and knew better than to reveal any secrets, personal or otherwise. Cyrus admired her for it. He placed the glasses back on the bridge of his nose.

"I guess that's it then. Thank you for your help, young lady. Have a lovely day."

She fought off the frown beginning to form on her face, but only partially succeeded. "You too, Doctor. Good luck."

Once outside, he ripped open the brown paper. As expected, he found a cassette tape. He climbed into his Chevy Impala. He wanted to get home and listen to the recording. During the ten-minute drive, he contemplated what the small reel of magnetic tape might contain. He didn't want to jump to conclusions, though it looked as if the chips had already found their final resting place.

Normally, his work at the lab took precedence over any other concerns. The fact that he'd taken a rare personal day to resolve his romantic entanglement troubled him. As he parked the car and walked inside the house, his mind imagined the sounds of the dogs welcoming him. The thought that Matthias might be in the kitchen preparing coffee and a snack crossed his mind. But no smell of freshly ground Colombian beans or an aroma of sizzling honey-cured bacon frying up in the pan greeted him. He felt devastated.

Slipping the cassette into the tape deck, he hit the play button. Settling on the couch, he removed his glasses as the voice of the man he loved filled the living room.

"Cyrus, I'm so sorry to hurt you, but I've come to realize that we have too many differences between us. It's better for me to leave now, rather than wait any longer and drag it out. We've had a great relationship and I still love you. This separation has been brewing for several months. In time, you'll come to realize that this is the proper decision. The fault is mutually shared. I care for you, but can't be with you. In a week or so, my lawyer will call and sort through the financial entanglements."

The hiss of the magnetic tape took the place of the sound of Matthias' melodious voice. His lover left no contact information behind, only his goodbye. Their relationship had lasted close to three years. Cyrus' heart had been ripped into tiny pieces. Absolutely nothing that he could do would change anything. He needed to get to the lab and immerse himself in his work.

CHAPTER FOUR

Whatever Happened to the Revolution?

Oakland, California, August 14, 1968

George Taylor owned a three-bedroom home in the Fremont section of Oakland. A good pal and business associate of Dan's traveling companions, their commercial alliance included the sale and distribution of illegal weapons and various pharmaceuticals.

A fascinating assortment of individuals entered George's portals. A melting pot of miscreants and outlaws, his customer base existed just beyond the fringes of society. Well-adjusted to living outside the law, these people exulted in their ruthless reputations.

The clientele consisted of motorcycle gang members, violent revolutionaries, and hardcore criminal types. With highly questionable pasts and little in the way of optimistic futures, George's customers rolled in and out. A sizable number had spent time in prison or drug rehab facilities and probably well on their way to returning.

So far, Dan's introduction to the "left coast" had been underwhelming. The answer to his problems couldn't have been more obvious. Why not experiment with psychedelics, and see what degree of emotional impairment he might create for himself?

Locating the proper medicinal aids couldn't have been simpler. George's arsenal contained a veritable smorgasbord of mind-altering drugs. His hospitality knew no bounds and at a deeply discounted price, supplied his guest with the latest batch of Owsley's "White Lightning."

Holy cow! Dan couldn't believe all he'd missed while out of circulation. Smoking a joint or two had been an experience he'd thoroughly enjoyed, but that high lasted only a couple of hours. Dropping a tab of acid would give you a twelve-hour slice of psychedelic wonderment. "Tripping" had a more pronounced effect. Once the chemicals entered the bloodstream, any inhibitions melted away. The soul crossed over into an unexplored universe.

He and George sat on the concrete steps in the backyard. "Hey, Danny boy," his host sang out. "Tell me about Ben growing up in Brooklyn. How crazy did he act back then?"

Dan laughed. "I don't know, how crazy is he now?"

"Pretty nuts," George avowed. "Can I ask you something else?"

"Sure, go ahead." Dan noticed a small flock of birds flying by overhead.

George poked him. "Hey, pay attention, man! Did you hang with him when he waited for girls outside the Women's House of Detention in Greenwich Village?"

"What? No. I must have missed that one." Dan's lips felt numb. The effects of the LSD had definitely kicked in.

"Really?" George sounded disillusioned. "Too bad. Ben clued me in. He told me that he figured it would be an easy way to get laid. The chicks getting released would be so horny, he'd just have to say hello and wham! He'd be home free."

Dan cracked up. "Glad I missed it. I must have been in the Army. That plan doesn't sound like much of a plan. I don't think girls are that easy. Besides, how can you trust them? They're inside for a reason. So, tell me. What happened? Did his plan work?"

George laughed. "I think one almost took his nuts off. She robbed him."

"You see. "Dan felt a huge surge of energy. The LSD rushed through him.

August 21

Unfortunately, drugs have side effects. Once the acid's mind-altering powers fade, brain fog sets in. The expense for each psychedelic journey is the bending and twisting of the serotonergic neurons and elimination of a goodly amount of frontal lobe brain cells. With a pool of a hundred billion or so available, Dan figured he could stand to lose a few million and still be okay. Wrong!

Under the magic spell of LSD, Dan's mind filled with a color spectrum of rainbow insanities that included cyclical illusionary visions of hysteria and euphoria. Only a tiny stepping stone in the introduction to the Timothy Leary school of chemically induced paradise and the start of his climb upward, or so he thought.

The next phase in Dan's re-education: the rental of a modestly furnished one-bedroom apartment on Dwight Way, just off Telegraph Avenue, in Berkeley. With their meager supply of clothing and toiletries stashed in the trunk, George dropped his three freeloaders off.

As the new apartment dwellers unpacked, Ben pulled down the oven's silver door and laid a black pistol on the top shelf.

Dan freaked. "What the hell is wrong with you? What are you gonna do with that thing?"

"Don't worry about it. The safety's on. Besides, it's only a twenty-two," Ben teased, snapping the door shut. "We'll need it for protection against break-ins. There's a lot of sick people out there."

Dan didn't agree. What if his friend knew something he didn't?

Firing a weapon no longer figured as a line item on Dan's to-do list. No more gun-toting for this fellow, he'd promised himself. The army had taught him target detection and taught him to hit a bull's eye at a hundred meters. More importantly, his military service taught him the true value and sanctity of human life. Never again would he take part in any acts of violence or physical aggression. There would never be the need to grip an instrument of destruction and discharge a round.

August 23

Thus far, Dan's return to society hadn't worked out the way he'd envisioned. While overseas, "The Summer of Love" had transitioned to autumn. The heat and promise of last year's optimism suffered defeat at the hands of the frosty winter of cynicism and enmity. He decided to stay positive, certain that the good times still existed. He needed to find them.

As he and his two roommates stood against Pepe's Pizza's plate glass window munching on their slices, their eyes focused on the action along Telegraph. Not quite as populous as the streets of New York City, plenty of warm bodies filled the streets. The last of their lunch went down and he and his two buddies joined the foot traffic.

Dan noted a good number of young folks moving along the sidewalks. A murky atmosphere of desperation surrounded a number of them. The rich and powerful would probably categorize these Berkeley residents as the dregs of society. People dressed in business attire walked at a faster pace, scurrying in and out of the crowd. Occasionally, a smiling "flower child" would throw out a peace sign.

Dan dropped a quarter into a beggar's cup. He felt betrayed. He'd expected much more in this bastion of social change and enlightenment. Whatever happened to the revolution?

They entered the grounds of the University of Berkeley campus. Pedestrians filled the concrete footpaths. Dozens of people sat on the lawns surrounding them, just kicking back, taking in the sun. Others sat in small groups, enjoying conversations. Suddenly, Bill stopped and gently grabbed hold of Dan's arm.

"Guys, hold up a minute." He pointed at a group leaning back against a huge tree trunk. "I see someone I know."

Bill steered them over. "Hey, Dan, this is Mary. Her old man plays sax with The Sensational Satisfactions. I told you about him.

Bill gave her a tiny kiss on the cheek. "Hey, girl," he purred, "how you doing?"

Mary beamed. "Great. It's good to see you. Why don't you guys grab yourself a piece of turf and hang out?" She patted the grass next to her.

Dan flopped down with his friends. Someone passed Dan a joint. A bit paranoid, he checked around him before taking a short hit. He exhaled and passed the joint over to Ben.

Dan looked over at the guy who handed him the doobie. "This stuff is smooth, man. Thanks"

He extended his hand. "I'm Dan. How you doing.'"

"I'm Sal. Yeah, good meeting you."

Sal frowned, noticing the military footwear. "What the hell is that? Jungle boots? Are you nuts?"

Dan never thought much of it. He wore them as a badge of honor. "Yeah. I just got back from 'Nam last month."

Sal shrugged. "That's just great." His voice elevated. "Hey people, we got us one of them certified baby killers, right here."

He turned his full attention to the ex-vet. "Did you have fun over there? How many people did you get to kill?"

Sal stood up and waved his arms, looking to draw attention. "Another of LBJ's psycho killers. Check him out."

Crouching down, Sal pointed at his target. "What are you doing around here? You working for the government? Don't bullshit me! You probably are. Why don't you take a hike?"

What's this guy's problem? Dan held himself back, knowing violence should never be the answer. His generation wanted to find its way to a better society and he planned on being part of it. He carried around guilt for his military service but had no reason to apologize for it. "Sal, get off my case. They drafted me, man. I didn't have a choice. I hated the fucking army. I want to make love, not war, man."

Sal cracked a tiny grin. "Okay. I can understand that. Forget it. I don't mean to get on your case, but there's a lot of crazy stuff going down. Yeah, a bunch of bad shit, man. The pigs keep busting heads."

Sal lit up another joint and handed it to him. "No hard feelings, man. Things are cool. Besides, I wouldn't want you to go psycho on me."

Dan tried not to overreact. "That's funny. Hey, no problem, bro, just water running off my back." He swiped at his left shoulder to illustrate the point. "Ain't no big thing."

But, it happened to be a big deal. So far, nothing had gone according to plan. He'd been in California two weeks and still trying to gain a foothold.

Dan tried to block out Sal's ribbing. He concentrated on the dozens of people moving along the concrete walkways. He found amusement in the fact that each person, though part of one society, inhabited his or her own separate world, oblivious to the others.

The sound of Sal's annoying voice intruded on Dan's meanderings. "Hey, Bill, did your friend ever trip? He looks kinda lame to me."

Dan had taken enough of this guy's crap. "Hey, Sal, I'm sitting right here, man. If you got anything to say, talk to me. I'm trying to stay cool, but I think you and I are about to have a problem."

Sal hopped up. "You're the one with the problem, dude, just another tool of the establishment. What are you gonna do, smack me? Go ahead. Hit me."

Dan stood nose to nose with his tormentor. "Fuck you, scumbag!"

Ben jumped in between them. "Be cool, guys." He pushed Dan back down. "Sal, you're messed up, man. This dude happens to be good people."

Sal shook his head. "Okay, fuck it. Your pal is still lame. He doesn't know shit from Shinola."

Dan glared. "Maybe I don't know what's going on, but I know when someone's an asshole."

"Fuck off, dick!" Sal spun away and headed toward a pair of young women sitting several yards away.

Sal happened to be right in one respect. Dan had tripped only a few times and had no expertise with hallucinogens. For his opinion to count, he needed to gain people's trust. If doing more drugs could create such acceptance, so be it. He'd concentrate his energies on converting himself into a psychedelic warrior.

August 25th

Dan gawked as Todd's tenor saxophone shapeshifted into a large loaf of Italian bread, then, seconds later altered into a duck-billed platypus, snout side up. Crazy! The Sensational Satisfactions rocked it, but he couldn't move, transfixed to the spot. The two trumpets and Todd's saxophone seemed to possess a gravitational field all their own. Pulled into their orbit, Dan's body fought the magnetic attraction. Even with his feet planted on the dance floor, he feared that one of the horns might suck him up onto the stage and pull him inside its bell. Flailing his arms and legs to the beat of the music, he danced away, and out of range.

The "Satisfactions" had opened the show at the Avalon Ballroom, an old building in the Polk Gulch section of San Francisco. Dan and his buddies dropped tabs of blotter acid before they squeezed into the band's psychedelically festooned bus. Serving as roadies, the three helped the group set up the equipment. He'd lost track of his friends earlier. Right now, his thought patterns and pictorial visualizations defied rational explanation.

As he boogied about with his inhibitions stripped away, he watched with curiosity as dozens of other dancers squirmed around him, rotating their limbs at varying speeds and angles. The pungent aroma of marijuana smoke filled the air. A braless girl with long brown hair and oversized breasts danced into view.

Her boobs escaped the strongholds of her low-cut top and bounced around freely as she gyrated. Dan watched as she twisted her head left, then right, and spun around again and again. Her undulations struck a chord. His wigged-out brain registered fascination.

A sudden chill ran through him. His attitude shifted. Cringing in horror, he visualized that a huge-breasted serpent danced in the woman's place. In his chemically induced state, he watched the huge breasts grow into gigantic melons. Green palm trees suddenly filled the ballroom. "I'm in the Garden of Eden," Dan yelled out. No one paid attention.

Maneuvering away from the dance floor, he stepped onto the carpeting that bordered the crowded concession area. He saw Ben, sprawled out on the floor outside the entrance to the men's bathroom.

"Four score and seven years ago," Ben yelled, staring at his left palm.

He noticed Dan and pushed himself up to his feet. "Look at this. Crab cakes, crab cakes," he screamed, pointing a forefinger at his right hand.

Dan grabbed hold of his friend's shoulders and shook him. "What's going on? It's just your hand. You're all right."

He shoved his palm up to Dan's face. "Shit. Don't you see it? It's a crab. Watch out. The claws can rip your soul apart."

As stoned as they both were, he seemed to make perfect sense. Nothing mattered, but everything did. Dan moved his head in time to the music and lifted his arms, spinning away.

He found himself in the bathroom, gaping in the mirror at the image of a young man with wild eyes and an even wilder, multi-colored beard. After a few seconds, the features altered. The frightening image of a werewolf took his place.

Gazing into the enormous blue eyes, the face took on a frenzied expression. The image converted once again. The peace-loving Jesus emerged. With the man-eating lycanthrope departed, Dan's terror morphed into relief and hysterical laughter.

Had he experienced a remarkable or profound event? No, not quite. Like so many self-medicators, he'd transformed into another disoriented traveler, floating along on the river of surrealism.

*   *   *

One afternoon, his roomies showed up at the apartment with shiny new motorcycles. Dan paid the rent and footed most of the bills, and wondered where they found the cash to buy such expensive toys.

"My dad sent it to me," Ben explained. "I had a bunch of Series E-government bonds from my bar mitzvah. They matured, and he sent me the money Western Union."

The story sounded plausible enough and he let the matter slide. "That's cool. Do you guys want to go get some pizza? I'm hungry."

Ben shook his head. "No, that's okay. We're gonna go ride into Oakland and see George, show him our new bikes. We'll catch up with you later."

Dan walked downstairs with them and watched them as they each did a wheelie and rode off.

He headed to get a slice at Pepe's.

*   *   *

The doorbell rang. Figuring his friends had arrived back early, Dan pulled it open without checking.

Surprised, he found a stocky, dark-haired woman standing on the welcome mat. A pair of large guys flanked her. None of three looked happy. "Where the hell is Ben?" She demanded to know. "That asshole and his scumbag buddy ripped me off."

Dan swallowed hard. "You missed him. He and Bill took off on their motorcycles."

She laid her body weight against the partially opened door. Dan's shoulder ached from the pressure against it.

"Those dipshits stole my mescaline, and I don't give a fuck!" she shrieked. "Where the hell did they go? Don't you fucking lie to me."

Dan's stomach churned. "Look, I have nothing to do with those two. They just crash here. I don't know anything about your mescaline. They went for a ride. They didn't say when they'd be back."

She jabbed her fingers into Dan's cheek. "You better tell those two that I'm going to find them and get my money."

Dan felt queasy. "Yeah. I'll let them know."

"Okay. You tell them I'm coming back tonight. There better not be any excuses."

She backed away from the doorway. "Come on, let's go. This dumb schmuck doesn't know shit. The fucker's lucky we don't take it out on him."

Dan breathed easier. Her supposition made sense. He didn't know shit about her drugs and definitely didn't want to be home when she and her goons came back. He packed a bag and thumbed his way to El Cerrito. Fortunately, he had a 'Nam buddy who'd probably let him stay a few days.

*   *   *

As the sun dipped below the western horizon, Dan, tripping like a champ, found himself staring at the cruise ship docking at Pier 39. Attracted by the activity, he moved closer. He bumped a dude standing at the railing. The guy turned and took one look at him. "Hey! I can tell. You're tripping, right?"

Dan analyzed the speaker. He looked a couple of years older, several inches taller and had a muscular build. A huge grin spread across his rugged-looking face. He brushed back his long brown hair. Distracted by the sound of a boat cutting through the waters, Dan turned back toward the bay. He felt a tap on his shoulder.

"Hey, buddy, I'm talking to you. What kind of acid you take?"

With any filters rendered inactive by his medicinally enhanced state, Dan didn't hold back. "Owsley, man. I'm on my third tab. It's good shit, man. I'm so stoned."

The big guy nodded. "Uh-huh. Gotta be. Owsley's the best. Maybe, you have another hit?"

Dan dug in his jeans. He pulled out the last tab and handed the white pill to his new buddy.

"Thanks, man. Cheers." He laid the dose on his tongue and swallowed.

"I'm Harry." He offered his hand.

"Dan, from the Big Apple."

"Cool. I'm from Minnesota, just outside Minneapolis. I've been here for almost seven years."

The two leaned against the wooden railing and watched the passengers walk up the gangway.

Harry noticed Dan's jungle boots. "Vietnam? I respect that." He pointed toward the bay. "That's Alcatraz. I spent fourteen months locked up, right out there."

"No shit. What'd you do?"

"I got busted with a pound of weed. They convicted me of possession with intent to sell and gave me five years."

Dan tried to whistle, but no sound came out. "Shit. Five years? That's a long time. How'd you only serve fourteen months?"

Harry stared at Dan for a few seconds. He turned away and walked toward one of the tourist telescopes. "Come here. Check this out."

He dropped a quarter in the slot. "Just look through this. Believe me, the last place you want to end up is out there. It's hell on earth."

Dan looked through the dual eyepiece. He saw the small rock island. Dan lost focus and tracked a seagull through the telescope. The sound of Harry's voice brought him back to earth. "Can you imagine what it's like getting stuck out there, man?"

Dan's eyes found the prison again. "Wow, Harry, that place looks rough."

"Rough ain't the word, fucking awful's more like it. It's closed now. But no shit, Dan. You wouldn't want to be an eighteen-year-old stuck inside that rock, with hardcore criminals all around you. They're just looking for their chance to fuck you over."

"I can only imagine how bad you had it. I know it's not the same. But, serving in Vietnam felt like being in prison, except people kept shooting at me."

Harry didn't laugh. He gave Dan a hard look and turned back toward the bay. He let out a moan. "You know I love standing here."

He took in another deep breath. "I love that salt smell, don't you?"

Dan looked up at the sinking sun. A gust of air off the water pushed against his face. "Yeah man, the air smells fresh and clean."

A smile broke across Harry's face. "You know, Dan, I'm a lucky guy. Things could be way worse for me."

"Yeah, I guess."

Harry turned and strolled along the railing. He walked back toward Dan, but stopping abruptly and turned. He stared out at the bay waters. Digging his hand into the back pocket of his jeans, he pulled out a wallet. "Dan, I want to show you something."

Harry extracted a small color photo and handed it to him. The picture of a small boy with short platinum blonde hair looked up at Dan.

"That's my kid."

"Wow! He's cute." Dan handed back the picture.

"Yeah, thanks. I knocked up my girlfriend during my senior year. I dropped out and got a job stocking shelves in a grocery store. We got married, but it didn't work out. Her parents hated me. They got a judge to annul the marriage before she had the kid."

Harry looked out at the water again and sighed. "They still live in Minnesota. My son's eight now. His mother's remarried and I don't get to see him at all. That rips me up inside."

He rubbed his shirtsleeve against his eyes. "I gave up my rights as a father when they locked me up. I figured the kid would be better off without me."

Dan had known Harry for only the better part of an hour, and he really felt for the guy. The dude had been divorced, spent time in prison, and given up his kid. Boy, he'd had it rough!

"Wow, Harry, that sucks the big one."

"Yeah, I know. Listen, I told you I spent time in prison, right? Well, I'm lucky that I'm still alive. I don't talk about it much, but I need to share it with somebody."

He locked eyes with Dan. "You want to know the reason why they let me out early?"

"Uh-huh, sure."

"Okay. I'll tell you. I saw two gang-bangers shank a dude in the shower. Their victim started screaming bloody murder, and the guards showed up quick. The guy ended up dying. The killers knew I saw the whole thing. I told them I'd keep my mouth shut, but I knew they'd ice me next. It scared the shit out of me. I didn't know what the hell to do."

Harry drew in a deep breath. "It's not too easy to talk about." He turned and looked out across the water.

"That's a crazy fucking story, Harry. What ended up happening?"

Harry swiveled back around. "You know how I got my sentence shortened?"

Dan shook his head. "No. How?"

"I became a rat and testified against them. The warden wanted to nail them and promised me an early release. So, I did it. What other choice did I have? I knew I'd end up with my throat slit, otherwise."

"You did the right thing. Whatever those guys got, they deserved."

The two rambled on. They left the wharf and headed west.

* * *

With the drug coursing through them, the pair lost any concept of time and unmindful of their location.

Dan noticed the sky beginning to brighten and the sun peeking over the horizon. "Harry, I'm beat. I need to get some sleep. What are you going to do?"

"I don't know. I have nothing happening. Is it okay if I tag along?"

Dan hadn't been back to his apartment for a week. This would be a good time to reclaim it. His friend's size filled him with confidence. "Sure thing. Let's figure out where we are." He pointed to the street signs at the corner of the block. "Bay Street and Columbus."

Harry laughed. "Holy crap. We're almost right back where we started."

Though their feet covered close to ten miles, they'd circled around and now stood less than half-a-mile from the wharf.

"That's crazy, man." Dan stepped off the curb and stuck out a thumb. "How about we hitch a ride over the bridge?"

"Right on, man!" Harry hopped onto the asphalt surface and waved his thumb.

They didn't wait long. Within several minutes, a tan Lincoln Continental pulled up. The passenger window slid down and a voice called out. "Where you fellows heading?"

"We're trying to get to Berkeley," Dan answered. "You going across the bridge?"

The power door locks popped open.

"That's perfect. Hop in. I'll be glad to drop you off. One of you can climb in the front."

Harry slid into the back. Dan pulled open the front door. A stack of black books sat on the front seat.

The driver pulled several of the thick books closer to him. "That's okay, son. Just stack the rest on the floor."

He wore a wrinkled gray suit and white shirt. His black tie hung loosely around his neck. An elastic band held together his red ponytail. Dan guessed his age as late thirties or early forties. "Sure thing, sir. Thank you for stopping."

The gold print on the book covers advertised The New Testament. Dan stacked them carefully between his feet.

In the back, Harry, a bit rougher, pushed the Bibles out of his way and laid back.

"I'm delivering the books to the church," the driver explained.

The hairs on Dan's neck raised. "Are you a minister, sir?"

"Yes, a pastor. But, you call me Brother Jim, not sir. And what about you two gentlemen?"

"I'm Dan. That's Harry in the back, but no one confuses us with gentlemen." He thought better of his remark. "Sorry, Brother Jim. I didn't mean to sound like a wise guy."

"Oh, no need to apologize." The sound of his voice immediately put his passenger at ease.

The events of the last few weeks had given Dan reason to question his concept of Godliness. The presence of this man of God brought significant thoughts to the surface. He realized how blasphemous he'd been acting since coming home. The LSD had affected his rational thinking. He felt the interior void waiting to be filled.

As the car stopped for a red light, the pastor turned toward him. "I've noticed that you seem conflicted, my son. Can I be of assistance?" His manner and words felt reassuring.

Dan fought off tears. "Yes, Brother Jim. I'm confused. I came home from Vietnam last month and I'm lost."

The traffic light changed. Brother Jim guided the car across the intersection and pulled over to the curb. He shifted into park.

"What you're experiencing is nothing new, Daniel. Confusion has ruled the world since the days of Adam and Eve. Life can be a beautiful journey or one filled with unhappiness. It's your choice. Allow no hate into your heart. Remember, God is always with you. Once you accept that, living will be joyful."

His words made sense to Dan. "I know you may think I'm foolish, but I believe that God protected me in Vietnam. Having the opportunity to be away from society helped me understand the unrest taking place in America. So many people are traveling down the wrong road. I know I'm meant to do good things, to help my generation, but, I need to find my own path first."

Brother Jim placed his hand on the neophyte's shoulder. "You're a good man, my friend. I have a story I'd like to share with you."

Daniel shifted around to check on Harry, oddly silent for the last several minutes. His head rested against the side window, with eyes shut. Dan smiled and twisted back around.

The pastor turned on the fan. "I grew up in Chicago. It's a good place, but things can get rough."

Dan shook his head. "I'm from New York. I know how big cities can be."

The pastor winked. "Anyway, one Saturday afternoon about ten years ago, a group of teenagers walking through a public playground, stumbled across a derelict. He was fast asleep, his body balanced precariously on a damaged wooden bench. The group stopped in front of him.

"'Hey guys, will you look at that,' the largest one shouted, pointing to the spout of the whiskey bottle protruding from the side pocket of the slumbering man's green fatigue jacket.

"'Just watch this,' the big guy snarled as he inched closer to the gnarled wood.

"The three others watched him.

"'Hey, Rick, what you gonna do?' One of them asked

"The big guy gave him an elbow in the ribs. 'You just watch and learn, Bobby.'

"Rick reached across the sleeper and removed the container of booze from his pocket. He unscrewed the cap. Placing a foot on the end of the bench for balance, he pulled down his fly and aimed the stream into the pint bottle's narrow opening. He shook the mixture. Replacing the cap, he slipped the flask back into the fatigue jacket."

The pastor took a breath and before continuing his story. "'Get the hell up, asshole,' Rick yelled, poking a foot into his ribs.

"As the vagrant stirred, the four young men moved away from the bench. The drunk dug into his pocket and pulled out his liquid stash. Twisting off the cap, he took a big swig from it. As the blend of tart, acidic liquid, and tepid booze hit his taste buds, the disgusting truth found its way into the booze-filled brain. He coughed out most of the mouthful.

"'You're assholes,' he screamed. 'Leave me the hell alone.'

"Unsteadily, he pushed himself up to his feet and tried to grab hold of any one of the bullies. They easily avoided him.

"Losing his balance and lurching forward, the drunk went sprawling, landing face-first on the concrete. His right cheek scraped against the uneven pavement, reopening an old scab. Blood began to drip, trickling down his face and into his scraggly beard. The rest of the contents of his whiskey bottle spilled out on his jacket, adding its contribution to the filthy fabric.

"The four thugs, no longer amused by the plight of the destitute tramp, double-timed it through the playground gate.

"The drunk sat up. 'It's not fair. It's not fair,' he repeated, over and over.

"Tears ran down his face. Using a dirt-encrusted rag, he dabbed at the wound. Hopelessness and utter desperation filled him. He questioned how he could have allowed himself to sink to this lowest of levels."

Brother Jim looked deeply into Dan's eyes. "So, what do you think?"

"Wow. What schmucks."

The pastor chuckled. "Do you know why I told you that story?"

Dan thought about it for a few seconds. "I bet you're gonna tell me that you're one of those guys?"

"No," he chided. "That poor soul, that pitiful outcast was me. Forlorn, and totally lost, I had little hope and no belief in any future. That day changed it for me. God's message finally came through clearly. He spun me around and lifted me. I felt His love and understood His word."

"How did you get that way in the first place?" Dan asked, caught up the story. "What made you drink so much?"

Jim sighed. "Hold your horses. I'm getting to that."

He slouched down and seemed to relax. "I majored in journalism at the University of Kansas. After graduation, my dad put up the money, and a friend and I created a monthly sports periodical. We called it *The Wichita Whistler*. It went from nothing to a subscription base of seven thousand within our first year. We banked a half-million dollars in advertising by our third year. Our paid subscriptions grew to twenty-five thousand. That's when trouble came along. A large East Coast newspaper offered to buy us out. We refused.

"That turned out to be a huge mistake. They sued us over a bogus copyright infringement issue. Our lawyer had us file a countersuit, but, in the end, deep pockets won out. Our company folded. The judge awarded the plaintiffs damages, including the use of our paper's name. I had to file for personal bankruptcy and move back home with my parents. That's when I began drinking. My family tried to help, but they eventually gave up. I moved out and started living in my car in a Wal-Mart parking lot. When the bank repossessed it, I slept in the street. When it became too cold, I spent the nights in homeless shelters."

The preacher stopped and wiped his mouth.

His pause gave Dan an opportunity to comment. "My God, that's awful, Jim. That must have sucked. How did you live like that?"

"Almost two years. That day in the park changed my life."

"Wow! That's a long time to be living the street life."

Dan wondered how the pastor could have gone "cold turkey" and put a stop to the vicious cycle. "What happened next?"

"My young friend, I'm lucky that my family still cared about me, even after the grief I'd caused them. My parents gave me a second chance and paid for a rehab clinic. This time it worked. I'm more than nine years sober."

"Wow, Jim, that story is truly amazing. What happened after rehab?"

"I went to work for my dad. He owned a limousine and truck-rental service. I became a dispatcher, eventually, a minor partner.

In fact, this Lincoln is one of the company's cars. It's recycled, two and a half years young with only sixty-eight thousand miles on the odometer."

Dan's head ached. Could this guy truly be a pastor? Too many dots still needed connecting. "How did you become a man of religion?"

"It's a relatively simple scenario. Four years ago, my father passed away and left the business to my brother and me. I sold him my interest and moved out of Chicago. I moved to the Bay area. It's been almost two years since my wife and I opened the ministry in Berkeley. It happened after we went on a vacation to Oregon. That's when we decided to make the change."

"What motivated you?" Dan asked.

"I'm getting to it. You see, Alice and I decided to camp out in the Rogue River Canyon. We survived an up-close and personal meeting with a three-hundred-pound black bear. It ate most of our supplies and scared the bejeezus out of us, but he left our camp and went back into the woods. Right then, Alice and I understood what we needed to do. We wanted to make a difference and add true meaning to our lives. Within two months, we created The Ministry of Collective Harmony and Spiritual Balance and put some money down on a small piece of property on Shattuck Avenue, in Berkeley."

Dan felt the minister's strength. "Your story is incredible. I'm so happy that you picked me up."

The pastor nodded. "I don't believe in chance, Daniel. God arranged our meeting. The good Lord brought us together for a reason."

Jim laid a hand on his shoulder. "It's up to you. You're a co-creator. Along with the Almighty, we'll mold our destiny. We've both been to the valley and climbed out from it. There's a mountain of happiness and prosperity awaiting both of us. We can scale the peak together."

Dan's sleep-deprived mind couldn't grasp the rudiments at the moment, but the seeds were sown, and moisture added to the soil. The pastor started the car and maneuvered the Lincoln back onto Market Street. His passenger's eyes slowly closed. Dan fell asleep before they exited the Bay Bridge.

*   *   *

Dan's eyes popped open as the car came to a stop. Yawning, he stretched his arms and legs.

Brother Jim tapped him on the knee. "We're at your place."

"Thank you. I appreciate the ride."

"It's my pleasure. Don't forget, if you ever need a place to crash, call me. Here's my card."

"Thank you. That's nice of you, but I got my own place."

"That's fine. Then, make sure you come and visit."

"I'll try."

Dan leaned over the seatback and shook his friend. "Harry, come on, get up."

Harry rubbed his face and sat up. "Where are we?"

"My place. Get up. You can crash out upstairs."

The big Lincoln pulled away.

Harry looked up at the four-story apartment building. "What floor do you live on?"

"Why? You afraid of heights, big dude?"

"That's funny. I'm just curious."

Both men, still not fully recovered from their acid trips, plodded through the lobby. The Otis elevator had seen better days. The lumbering motor protested loudly as the traction cables delivered the car to the lobby.

Inching its way up, the car made it to the third floor. The heavy metal door slowly slid open.

"Okay, this is it, Harry. Just follow me. I'm in 3B."

Dan's feet skidded to a stop. Strips of yellow crime scene tape blocked the door to the apartment. "Oh, shit. What the hell is this, Harry?"

"You tell me, brother, but this is not good. Maybe, one of the people on your floor knows what happened."

Mr. Keegan, the talkative old guy in 3G, loved the opportunity to divulge whatever he knew. "I heard that two people got shot." His mouth twisted into a sneer, revealing his missing front teeth. "I'd gone out shopping. When I came home, I saw the ambulances pulling away."

Dan felt faint. "What happened to the two guys who live with me? Do you know what happened to them?"

Mr. Keegan loved a captive audience. He cleared his throat and leaned on his cane. "The building superintendent told me that the stupid looking one with the big nose and New York accent got stabbed a couple of times, but he'll live. He's the shooter. I don't know if anyone got killed. The other one, Cochise, he got away down the fire escape. The police are looking for him. Both of them are in a heap-a-trouble."

Dan had heard enough. He pulled out Jim's business card and read the address on the bottom. Time to get out of Dodge.

CHAPTER FIVE

The Formula for Success

Sandy Springs, GA,
Monday, February 27, 1984, 06:43 P.M.

"*Brinng, brinng.*" Cyrus placed his coffee cup on the kitchen table and lifted the telephone's handset from the wall. "Hello. This is Cyrus."

"Please hold for Malcolm Hirsch," the curt female voice ordered.

He slid over to the large picture window and gazed at the reflection of the setting sun on the Chattahoochee. The waters rippled past a barrier of rocks as they flowed southward on their way to Florida, and ultimately spilling into the Gulf of Mexico.

The scientist loved his piece of property. The river bank began only a scant fifty feet from the back door and the sight of the wild ducks and Canadian geese always put a smile on his face. When life's trials and tribulations took their toll, he could sit on the back deck and enjoy the "Hooch's" cycle of life.

His numinous moment of reverie ended when the voice on the other end of Alexander Bell's ingenious invention intervened.

"Good day, Doctor Markum. This is Malcolm Hirsch. I'm an attorney. I'm calling from San Francisco on behalf of Matthias Desjardins' estate. Did I catch you at an inconvenient time?"

"No, it's fine. I just finished dinner. Why are you calling, Mr. Hirsch? Is Matthias okay?"

"No, unfortunately. I'm sorry to say, he's not."

Cyrus hadn't spoken to Matthias for several months. Their last contact had been the exchange of Christmas cards in December. After their acrimonious parting years earlier, the former lovers had ironed out their differences and carried on a platonic long-distance friendship.

Matthias, having admitted the truth several years earlier, fessing up that a younger man, Antonio Vargas, had been the mitigating factor in the dissolution of their former partnership. The tendrils of pain created by his lover's treachery had time to untwine over the years.

"Doctor Markum, have you been listening?"

"Yes, Mr. Hirsch. Excuse me. Please, tell me, what happened?"

"Err... I'm sorry to be the bearer of bad tidings. Mr. Desjardins passed away on the twenty-third of February."

Cyrus collapsed on a chair. Thoughts of Matthias swirled in his head. Unable to ever fill the emptiness in his heart, the memories of the man that once shared his life lingered. Images of his only love snuck into his dreams occasionally and this dreadful news cut to the quick. He caught sight of the calendar mounted to the right of the clock. He repeated aloud the day and date of his death: "Thursday, the twenty-third."

"Doctor Markum, are you speaking to me? I know this must come as a shock."

"That's an enormous understatement, Mr. Hirsch. But what does his passing have to do with me?"

"That's an excellent question. I'm the executor of Mr. Desjardins' estate. My call is meant to alert you that you're a major devisee in his last will and testament."

Cyrus rattled his cup on the tabletop. "Really?"

"Yes, Doctor Markum. You'll need to clear your schedule. It's in your best interest to attend the unsealing. That will be in my office on Thursday morning of next week. Expenses for your visit will be prepaid. You'll also be reimbursed for any unexpected costs. Just save any receipts."

Cyrus stood up and paced around the room. "What? Why did he name me?"

"That I can't answer. Suffice it to say, you're the recipient of a sizable inheritance. Mr. Desjardins happened to be quite a successful entrepreneur. The net worth of his estate is valued at more than one hundred million dollars."

Money didn't mean that much to a man of science. Cyrus thought back to earlier times when he and Matthias shared their love. Happiness abounded in those days. Now, the thoughts of his former lover's death wrenched his heart apart for the second time.

"Your news is disturbing, Mr. Hirsch. How did he meet his demise? Was it an accident of some sort?"

"I'm sorry, Doctor Markum, but I'm not privileged to share that information. There's no need to trouble yourself with the details. All will be explained in time."

Cyrus found his answer odd but didn't press further.

"I'll see you in person in a few days. Please hold for my law clerk, Jennifer. She will relay the particulars."

A clicking sound punctuated the dialog. The unmistakable sound of Tony Bennett's highly distinguishable voice followed. "I Left My Heart in San Francisco" came through the tiny speaker pressed against Cyrus' ear. If he wasn't so upset, he would've snickered at the ironic choice of music on hold. After several seconds, a woman's voice swapped places with Tony's.

"Hello, Doctor Markum? This is Jennifer Stanton. I have taken the liberty of arranging accommodations for you at the Omni Hotel. It's in the heart of the financial district and the most exclusive in San Francisco. You'll be only a block from our offices. The hotel is also within walking distance of the bay. I'll book your flight and have a limo meet you at the airport. Wednesday, March 7th through Sunday, March 11th, will that be suitable?"

March 7

The hands on the clock in the San Francisco air terminal showed half past noon. With today being Wednesday, Cyrus' analytically programmed mind calculated that thirty minutes had passed since the precise instant of midweek. An insignificant detail for most people, but he preferred to stay mindful of his immediate reality.

As he followed the arrows that pointed the way to "Exit and Ground Transportation," two chanting young men with shaved heads danced into his line of sight. Clothed in the traditional Hare Krishna orange outfits, one tapped on a small drum. The other clanged on small finger cymbals, a pair in each hand. They moved energetically and looked to be truly enjoying themselves as they sang.

He felt envy for the religious minstrels. How could they be so happy when grief filled him? With thoughts of Matthias vividly imprinted in his mind, the carefree cheerfulness of Lord Krishna's disciples served only as a painful reminder of happier times.

With the sound of music fading in his ears, Cyrus found the area designated for limo drivers. Several men waited there. Each held up a placard. One, an African-American male, about six feet tall and dressed in a dark gray chauffeur's uniform with matching cap, supported a white piece of cardboard with Dr. Markum's name scribbled on it in black marker.

Cyrus raised his hand. "Hello, I'm Doctor Markum."

He placed his small red Samsonite suitcase on the floor and shook hands with the driver.

"Welcome to San Francisco, Doctor. Did you have a good flight?"

"Yes, I did. Tiring, but okay."

"My name is Omar. We'll be heading to your hotel now, if that's okay with you, sir?"

"That's perfect, Omar. I'd like the time to relax and unwind."

The driver picked up his client's bag and pointed toward the exit.

As the tan Lincoln Town Car pulled into traffic, Omar looked up at his passenger's reflection in the rearview mirror. "It's awful about Matthias. I've worked for Mr. Desjardins for almost three years now. I understand that you two shared a close relationship at one time."

"Yes, that's true. The two of us had a good friendship." Cyrus sighed and gazed out the window. "Ah yes, we did have great times together." He sighed as the past snuck up on him once more.

He felt a bit at a loss. Omar had intimated that he might know of the romantic nature of their bond.

The doctor leaned forward. "His death troubles me deeply, Omar. I've always cared for him and I'm saddened by his passing."

"Such a tragedy, sir, even though we expected it."

Cyrus saw his opportunity to probe more deeply. "What do you mean expected? What medical condition did he have? You would think, with all his money, he could get the proper care?"

"Those are good questions, sir. The doctors argued over the diagnosis. The top specialists examined him, but no matter what they tried, he grew worse. They thought he had bone cancer and complications of pneumonia caused his death. The people closest to him doubted that. They figured it had to be something different."

Omar must have sensed he'd revealed too much. "But, I thought you knew this? Please don't let Mr. Hirsch know I said anything."

Omar turned up the volume on the radio. The interior of the car filled with the refrains of Frankie Goes to Hollywood. The singer repeatedly hollered his advice about learning to relax. Cyrus leaned back in his seat and paid little attention to the pleading, reflecting instead on Omar's words.

The talkative driver disclosed a number of interesting facts. What could this indefinable and mysterious ailment be? He had his suspicions but needed to test the limits of his own resourcefulness. Utilizing guile in conjunction with investigative skills would be essential. He'd need to establish a presumptive supposition, if for no other reason than to maintain a firm grip on his own sanity.

*　*　*

The seventeen-story Omni Hotel sat in the heart of downtown. Originally a bank and office building erected in 1926, it stood out as a San Francisco showpiece. The lavish 362-room hotel in the Nob Hill district, had been fashioned in Florentine Renaissance styling and dazzled both inside and out. The magnificent Italian marble lobby floors, luxurious hanging draperies, and Austrian produced crystal chandeliers, forewarned guests that they'd be contributing a substantial sum of money to the hotel's coffers.

Deftly navigated the vehicle, Omar guided the black stretch limo to the main entrance in less than thirty minutes.

"Please, Doctor, what I told you before, please keep it under your hat," Omar insisted, pulling the suitcase from the trunk. "I don't want to get fired,"

Cyrus understood his predicament. "Not a problem. My lips are sealed."

The driver looked relieved. "Thank you so much, sir. I owe you."

Cyrus followed him through the main entrance and into the huge lobby. While Omar engaged the hotel manager at the front desk, the first-time guest took the opportunity to admire the flamboyant fineries of the atrium.

Omar handed Cyrus the room key card. "We're all set, Doc."

"Okay, that's great. Thank you."

"Mr. Hirsch is having a dinner party in Matthias' honor tonight. I'll be back to pick you up at seven-thirty. That's okay with you?"

"Sure, that'll be fine." Cyrus checked his watch.

"Very good, sir. You'll be dining at the Fior d'Italia on Mason Street. The food is delicious. Don't eat too big a lunch. You gotta leave room for dessert. I promise you won't be sorry. You can sign for whatever you like at the hotel. Just have them bill it to your room."

"I got it, Omar. Seven-thirty."

"Yes, sir, see you then." Omar tipped his cap and turned toward the exit.

One of the bellmen hustled over and picked up the piece of luggage. "Right this way, sir." He led his guest to the elevator.

As it began to climb, the worker glanced at Cyrus and grinned. "My name is James, sir. If there's anything that you need, anything at all, just let me know."

Cyrus didn't answer immediately. He had an idea. Why couldn't he pay a visit to Precious Pattie's Winery? Maybe the bellman could help arrange it.

"I *can* use your help, James. I'd like to rent an automobile. Do you have any suggestions?"

"That's an easy one, sir. My brother is an assistant manager for Hertz. I'll call over there. You can give him your information over the phone. He'll have a car brought to the hotel. I'll just photocopy your license and you can sign the paperwork once he arrives."

The doctor smiled. "Fantastic, James, but speed is of the utmost importance."

"No problem, sir," he said with confidence. "Speed is my specialty."

The elevator door opened. He followed the bellman.

"Here we are, sir, room 437." James slid his passkey into the electronic door lock and switched on the foyer light.

Cyrus noted the spacious interior. James laid the suitcase on the luggage rack and pulled the cord on the red blackout curtains. The sunlight came flooding in.

"I'll call my brother right now. I'll have your car here within fifteen minutes."

Cyrus looked at his watch again: almost two. "That would be fantastic."

He had a bit more than five hours until Omar would return. At this time of the day, the ride to Livermore should take less than an hour in each direction. He should have enough time.

Within forty-five minutes, he noticed the sign showing Interstate 580, as he cruised through Alameda County. Determined, but grappling with a large measure of uncertainty, he wondered what he'd discover. Rumblings that a fatal disease had taken direct aim at the gay communities of both New York and San Francisco currently circulated in the medical community. He hoped to unravel the mystery of his former lover's death.

*   *   *

At the time of Jonesy's retirement, Precious Pattie's vineyards encompassed forty-two acres. Under Matthias' watchful eye, the winery had purchased adjacent properties and developed several hybrid grape varieties. Now, quadruple in size, the once modest winery included two separate tasting rooms and a twenty-thousand-square-foot production and storage facility.

The winery's automated production techniques served as a benchmark for the industry and the recipient of the special achievement award from The North American Viticulture Association for three years running. Cyrus gawked in amazement at how much things had changed since his last visit fifteen years earlier.

Maggie recognized him immediately. "Doctor Markum, I haven't seen you in a dog's age. How have you been?"

She looked quite different from when he'd last seen her. Thirty pounds heavier, her long brown hair was cut short and dyed blonde. She wore a light blue pantsuit, a hint of purple eyeshadow, a subdued application of rouge, and a touch too much red lipstick.

"Couldn't be better," he fibbed. "How about yourself?"

"It's been rough around here for the last few months. But I'm okay. It's so sad. Mr. Desjardins death came much too soon."

Maggie sniffled and grabbed a tissue from the box on her desk. She blew her nose and tossed the Kleenex into the bucket.

Cyrus waited for her to finish. "Even though we haven't seen each other in years, my love for him has never faded."

He thought back to that fateful day in the hills of Berkeley when he and Matthias first stared into each other's eyes. That seemed like a lifetime ago.

"Maggie, what about the funeral arrangements?"

"Oh, I thought you knew. The cremation took place last week. We're having the memorial service Saturday morning. His ashes will be spread over the lake behind the house, at the south end of the property." She grabbed another tissue. "That will be his final resting place. You're coming, of course."

Cyrus scratched his cheek. "Of course."

Maggie dropped the Kleenex in the trash. "The word around here is that you're going to be the new head honcho. You must be excited."

The doctor looked shocked. "Where on earth did you get that idea?"

Now, Maggie's turn came to be caught off-balance. "You're joking, right? Everyone knows that you're going to be the major shareholder."

"That's ridiculous. Nobody's told me anything. Why me? What about his boyfriend or his family in New Orleans?"

"I don't know the details, but that's the word along the grapevine."

She giggled at her play on words. It went over his head.

Cyrus struggled with her piece of news. "I know nothing about grape growing or winemaking, let alone running a business. I'm a man of science. I certainly have no interest in learning the practical aspects of winemaking!"

He needed to stop his complaining. Maggie didn't need to hear any of this. But, she'd opened the shutters of sensibility and allowed a torrent of light to break through. He'd drive to the estate and see if he might discover any details from Matthias' boyfriend.

*   *   *

56

Cyrus put the car in park. He found a stylized five-bedroom home built in the Spanish colonial style, with a statue standing at the center of a garden. To the left of the main house sat a two-story garage. Three white bay doors accommodated entry for vehicles.

He noticed a white van sitting beneath one of the open doors. The black print below the curtained double glass windows read Shining Light Home Hospice and Palliative Care. That seemed odd.

As he walked toward the residence, the screen door swung open and a young man carrying a medical bag, stepped halfway outside but stopped abruptly. He turned back toward the interior of the residence. A woman in nursing garb was visible standing just inside.

Neither party noticed Cyrus, who paused several yards from them and listened as the doctor provided instructions: "Please continue the morphine, ten-milligram every four hours. If Mr. Vargas shows any sign of discomfort, you can increase the dosage to fifteen. If that's insufficient and he's still uncomfortable, I'll have you boost it to twenty milligrams. Contact me first."

"Yes, I understand. I'll call you if there's any change," the nurse replied.

"If there are any further indications of dyspnea or chest distress," he added, "you may increase his oxygen intake from four liters to six."

Cyrus grasped the circumstances immediately. Why would Matthias' lover be sick? From what he ascertained from the conversation, death sounded imminent.

The MD stepped from the doorway. His symmetry suffered a slight hitch when he spied the unexpected gatecrasher. "Hello. Can I help you?"

"Yes. I'm Doctor Markum. I'm a friend of Mr. Desjardins and your patient." He'd stretched the truth a mite, but the statement served its purpose. "I'm here to see how Mr. Vargas is doing?"

"Ah, I see. I'm Doctor Goodman, the on-call physician. I'm here performing a routine check on the patient. What's your medical specialty? Are you here in a professional capacity?"

Cyrus waved a hand. "Oh, no, my expertise is in the field of molecular biology. I've traveled from Atlanta. My visit is purely of a personal nature. I happened to be good friends with the deceased and his partner, Antonio. From what I've overheard and with the van's markings, it seems Antonio's condition is terminal."

Doctor Goodman frowned. "Unfortunately, your observation is correct. I wish I could do more for him. There's no remedy for his malaise. He's receiving corticosteroids through his IV drip, but his condition has shown no improvement. Mr. Vargas probably has only days to live. Little is known about Kaposi's sarcoma and Pneumocystis pneumonia. There's no cure or course of treatment."

Dr. Goodman shook his head, upset that he could do nothing for his patient. He looked up at the passing clouds and sighed. "You can go in and see him."

"Thank you. I will."

The MD held open the screen door. "So nice to meet you. I'm sorry about your friends."

The two men shook hands. The physician walked to the garage and climbed into the passenger seat of the van. The engine turned over. Cyrus watched as the vehicle backed out.

"Come right this way," the young nurse instructed. "My name is Allison. If you have any questions, don't hesitate to ask."

"Ah, yes. I'm Doctor Markum. Thank you for your kindness."

Allison led Cyrus into a bedroom that presently served as a transitory infirmary. On the left side of the room, hung beige curtains covering the two large windows. No sun came in directly, but the reedy fabric permitted adequate lighting to filter through. A hospital bed sat perpendicular to the far wall. Its male occupant, lay trundled in a sheet. His upper shoulders, neck, and head jutted out from under the white fabric.

An oxygen mask concealed his nose and mouth. His right arm lay exposed, allowing the catheter to feed the vein in the pit of his elbow. A rolling metal cart with a canister secured to it, fed life-giving oxygen into the mask. Two IV bags hung from the top of the holder. Liquid slowly dripped into the clear tubing. Cardiac and blood pressure monitors sat on a wooden shelf just above the patient's head. Three thin wires ran from each of them and vanished beneath the sheet.

A bald nursing assistant sat next to the bed. Attired in green scrubs, his dark chocolate skin glistened. Black-framed glasses balanced on the bridge of his nose. A table lamp provided the illumination for the hardcover book that sat on his lap.

The attendant looked up. "The patient is resting peacefully, Allison."

"That's good, George. This is Doctor Markum. He's a friend of Mr. Vargas."

The attendant laid the book on the table next to him and stood. Cyrus offered his hand. "It's nice to meet you."

"Good to meet you too, Doctor. He checked his watch. It's time for me to get Mr. Vargas' vitals."

George slipped on latex gloves and walked around to the far side of the bed. He checked the oxygen and IV feeds of his comatose patient. Antonio's left shoulder twitched every few seconds. Even though the oxygen mask covered a good part of his face, purplish colored nodules were visible on the exposed areas of his face and neck. The patient looked noticeably gaunt.

Cyrus believed he understood the nature of the illness and, unfortunately for Matthias' lover, the evidence he sought. He scanned the room and took note of the two popular Andy Warhol prints hanging on the wall across from Antonio, the one on the left of the blond-haired Marilyn Monroe, the second, a likeness of the balding Chairman Mao.

An ebony avant-garde sculpture sat on the tan carpeting. Standing four feet in height, the piece featured a reedy man awkwardly balancing his derriere on a jagged rock. The fingers of his right hand cupped his chin, his facial features were captured in a wistful pose. *Yes, it's so true,* Cyrus mused. *Life can be confusing. Does anyone know the true meaning? Is there anything more than a scientific explanation for this earthly existence?*

* * *

He arrived at the hotel with forty minutes to spare. After showering, Cyrus donned a pair of khaki slacks and a beige dress shirt, then slipped on his brown "Members Only" jacket. Taking a last look at himself in the large bathroom mirror, he closed the light. As the elevator descended, he checked his watch: seven minutes to spare. He stepped out from the compartment and onto the lobby's marble floor.

Omar, having arrived early, stood at the front desk joking with the clerk. He stopped when he saw Cyrus. "Good evening, Doc. You look mighty sharp tonight. Are you ready for some fine food?"

"Sure, but honestly, I could use a glass of wine." Cyrus tightened his lips, troubled that the remark might have seemed insensitive.

Omar, paying no notice, didn't miss a beat. "We'll be at the Fior d'Italia before you know it." He pulled open the rear door. "The restaurant's only five minutes away. We'll be early. Would you like me to cruise around a little?"

"Outstanding idea, Omar. Why don't you stop by Washington Square Park? It's on the way. I'd like to see the cathedral."

"You bet, Doc. Fasten your seat belt and ready yourself for takeoff." Omar winked at the rearview mirror.

The car pulled into traffic. Cyrus glimpsed his watch as the park came into view. He had fifteen minutes.

Omar parked in front of the church and came around to open the door. "Take your time, Doc. I'll be right here waiting."

"Thank you. I'll be back shortly."

The majesty of Saint Peter and Paul's Church rekindled fond memories of happier times. The twin steeples also reminded him of a less fortunate pair, one not constructed of concrete and steel, but fashioned from flesh, blood, and bone. Earthly constraints no longer bound Matthias. Poor Antonio lay in a medically induced stupor, and would soon join him.

Scientists, visceral pragmatists, and doubters of theologian philosophies disbelieved in an afterlife. If heaven is real, show us the hard evidence, they challenged. No one had yet come forward to assuage those doubts.

* * *

The limo pulled up to the entrance of the Fior d'Italia restaurant. Omar opened his passenger's door. "I'm not going in, Doc. I'll wait for you in the parking lot."

Cyrus stepped out on the sidewalk. Thanks, Omar. I'll see you a little later."

He pulled open the door and instantly greeted by the maître d.' "Good evening. How are you, sir?"

"I'm good, thanks. I'm here for Mr. Hirsch's party."

"Ah, yes. Please, right this way."

Ushered into a small room at the rear of the establishment, Cyrus found two middle-aged men and a young woman sitting around a rectangular wooden table. One of the men, bespectacled and balding with a thin black mustache, dropped several sheets of paper he'd been looking over.

He stood and extended his hand. "Ah, Doctor Markum. I'm Malcolm Hirsch. This is Jennifer Stanton. You spoke with her on the phone."

He gestured toward the other man at the table. "I'd like to introduce Bartholomew Sutton. He's a senior vice president with Wells Fargo Bank. He'll be handling the trusteeship and subsequent disbursement of funds."

The two men shook hands. Cyrus smiled at the young lady.

The attorney collected his papers and slid them into the brown attaché case resting near his feet. He pointed to one of the chairs. "Please sit, Doctor Markum. What are you drinking?"

"I've been looking forward to a bit of white wine, Mr. Hirsch, say a glass of Blue Nun."

The lawyer let out a hearty laugh. "Blue Nun? C'mon, please. You're in California. I can't believe you'd want a German wine and a cheap Liebfraumilch, at that. Your tastes will need to keep pace with your financial resources. Allow me to order a vintage from a local vineyard?"

Cyrus had no real preference. "I'll leave it to you, Mr. Hirsch. Go ahead and decide."

"I think that a ten-year-old bottle of Pinot Gris, a delicate and flavorful variety, produced by our own Precious Pattie's, would do nicely."

The lawyer chuckled. "Once you hear what I have to say, you may want to order a second bottle."

That sounded a bit portentous to Cyrus. "Why would I need so much to drink? Is there a problem?"

Mr. Hirsch howled with laughter. He grabbed hold of his bifocals to keep them from falling off his nose. "On the contrary, Doctor Markum. I didn't mean to startle you. I simply meant that the wine will be a toast to your good fortune. Unfortunately, it's due to Mr. Desjardins' untimely passing, but let's not put a damper on our celebration. We should enjoy ourselves. Our departed host would want it that way."

The clattering of heels scraping against the wooden floor in the hallway distracted Cyrus. He turned as a group of women entered the room. He recognized Aunt Claire immediately.

Before Malcolm had the chance to make introductions, Cyrus hopped up. Claire walked straight over and hugged him. The doctor and the restauranteur hadn't seen each other for years, but the two had bonded almost a decade and a half earlier when he and Matthias visited New Orleans.

"I'm so sorry for your loss," he commiserated. He hugged her and planted kisses on both cheeks.

"Oh, Cyrus," she sobbed. "I'm so happy to see you, even with such a heavy heart. I've missed you."

The ticking clock had been kind to Claire. Though she'd rung almost three-quarters of a century of living in the register, her sheen had faded little. Her color-enhanced auburn hair, fashioned nicely into a Princess Diana cut, looked quite natural.

"Claire, it has been such a long time, too long," Cyrus cooed.

She hugged him again. "You remember my daughter, Marie, and her daughters, Millie and Maryanne?"

He took in the three generations of ladies. "Your family is beautiful. And, you look magnificent. You haven't aged a day."

The matriarch blushed.

Cyrus reached for her daughter's hand. "Hello, Marie. It is so good to see you again. You have my deepest sympathies."

Marie had inherited her mom's genes. Her tight girlish figure filled out her dress admirably. Matthias always filled with pride when he spoke about her. As a budding debutante, she'd had several suitors from well-heeled families pursuing her. With little interest in any, she'd spurned any advances, and instead, fell for a local jazz musician. The syrupy sounds dripping from his shiny brass flugelhorn captured her heart.

Never interested in the quest for material goods, she went for spiritual substance rather than an assured life of luxury, though her husband found success on his own.

Marie, who entered the world with a veritable golden spoon protruding from her lips, grew into a special person. She advocated for the homeless and the less fortunate and spent her time raising money through her foundation.

Now approaching fifty, you'd think she was fifteen years younger. Cyrus watched as she moved lithely to her seat.

Both Marie's daughters hadn't been shortchanged. Millie, the elder by two years, wore her blonde textured hair short and carried a gregarious smile. Her bright brown eyes and a tiny upturned nose complemented her attractive look.

Maryanne, who'd just turned twenty-three, looked the part of a Bayou beauty queen. Cyrus imagined she'd already broken many a heart. Her long brown locks spilled down past her shoulders and onto her ample bosom. He would bet that men couldn't resist turning their heads to catch a glimpse of her as she passed. The girls had been mere children the last time he'd seen them. They'd matured nicely.

*   *   *

He'd been Ill-prepared for the lawyer's revelations, and Cyrus used alcohol to soothe his state of bewilderment. By the time he'd emptied his fourth glass of wine, the newly minted millionaire's face was numb.

Omar helped his client climb into the hotel elevator and supported him into his room. The doctor kicked off his loafers as he fell onto the king-sized bed. He moaned softly and rolled over on his stomach. After less than a minute his breathing slowed. Sleep encircled him.

*   *   *

"Cyrus. Wake up."

Was this voice a part of a dream? He didn't think so.

He bolted upright.

"Cyrus, my son. Come to me."

He felt chills running through his body. That voice, it sounded like his mother.

"What? Who's there?" He questioned, looking around the hotel room, searching, but to no avail.

"Cyrus," the voice called out, now even louder. "Please! Stand up. Come to the window."

No longer feeling the effects of his drinking, he bounded up from the mattress and pulled aside the maroon window curtain. His entire body tingled. Slowly, his feet lifted from the floor. He felt no control over his limbs and watched in wonderment as an unseen force supported him, guiding his body through the open window.

He felt no fear as a refreshing draft of air caressed his body as he ascended. It had been nighttime when he'd laid his body down, but now brightness filled the sky. The sensation of tranquility flowed through him. No longer in an urban setting, the umbrella canopy of a dense forest had sprouted beneath him. The sharp, yet sweet aroma of pine needles smelled refreshing. As he cruised above the treetops, Cyrus knew with absolute certainty that he'd connected with the Supreme Being. For the first time in his life, he felt one with the universe.

He breathed normally. He could manipulate his arms and legs, but couldn't control his flight pattern. His celestial body gradually picked up the tempo and glided downward. The forest thinned out. Plump cows, busy feasting on the rolling meadows, replaced the lodgepole pine trees and Douglas firs.

Brusquely, the blue sky darkened. A booming thunderclap, accentuated by two jagged daggers of light, sliced through the heavens. The transitory brightness outlined the silhouette of a white structure below him. The outline of a rubicund cross, emblazoned on its flat roof, visualized momentarily.

Several more lightning strikes split the darkness. The distant rumblings of thunder followed a second later. The sky turned crimson. His neck hairs stood at attention. Fields of goosebumps erupted on both forearms. Aside from the breeze's soft whispers, all remained eerily silent. A hazy blue light sprang through the building's dozen windows.

Ever so slowly, Cyrus' body descended. Now upright, he hovered in front of one of the windows. He strained his eyes, but could only see shadows.

"Look to your soul for guidance," the unseen female directed. "You must learn to live in the now. Your purpose is here to behold."

Cyrus grappled with overwhelming bemusement. That voice! The intonation and timbre sounded so familiar.

"I'm not afraid," he barked, wearing his bravest face. "Mother! Is that you?"

It seemed impossible. Congestive heart failure had taken her six years earlier. He'd wanted to be with her, but he'd been stranded on the African continent. The Ethio-Somalia war raged, and flights were canceled. The guilt still gnawed at him.

"Please, answer me. Is that you, mother?"

"Brother, it's me, Leonard," a child's voice answered. "I'm with mom. Join us."

"This can't be possible. It isn't real," Cyrus bellowed. You're dead."

As the blue mist dispersed, the outline of a small boy became visible. He motioned with the fingers of his right hand. "Float through the window. Come to us, Cyrus."

A bright white light shone through the cobalt clouds obscuring Cyrus' view. A pulsating green light outlined the miniature figure. His little brother looked exactly the way he remembered him before leukemia drained his life away.

Behind the pint-sized orator stood a female. Her hands rested on Leonard's shoulders. Her rosy cheeks and smiling face had replaced the paleness of the withered old woman he last remembered. Recently, he'd pulled out black-and-white photo albums from her high school graduation. There she stood, in the flesh, and looking even more robust.

How could she and Leonard be here? Yet, here they were, looking fit and healthy. Cyrus' feet slid through the open sash window. Waves of uncontrollable emotions gushed through the astral wanderer as he took his place beside his departed loved ones.

His mom stroked his cheek. "My son, there's no need for tears. Leonard and I are both at peace. There's no pain, only happiness."

How could this be happening? Why did the scent of Chanel No. 5 perfume, the fragrance his mother always favored, hang in the air?

"Your brother and I are your chaperones. We're here to guide you. You've been chosen to do vital work for humanity."

"What work? I've been doing my part. I work hard every day."

"That's true, my son, but there is a mission ahead for you."

The last twenty-four hours had been an emotional roller-coaster ride. He felt as if water droplets and ice crystals were fogging his head. "I don't understand. What work?"

His brother slight fingers folded around his hand. "Come, follow me. Let us show you."

Cyrus trailed his loved ones through a doorway and into a large windowless room. A row of beds sat on either side of a narrow center aisle. Each one was occupied by an emaciated male who appeared cataleptic. Purple sores stood out on their faces.

The sound of an alarm bell startled him. Two females, their bodies covered with scrubs, surgical gloves, and fabric masks, rushed to one of the bedsides. The overhead ECG monitor showed an electronic flatline. One of the nurses pressed the tips of her fingers to his carotid artery.

He gaped as the esoteric spark of existence escaped through the chest of the victim of artificial selection. A whooshing noise filled the room as his life-force shattered, flinging atomized particles into the air. The scent of ocean spray wafted into Cyrus' nostrils as the living soul pulled itself free of its earthly body. Ever so slowly, it ascended toward the ceiling. With arms pinned to the sides of the spirit body, the expression of absolute joy covered his face. A reassuring awareness of peacefulness came over Cyrus. He looked at his mother and Leonard. They both wore expressions of tranquility.

An MD, clad in scrubs and sterile safety garb, rushed into the ward. He pressed his stethoscope to the stricken soul's chest. The physician furrowed his brow and pulled the white sheet over the patient's face. One of the nurses turned off the heart monitor.

The doctor checked his watch. "Time of death, eleven fifty-five p.m."

The second nurse made a note on the chart.

Cyrus' eyes wandered to the wall clock at the center of the ward. Five minutes short of midnight. The deeds of his past or any hopes for a future no longer mattered to the cadaver's earthly existence. The reasons for this journey were becoming clear. He knew he must begin to live in the now.

"Cyrus." His mother's voice startled him. "That soul succumbed to complications caused by the HIV virus."

This news came as no surprise, but her comment delivered the complete clarity he sought. His earlier detective work had helped provide the payoff. Both Matthias and Antonio suffered the effects of this incurable and life-sapping disease. With no longer any doubt in his mind, Cyrus made a promise. From this point onward, developing the cure for the HIV retrovirus would rule his life.

CHAPTER SIX

Awakenings

The LED on the digital clock radio showed just past six. Cyrus rolled onto his right side and pushed himself up from the bed. *Ouch,* his head ached. He stood and pulled back the curtain. He looked out at the street, hardly any traffic at this time of the morning. The vivid memory of last night's astrophysical expedition ran through his head. *That dream... it felt so real.*

He shivered as the shower's icy water cascaded over his body. Adjusting the temperature and intensity, he thought over the sequence of events since he'd arrived in San Francisco.

The warmth of the water and intensifying cloud of smoky vapor felt refreshing. As the tiny pellets of water poked at him, a sneer blossomed on his face. He drew the green shower curtain aside and stepped from the stall. Pulling one of the Omni hotel's white monogrammed towels from the rack, he wiped at the white fog covering the mirror.

He stared at his image. "If you truly exist, God, please give me a sign."

He wrapped the towel around his waist. Pivoting away from his reflection, he stepped into the main room. Cyrus fiddled with the buttons on the television remote. The tube came alive. On screen, two women mimicked a male trainer's routine. They stretched and flexed as their instructor counted time. Mellow jazz played in the background. He threw the towel down on the bed and pulled open the dresser drawer. Out came his bathrobe.

The clock radio displayed the time: six twenty-three. He needed to be at the lawyer's office at nine. He'd have plenty of time to get ready and order breakfast. He pulled out a pen and notepad from his bag, then collapsed on the bed.

"Okay. Let's record the timeline of the epidemic," he said aloud. "I know that scientists isolated the retrovirus causing AIDS this past March." He scribbled that down. "I've read in a 1984 scientific journal article that Patient Zero, a male airline flight attendant from Quebec, is presumed to be the originator." He added that information to the sheet of paper.

He tapped the barrel of his pen against his forehead. "The CDC study estimates the Canadian resident with seven-hundred-and-fifty sexual episodes of male coupling over a three-year period. The presumption is that the disease incubated in New York City and traversed to California." Again, he added that information to his notes.

"Now, the supposition is that the virus originally traveled with Patient Zero from Africa, though the sampling of genetic sequencing has thus far proved inconclusive." He didn't bother to write that down.

Cyrus knew the CDC had been gathering information in both New York and Los Angeles. Just last month, several comprehensive reports claimed the bugs triggering the virus had been identified as either HTLV-III or LAV. Scientists hypothesized that the two might be the identical strain, as two independent research teams pursued the syndrome simultaneously. The smart money figured the teams might possibly be evaluating the same deadly ailment but using divergent designations. The FDA would soon issue commercial licenses to allow the drawing of blood to determine the presence of the antibodies that caused the AIDS infection.

Highly respected by his peers and superiors alike, he assumed he could gain an assignment with one of the two investigative teams if he desired. "Yes. I must attend to that as soon as I'm back in Atlanta," he announced, reinforcing his decision.

He glanced at the television screen. A young woman shared her recipe for chicken parmigiana and baked ziti. An instrumental version of "Volare" played softly through the speaker. The on-screen backdrop featured the Leaning Tower of Pisa. He remembered reading that during WWII, the Americans spared destroying the historic building, preserving the almost eight hundred-year-old structure. Both Cyrus' eyebrows raised. *What an odd hour for cooking an evening meal, though it did serve to stir his taste buds and strengthen the appetite.*

He picked up the phone and dialed.

"Good morning," a friendly female voice announced. "Room service. How may I help you?"

"Yes, good morning, ma'am. This is room 437, I'd like to have breakfast delivered."

"Yes, sir. What would you like?"

"Please send up a bowl of oatmeal, a banana, two pieces of whole-wheat toast, and a glass of tomato juice. Please add a pot of coffee."

He could certainly use a kick-start. "Please, ma'am, I almost forgot. Send a pitcher of ice water and two Advils. Thank you."

"Got it. Twenty minutes."

The line went dead.

Twenty minutes? That should give him ample time to shave and get dressed.

Back inside the bathroom, his Norelco razor made short work of the stubble. The neat little pop-up trimmer took care of his sideburns and eyebrows. He closed the carrying case and followed the trail of sound into the main room. As he secured the top button on the white designer dress shirt, a new show came on the boob tube. This one was a huge departure from the exercise show or the oddly-timed Italian cooking show.

A handsome young man pranced around the TV screen. His shoulder-length brown hair bounced on his shoulders as he emphasized his talking points. His blue dress shirt lay open at the neck. The short sleeves allowed a glimpse of a pirate's head tattoo on his interior right forearm. His expressive manner of speaking stirred Cyrus' attention. The doctor stopped tying the half Windsor knot. Instead, he let go of his tie and sat down on the edge of the bed.

The Bible-thumper stood on an emerald green stage and spoke from behind a belly-high white podium. A white cardboard banner hung across the upper portion of the black curtained backdrop. The inscription declared: "There's only the now. Live in the moment."

That concept struck a resplendent chord within Cyrus, the message so similar to his mom's during last night's astrophysical pilgrimage.

Could this be a large dose of the validation he sought? Or, might this charismatic preacher be just another religious charlatan? Whatever the reality, this espousing leftover from the sixties commanded attention. His message came across the airwaves filled with intensity and sincerity.

"The Ministry of Collective Harmony and Spiritual Balance," the name of the church, covering the front facing of the lectern. The camera angle shifted. A panoramic shot disclosed several hundred chairs, half of them occupied. A second camera showed the faces of the congregants. Whites made up two-thirds of the audience. A few Asians, a smattering of Afro-Americans, and several Latinos spiced up the mix. Most were primarily young, casually dressed, and aside from a few small children, wide awake and enjoying the sermon.

Cyrus sat mesmerized. On screen, the curtain slipped open. Any babies still asleep, awakened with the sound of a bass drum, snare, and hi-hat breaking through their world of dreams. The preacher hopped behind a mahogany Hammond organ. A tall, goofy looking guy smacked his fingers against the strings of a bass guitar. A young woman strummed on an acoustic.

The people in the audience got busy clapping. A good number rose to their feet and shook their bodies. Cyrus listened intently, straining his ears to decipher the words of the preacher's song.

Two loud thumps on the door interrupted his effort. "It's Larry from room service. I'm here with your breakfast."

Cyrus rushed over to the courtesy closet and slid open the wooden partition. "Be right there. Just give me a minute."

He ripped a pair of black trousers from a hanger, slipped one leg in, then the other. Maneuvering around the bed, he grabbed the brass doorknob, his eyes affixed to the television.

The worker rolled the cart into the room. "Good morning, sir. Where would you like me to leave it?"

Engrossed in the show, Cyrus only waved a finger. "Right over there is fine. Here you go."

He handed Larry a five and scribbled on the bottom of the bill. "Thank you very much, sir. Will there be anything else?"

"No. No, thank you. Just close the door behind you."

His attention drifted from the television as he surveyed the items arranged on the cart. He filled the tall glass with water and added three cubes of ice. He tore open the Advil wrapper and swallowed. He washed them down, then, sliced off several small pieces of the banana and stirred them into the oatmeal. Grabbing hold of the spoon, he swiveled the chair around and pulled it within a foot of the TV. He ladled a spoonful of the warm cereal into his mouth. The song had finished. The pastor began his sermon:

Open your mind and receive God's gift of love, people,
Allow the communal soul to enter, and share in the joy of life,
God is within each of us.
He's here with us now on earth and not far in heaven,
Be joyful and share your special gift with the world.
Let the Christ spirit abound within.
Let it lift you to where you've never been before.

A camera panned over the appreciative crowd. Just as the credits rolled up the screen, the telephone ringer began chirping. In a reflex action, Cyrus turned quickly and accidentally smacked the coffee cup. It flew off the tray and hurtled to the carpet. He retrieved it, but the damage had been done, both with the mess and the on-screen credits.

When he refocused, the names of the two camera operators and the sound engineer rolled by. He'd missed the most important information, the name of the preacher. Luckily, the last graphic that ran down the screen showed: The Thirty-Eighth State Broadcasting Company, Aurora, Colorado. He grabbed his pen and notepad and jotted that down.

The ringer sounded again. He knew who it would be.

Cyrus held it to his ear. "Hello."

"Good morning, Doctor. It's Omar."

"Good morning, Omar. Be right down."

Cyrus dropped the handset into the base. He adjusted his tie and slipped into his sports jacket. Stuffing his valuables into his pant pockets, he pressed the off button on the remote and threw it on the bed. He picked up his pen and pad and placed them inside his small leather carry bag. Looking around the room one last time, he shut the lights.

At last night's dinner, Mister Hirsch advised him that the lion's share of Matthias' estate would be his. Today's official disposition of assets and property were merely a formality. As he strode toward the elevator, he knew a brand-new phase of his life had already begun.

71

CHAPTER SEVEN

The Visionaries

Aurora, Colorado, August 1988

The Ministry of Collective Harmony and Spiritual Balance developed a following of almost a quarter of a million devotees in it's little more than two decades of existence. March of 1967 saw the original Berkeley church open its doors. Ten years afterward, the Aurora, Colorado facility came into being. The new Boulder worship center performed its first service this past April.

The tiny red brick building where Brother Jim and his wife originally set up shop was now a state-of-the-art facility. Over the last two-plus decades, the influx of generous donations bolstered its evolution. The original ten-car Berkeley parking lot could now easily accommodate more than five hundred. Each church in Colorado provided space for close to eight hundred vehicles. Construction crews had broken ground in Chattanooga, Tennessee, and a property just outside of Fayetteville, North Carolina, now under consideration as a fifth location.

Dan's band, the Souls of Creation, placed albums on the Billboard Christian/Gospel's top one hundred chart, twice over the past three years. With increased awareness of MCHSB, the acronym for the Ministry of Collective Harmony and Spiritual Balance gloried in their unprecedented growth spurt.

* * *

The call came into the Memphis hotel room in the early morning hours. Dan rolled over and grabbed the handset. The clock radio on the nightstand showed: 3:23. Joanne sat up and ran her hands through her hair.

Dan and Joanne's eyes met as he answered. "Hello. Who's this?"

"Dan? It's Alvin. I'm sorry to call you so early, but I have terrible news."

Dan sat up and took his wife's hand. "What's wrong?"

Alvin whimpered. "It's Brother Jim. He's dead."

"No! That can't be. How'd it happen?"

"An accident. He fell in the bathtub. His wife discovered his body after she came home from the Saturday night women's meeting."

*   *   *

Jim's fall caused cervical fractures of the C2 and C3 vertebrae. The official Aurora medical examiner's autopsy report listed asphyxiation as the cause of death.

Each of the three church ministries performed a memorial service. The MCHSB's founder's ashes found its final resting place in the waters near Fisherman's Wharf in San Francisco.

The church faithful believed the pastor's spirit hadn't perished, but now existed in the celestial realm. His chi would continue to thrive. Only the physical manifestation, his corporeal shell, had departed this earthly plane.

Daniel sang Jim's praises quite eloquently at the Aurora service:

"Jim Bridger and I first met when I was a lost soul and unaware of my true self and purpose. I had not yet discovered the importance of the Holy word. That encounter changed my life."

Dan paused, overcame with emotion. He wiped his eyes. "We've suffered a tremendous personal loss. The world has lost a great leader. With Jim no longer here to provide spiritual guidance, I pledge to each one of you, I will carry his torch. His shoes are too big for anyone to fill, but I'll do everything possible to emulate his goodness and teachings."

Part of that philosophical doctrine subscribed to the belief that every human being happened to be a child of God and espoused that Jesus, the enlightened one, was to be revered as the truth and guiding light. The church practiced the laws of optimistic vibrations and positive attraction, accepting that in time, negative energy would scatter and disintegrate. Naysayers might argue that the explanation an oversimplification of a mystical theorem, but the concept fit well as a major part of their gospel.

Under Brother Jim's tutelage, Daniel's spirituality had flourished. Over their two decades together, his musical talents also mushroomed. Jim's acolyte, a valued spokesperson for the church and televangelist for their cable broadcasts, released his first album, *A Galaxy Filled with Love,* in the summer of 1970. The music rippled the waters of the Christian music world. The album sold more than a quarter million copies. The first single, "Walking into the Light," crossed over onto the pop music chart and reached the number twelve spot.

Over the years, the honeyed harmonic blends and catchy hooks attracted a large enough following to spawn seven more albums. Dan handled the male vocal parts in the recording studio, playing keyboards and electric guitar parts as well. Max added his soulful bass guitar to the acetate reels while Bud contributed thoughtful percussion. Joanne strummed her twelve-string acoustic and sang soprano and alto.

In June 1971, Jim officiated as Dan and Joanne exchanged vows in the Berkeley chapel. Since that day, their mutual infatuation grew ever stronger. God blessed the couple with fraternal twins, Cooper, and Iris, in May 1972. The month following their birth, Joanne's parents relocated to Berkeley, a Godsend for the entire family.

As the children matured, their footprints overshadowed those of their parents. At eleven, the twins created the Harmonic Balance Youth Council. They recruited fifteen members and dubbed the group, The Hummingbirds. They held bake sales, washed cars, sold lemonade, and even traveled door to door, to generate funds to aid the indigent. The gratitude of the many they helped served as reward enough for the inspired young people. Their efforts didn't go unnoticed. The Hummingbirds became an integral part of the church's organizational philosophy.

The twins, also gifted students, both skipped the seventh grade and would graduate high school a year early. Iris, with her curly blonde locks and amazing figure, was even more gorgeous than her mother.

"You better be careful," Mister Sylvester, her guidance counselor, warned Dan on only her second day at school. "Now that your daughter's entered Central High, you might want to carry a big stick with you to keep the boys away."

Her dad laughed. "Ah! Like Teddy Roosevelt, except I'm not known for walking or talking softly."

The school administrator eyebrows raised. "That's a good one, Reverend. I get it."

Possessing a dynamic personality, the feminine wunderkind oozed energy. But, Daniel knew she could be tough and take a stand if she believed she had right on her side. The young woman had a special spark.

Her sophomore year, she and her mother had a sit-down. "Mom," Iris informed her confidently, "I know what I want to do with my life."

"What's that?" Joanne asked, unsure of what her daughter's next statement might be.

"Well, the idea of screenwriting and movie production intrigues me. I want to attend Colorado State after graduation."

Her mom wasn't surprised. "I think that you'll be successful in whatever you do. Your father and I express our energies through music. Your choice makes perfect sense."

Cooper, on the other hand, persuaded his parents to allow him to join their band. Even more gifted and musically blessed than his antecedents, the Souls of Creation already included two of his tunes on their last album. The band opened their latest series of shows with "The Lord Sings through My Heart," one of his latest compositions.

At six-feet-two, he stood three inches taller than his dad and believed wholeheartedly in the beneficial effects of physical fitness.

"I'm not obsessed, I'm addicted," he claimed one morning when his dad asked why he always woke up so early. "Come on, Dad. It gets my blood percolating. There's nothing wrong with that!"

As the sun shared its morning light, his lithe body coursed along the dirt road that snaked around the lake. Aerodynamically styled, his close-cropped brown hair and rippled muscle tone proclaimed the need for speed. The Central High track team won state the past spring because of Cooper's work ethic and fleetness.

His intrinsic ability to create and interpret music compelled him to reject scholarship offers and pursue his true love.

Joanne and Daniel couldn't have been prouder. Their children trusted in goodness and valued the sanctity of life. The twins understood that each proton and nucleon in this physical world were a magnificent piece of God's mystical puzzle. Empowered by the Holy Spirit, the two sixteen-year-olds ran far ahead of the curve.

*   *   *

"My route to ordination has been a circuitous one," Dan confessed to the reporter from the Aurora Crier. "Before taking an active role in the church, I went on a bumpy roller-coaster jaunt."

Janie Magnuson scribbled down his answer on her pad. "How so?"

"Well, in May of 1969, I drove cross-country from Berkeley to New York City. Joanne lived there with her parents. I convinced her to come with me. That part was easy."

Janie broke in. "Why do you say that?"

"Her parents turned out to be more of a problem. It took several weeks, but they came around to my way of thinking. August twelfth, I remember the date. The two of us climbed into the green and white Volkswagen minibus and headed to Madison, Wisconsin."

Janie flipped the page. "Why Wisconsin?"

"The Berkeley of the Midwest, that's what they called it then. Hippies still bopped around there."

The reporter nodded. "Oh, I see."

Dan took a sip of water. "We rented an upper flat on Gorham, just off State Street. That's when we met Max and Bud and formed the original group. The band began playing local gigs and joined the Mifflin Street Music Collective. We staged street festivals, but playing for free doesn't pay the bills."

"Understood. So, what did you do?"

"Joanne found a job as an early shift waitress in a coffee shop. Max and I started a residential-painting business. Now, that dude happened to be a trip. The guy stood six-feet-six inches, had kinky black hair, huge gray eyes, and wore these big horn-rimmed glasses." Dan formed circles with his fingers and placed them over his eyes. "When we first met, I kidded him about how he'd escaped from the pages of a Bob Crumb Zap comic."

Dan pushed himself up from the chair. "Janie, would you excuse me for a few minutes? I need to use the restroom."

Janie's head bobbed. "Sure. That'll give me a chance to think of some more questions."

The bathroom break gave Dan the opportunity to reflect on those Madison days and that flat on Gorham. The attic became the rehearsal space. Max began crashing in the spare bedroom and eventually moved his stuff in. The real-life *Keep on Truckin'* hipster brought along his master marijuana blends and tight-joint rolling technique and generously shared both.

Bud, the percussionist, rounded out the foursome. His long blonde hair ran down the middle of his back. With his multi-colored beard and piercing watery brown eyes, he looked ready to board a ship, "hoist the sails," and navigate to the center of Lake Mendota. His persona inspired Dan to get that pirate tattoo on his arm.

A man of few words, Bud wore a constant and contagious grin. Limited public speaking skills did little to interfere with his dexterity and hand-eye coordination. His essential ability to use his drum kit as a creative and communicative bodily extension dazzled the eyes and ears.

The Milwaukee native delivered pizzas by day. His girlfriend, Gretchen, a German émigré and UWM alumni, worked at the university bookstore while she attended night classes in pursuit of a master's in psychology.

Since moving into their second-floor layout three months earlier, the residents experienced sporadic episodes of paranormal phenomena. Joanne visited the library and researched the history of the almost century-old structure. What she discovered surprised her.

William Brewster, a mathematics professor at the university, built the house in 1875. Two years after the inaugural date, an accident with a kerosene lantern took the life of twelve-year-old William Junior and destroyed part of the basement. Even though he had the property restored, the Brewsters, too pained by the loss of their son, moved out and sold the property.

Over the years, several families occupied the premises. The most recent, an elderly brother and sister. Last winter, the brother, suffering from pneumococcal pneumonia, had to be transported by ambulance to St. Mary's Hospital. He took his last breath a day later. A week later, the police discovered the sister's decomposing body after a concerned neighbor notified them that the mail had been piling up in the box. Since then, the first floor remained vacant.

Daniel and Joanne had experienced manifestations of two separate entities on several occasions. Though neither seemed malicious, sharing your home with apparitions could be disconcerting. Max also bumped into the ghostly roommates.

That's where Gretchen's abilities came in handy. Having a full work and school schedule, she'd never visited the Gorham residence or attended any of the band's gigs. With the bookstore closed for renovations, tonight, she accompanied her boyfriend to rehearsal.

The moment she stepped on the porch of the neat gray and white wooden home, her acute paranormal abilities stirred.

"Bud, I sense the spirit of a young boy. He's in pain," she confessed. "He's crying. I can smell smoke and see his clothes on fire. His death occurred a long time ago, but he's never left."

Bud paused in mid-step. "Wow, that's nuts, babe. I know, weird stuff's been going on. I thought I saw a ghost at last week during practice. I'd smoked some weed and figured it must have been my imagination. The other guys told me stories, but I never said anything." His lips puckered. "Let's tell them you're a psycho."

His girlfriend scowled. "Yeah. Really funny. C'mon, let's get up there. I wanna talk to them."

They climbed the stairs and walked through the open kitchen door. Before the people sitting around the table had a chance to greet them, Gretchen laid a hand on her boyfriend's shoulder and closed her eyes.

Max stood up and held out a joint. "Hey man, what's up? What's with your girlfriend?"

Before Bud answered, Gretchen, opened her eyes. "You have two spirits here. One is a young boy. He's been stuck here for many years. I also feel another, a woman who's recently passed. She's calling for her brother."

Daniel and Joanne exchanged glances.

"Wow! You're freaking me right out!" Max announced

Bud brought the joint up to his lips and took a hit. He blew out a cloud of smoke. "Yeah, man. She freaks me out too, bro. Can you believe it? She's on one of her bizarre ghost trips, man. She thinks your place is boo-coo haunted."

"Yeah, well it is," Dan confirmed. "We've all seen strange things here. Two nights ago, I woke up at three in the morning. I looked over my shoulder and saw a female standing over by the television. She looked like transparent Jell-O. I shook Joanne, but the ghost split before she woke up."

Dan reached for the joint. "I tell you, it scared the crap out of me. It was definitely a female. She had long hair but no facial features. I figure it must be the old lady that died downstairs."

Gretchen sighed. "The hyperplane is filled with earthbound entities. I can help. We need to perform a spiritual healing."

"You hear this, babe?" Dan squeezed Joanne's hand.

She looked up at Gretchen. "I've seen you before. You work at the bookstore, right?"

Gretchen nodded. "Yes, I do."

Her face went blank. "There are two souls living here with you. They don't know they've died. They like the familiar surroundings. Their spirits are stuck here. We can help them move on."

Joanne's eyes widened. "Oh, I'm ready. Do you want to do it now?"

"No, definitely not tonight, tomorrow. I need to get the supplies. But meanwhile, I wouldn't mind a glass of wine. What do you guys have?"

*   *   *

Gretchen and Bud brought along a package of white sage incense cones, several white candles in glass holders, and a box of Celtic sea salt. The Holy Redeemer Catholic Church contributed a bottle of holy water.

During the cleansing ritual, they'd need to access the basement and first floor, in addition to the second-floor apartment. In case of emergency, the rental agent had given Dan keys to the downstairs. Earlier in the day, he'd purchased five flashlights and a load of batteries from the Ace hardware store on State Street.

A little before nine, Gretchen and Bud came tramping up the stairs. Bud carried a paper shopping bag; his counterpart toted a brown shoebox. Waiting for them in the kitchen sat Joanne and Daniel. Max and his girlfriend, Rachel, stood near the sink smoking a joint.

Bud placed his bag on the kitchen floor.

Gretchen laid her box on the table. "Okay, people, everyone ready?"

"We're set," Dan answered, eager to start.

Max breathed out a large cloud of marijuana smoke. "Hey. Look at this, Gretchen." He pointed to his green tee shirt. The image of Merlin, hoisting his magical cane high above his head, stared at her. "I got this at the Salvation Army. It's neat, huh? Now we got us a little protection."

She waved him off. "Don't worry. We're good. We won't be needing his magic."

Gretchen's long brown hair cascaded in front of her face as she bent forward and lifted the cover off the shoebox. She threw her head back. "There's nothing to fear. No evil resides here." She placed a finger to her lips. "Okay, quiet. I need you to listen up."

"Do you have any small plates? I need them for the sage," she asked, handing Dan a few of the incense cones.

Joanne moved toward the cupboard. "Sure. I'll get them. How many d'you need?"

Gretchen wiggled the fingers of both hands. "Um, maybe ten. We wouldn't want anyone to burn their hands."

Rachel helped stack the plates on the table.

Gretchen picked a plate and placed one of the cones in its center. "Okay. Dan. You do the same thing with the other ones, and leave them on the table. First, we'll need to open all the windows. Bud and I will head up to the attic. You guys take care of this floor. Wait for us. Then, we'll go downstairs."

Once the windows were opened, the cool September wind gusted off the lake and whipped through the rooms. The temperature dropped twenty degrees. Bud and his lady still wore their jackets. The others, feeling the immediate temperature change, quickly added a layer of clothes.

The sound of Gretchen and Bud's footsteps resounded as they descended the stairs. "We're done upstairs," Gretchen informed the group. "If everyone's ready, let's head to the first floor."

Max took another hit on his joint and passed it to Bud. Daniel dug into his bag and handed out flashlights. The rest of the ghost squad gathered up the dishes and the balance of the supplies.

"Go ahead. Lead the way down, Dan," Gretchen suggested, stepping behind him.

"Me?" Dan gulped. "Okay, guys, follow me." He turned on the hall light. The sound of footsteps resonated in the narrow hallway. Unlocking the door to the first-floor apartment, Dan turned the knob and pushed it open.

The sounds of motion broke the interior silence. Max retreated a step. He landed on his girlfriend's sandal.

Rachel lifted her foot and wiggled her toes. "Ow! That hurt."

Max squeezed her upper arm. "I'm sorry, honey. What the heck was that noise?"

Dan aimed his beam down the hallway. "I don't know, probably roaches. Come on, guys. Everyone, turn on your flashlights."

Five narrow shafts of light moved over the floors and walls. The group worked its way through the foyer and into the kitchen.

"What's that smell," Joanne asked.

Max, quick with a quip, reacted. "Yeah, this place smells worse than stinky farts."

Nervous laughter filled the room.

"You should know," Dan giggled. "You're an expert on the subject."

"We need to get serious, people," Gretchen cautioned. "Let's open the windows and doors. Max, you go with Daniel and Joanne. Rachel, you can come with Bud and me."

"No way," Rachel croaked. "I'm scared. I want to stay with Max."

"No worries," Gretchen agreed. "We'll meet by the basement door once we're done. The rest of you start at the rear door and go through the bedrooms. Bud and I will head to the living room and work our way back."

Dan shined a light down the hallway. "Okay, got it. Let's go. We'll meet you in a few minutes."

In addition to the stale odor, the place looked a hurricane had blown through. Clothing lay strewn over the floors and furniture. When Daniel and his crew entered the master bedroom, the sound of scurrying little feet scraping across the wooden floor sent shockwaves through them. They aimed their lights at the sound.

"Look at those little fuckers," Max yelled.

A pair of brown rats scurried away from lights. They dashed across the room and found refuge beneath the bed.

Rachel shrieked. She clutched Max's arm. He pulled her closer and planted a kiss on her lips.

He laughed. "Now this is my kind of party. We should do this more often."

Joanne shuddered. "Count me out."

Dan remained cool. "My taste in entertainment is a little more conventional. But, at least we know what those sounds were. We've been lucky that those little suckers haven't paid us a visit upstairs. I'll let the rental agent know on Monday."

Max wasn't paying attention, too busy hugging Rachel.

Daniel maneuvered his beam around the floor. Fortunately, there weren't any more of the furry creatures. Satisfied, Dan raised his flashlight and found the windows. Joanne tiptoed over and opened one. Max opened the other.

With the windows in the living and dining room also opened, the air's kinetic energy picked up speed. A gale-force wind whistled through the flat. Gretchen shivered as she lit the white candles. It took her a few tries. She and Bud picked them up and placed one in each of the rooms. Dan followed with the cones of sage. Gray smoke and a skunky odor floated through the apartment. Dan opened the basement door.

Gretchen raised the flashlight and pointed at herself. Her face looked eerie in its glow. "Wait. We can't go downstairs yet. We'll need to walk around up here and drop salt into the corners of each room and sprinkle a few drops of holy water on the sills and in the doorways. Dan, you spread the salt. I'll take care of the holy water. Make sure you don't use too much. We need it for the basement and upstairs."

She handed Dan the bag of sea salt.

"Hey. We're going with you," Max announced. "We ain't gonna stand here in the dark waiting for a spook to pop out."

Dan snickered. "Sure thing. Just follow me."

Gretchen and Bud turned and headed to the front of the apartment. The rest of the party headed toward the back.

Gretchen's voice was carried along by the wind. "Our Father who art in heaven, hallowed be thy name…"

The sound trailed off as she turned off into a side hallway. The temperature had dipped another several degrees since they began the cleansing session. Daniel body trembled as he and his group moved methodically from room to room, dropping salt in the corners of each of them.

Their tasks didn't take long. The six participants stood at the basement door once again. Gretchen led the way down the stairs. Bud followed behind her. In his right hand, he carried a glass holder with a flickering paraffin candle. In his left, he balanced a small plated holding several sage cones. Dan trailed after him, Joanne on his tail. Max came next, then Rachel. As Gretchen and Bud reached the concrete, the sound of scurrying little feet greeted them.

Rachel shrieked.

"Ugh, more rats," Max hollered, clasping his girlfriend's hand, and guiding her down the last two steps to the basement floor.

The rats took refuge behind a pile of boxes stacked up against the far wall. Gretchen pulled out the small wooden table from under the stairway and dragged it to the center of the room. Bud laid his candle on it. He pulled out his lighter and lit three cones of sage and placed a plate on the table. Gretchen opened the two windows and added several drops of water to the sills. She began reciting the Lord's Prayer again. "Our father, who art…"

Daniel let the sea salt fall into each of the corners of the cellar. Max pushed aside the last of the cartons, allowing access to the final area.

Gretchen turned off her flashlight and stood by the table. "Please join me and shut your lights. I need darkness."

The other four lights clicked off. Guided by the dim candlelight, the others joined her.

"Please. Let's form a circle and hold hands," she urged.

Gretchen's eyes closed. Her body quivered slightly. "I see the boy. He is lonely and afraid. He's been here a long time. He died down here. His name is Billy. He's crying and calling for his mother."

A sharp tapping sound came from under the steps. Rachel recoiled in fright. Max reached his arm around her waist.

Gretchen's head turned toward the noise. "Billy, there's nothing to fear. You're safe. We're here to help you. Your mother is waiting for you. She wants you to join her. Go ahead, Billy. Walk forward. Walk toward the light. I know you see it. Let go of the past. Step into the light. Your mother is waiting for you."

Even through the dim light, every eye focused on Gretchen.

"He's passing through the void. He's walked into the light. He's with his family," she informed the others.

Max convulsed his body in mock dismay. "This is sure some freaky shit."

Gretchen's eyes closed again. "The female spirit, I see her. She does not recognize her passing. She's looking for her brother. Her name is Emily. She'd fallen and broken her hip."

Joanne shuddered. "My God, how awful."

Gretchen groaned. "Emily, your brother is waiting for you. He wants you to join him. You've nothing to fear. There's nothing here for you any longer. Walk toward the light. Your brother is there. Go ahead, Emily. Walk, walk into the light."

She paused. Then after several seconds continued coaxing her. "That's it, Emily, go ahead."

Several more seconds passed.

Gretchen body relaxed. "She's joined her brother. Your home is clear. Both the entities have passed over."

Inhaling deeply, she expelled a huge breath. Her shoulders sagged. "Whew, that freaked me out," she admitted. "Let's collect our stuff and go upstairs. We need to bless the rest of the house."

"You can turn on the flashlights. "Gretchen released an enormous sigh of relief. "My body is weary, but my spirit is refreshed."

* * *

That bit of mystical wizardry became their epiphany and would serve as the cornerstone of the band's future success. Inspired by Gretchen's special gift, the couple convinced their bandmates that their music should evolve. A few days after the spiritualistic episode, Daniel and Joanne played their latest composition, "Walking into the Light" for Bud and Max. The rhythm section loved the pure essence of the song and its progressive beat. The quartet never looked back. The band discarded the name: The Wolliwonks, and the Souls of Creation rose from the ashes, like a Phoenix.

Their bookings multiplied. The band traveled consistently to gigs in Milwaukee and Chicago. Their big break materialized when Bobby Samuels, a recording executive, and music producer showed up at one of their dates. In March 1970, as the band left the stage at DePaul University's Lincoln Park campus, someone thrust a business card into each of the band member's hands.

"Are you ready to become famous?" Bobby asked. "It's funny. My daughter attends this school and I flew up to spend the weekend with her."

Always on the prowl for new talent, he believed that Christian rock was about to take off, and the Souls of Creation possessed a special gift that needed only a small amount of shaping. The deal would be contingent on the band pulling up stakes and moving to the San Francisco Bay Area.

Max and Bud jumped at the chance. Joanne and Daniel thought about it a bit, but they both agreed, especially since Brother Jim had been on their case to move out to Berkeley.

Dan felt truly blessed. With his true love seated beside him, life seemed wonderful. The Almighty had saved him from a violent death in Vietnam for a reason. As he drove his Volkswagen bus westward, he thanked God for leading him to his destiny and sending him, Joanne, his twin flame.

She jotted down the poetic phrases that would become the lyrics for their newest collaboration. She kissed Dan gently on his cheek and sang it for him as they crossed into Nevada.

In big letters, at the top of the page, Joanne had inscribed the song's title: "Keep Striving for Perfection." The young lovers kissed. Laying the pen on the dashboard, she reached across the seat and tenderly squeezed his hand.

Eighteen years had flown by since that day. Their trust in God had deepened, and the love and belief in each other had grown ever stronger.

* * *

Dan grimaced and checked his teeth in the mirror. He wiped his hands on a paper towel and threw it in the wastebasket. He straightened his shirt and opened the bathroom door.

He smiled at the reporter. "Sorry, I took so long. Do you have time? I've got a long story to tell you."

Daniel sat back down.

The reporter grinned. "As much time as you need, Reverend."

CHAPTER EIGHT

THE BREAKTHROUGH

Los Angeles, California, June 11, 1989

The champagne corks popped. After three years of exhaustive research and personal sacrifice, Cyrus and his staff had their breakthrough. After half-a-dozen failed attempts, the aberrant gene, the conduit for the lethal HIV virus, had been identified. That villainous genome, responsible for hijacking the CD4+ lymphocytes, was corroborated by hard evidence and no longer a speculative hypothesis.

That devious HIV bug, adept at neutralizing the cells responsible for immune response and replicating its own genetic material, lay naked and exposed. Formula Seven, annexing the dormant CD4+ cells, allowed the body to triumph over the disease. The infected would have more than just useless prayers to fight off the incurable illness.

Charlemagne, Venus, and Neptune, three of the chimpanzee test subjects, exhibited a favorable response to the lab's latest antitoxin. Fifty-three days after inoculation, no trace of the HIV virus remained in their bloodstreams. Elated, to say the least, the doctor worked for three days to ready his corroborating paperwork. Hunched over his desk, he reread the final draft of the *Formula Seven* report, verifying transcription records and treatment timetables. He and his personal assistant would be departing LAX that evening at seven, flying to Atlanta to meet with the people at the CDC.

"Mom, you can be proud," Cyrus remarked aloud, folding up the last of his clothing and slipping it into his carry-on bag. "I've done it."

He looked forward to his stay at the Pine Lake cottage. "Oh. I almost forgot," he remarked, opening his bottom drawer, and tossing a bathing suit on top of his white shirt. *Why not take full advantage of the sunshine and luxuriate in his success?*

* * *

The first-class seats provided plenty of leg and elbow room. By the time the flight arrived at Hartsfield-Jackson, Cyrus had swallowed three cocktails and needed a bit of support.

The doctor yawned and stretched out in the back seat of the limo. "Wake me when we get there, Ronald. I'm going to close my eyes for a bit."

"Yes, sir. I will."

In less than thirty minutes, Ronald shook Cyrus' shoulder lightly.

His boss sat up slowly and looked at his watch. "Ah, it's nine, perfect. Please, pay the driver."

His assistant handed the driver two twenties. Struggling slightly down the gravel pathway, he juggled the two travel bags and a leather briefcase containing the dozen copies of the Formula Seven assessments.

Pausing at the cottage entrance, Cyrus reached above the door lintel. "Got it. Just where the agent said it would be."

"Very good, Doctor."

"I'm so excited, Ron. My discovery will save tens of thousands."

"Yes, sir. I realize that. I'm so happy for you."

Bright and cheerful décor greeted them inside the bungalow. Strategically positioned replicas of natural plants ornamented each of the rooms. Several large color photos and original paintings decorated the walls.

"Doctor, the layout is so charming."

"Yes, very nice," Cyrus replied perfunctorily, his mind focused on tomorrow. "You know, Ronald, once I submit my report and the government has the proof of the Formula Seven antitoxin, I will finally gain recognition for my brilliance."

"You deserve it, Doc. I'm so proud of you."

"Thank you. I'm so excited. I think my discovery will merit a Nobel Prize. Undoubtedly, I'll be awarded a presidential citation."

Cyrus continued fantasizing as he walked into his bedroom, irrationally envisioning a party for the menagerie of chimps on his triumphant return to Los Angeles. The hominids would celebrate with fresh fruit, he'd decided. It was too bad that they couldn't wash their food down with a sip or two of bubbly Champagne.

His enthusiasm abated slightly as he ran the toothbrush over his teeth. He pictured the thousands upon thousands infected with the HIV virus. Those without hope would now be given new leases on life and the AIDS curse eradicated for all time. Cyrus closed the light and crawled into bed. He tossed and turned, unable to sleep, visualizing tomorrow's meeting. It took an hour, for his mind to slow down and allow slumber to overtake him.

* * *

The car from the CDC waited outside, its engine idling. Cyrus swallowed the last of the coffee. His nerves felt as if they laid on top of his skin, but he remained filled with confidence. He had no doubt the science community would embrace his discovery. The incontrovertible evidence of the new drug that carried the sacred gift of life sat inside his bag.

Not since Jonas Salk's vaccine stemmed the tide of the crippling poliomyelitis epidemic had there been a finding of such magnitude.

His assistant placed his cup in the sink. "Can I get you another coffee?"

"No thank you, Ron. I'm ready to go."

* * *

Director Thaddeus Walton, CDC director, shook Cyrus' hand. "Your creation is ingenious and will be monumental in helping humanity. Your reputation is beyond reproach, but what you've brought us today is astounding."

The seven other men and the one woman stood up from the large table and applauded.

Mary Masters, the deputy director, couldn't contain her enthusiasm. "Doctor Markum, this innovation, Formula Seven, will save so many. I'm honored to be in your presence."

The doctor's heart pounded. "Thank you, but it's not me alone who can take credit. The team at the Crestfield Laboratory has toiled relentlessly to perfect the antitoxin. There's still more I'd like to accomplish. Many years ago, my younger brother died of leukemia. I've pledged to wipe out the disease. That will be my next project."

At fifty-three, Cyrus' genius was about to be recognized by the world. The thrill of his success felt indescribable.

Director Walton pulled the doctor aside. "I'll be flying to D.C. this afternoon and will meet with the undersecretary of health and human services. I'll provide the highlights of this morning's meeting. You should prepare yourself to travel. Once the people in Washington hear the details, they're sure to summon you forthwith. I'm certain the president will want to meet with you in the Oval Office."

"That's exciting, Director. What should I do in the meantime?"

"Bask in the glow of your success." He laughed. "Just wait for my call."

During the ride back to Pine Lake, the car passed a sandwich shop on Chamblee-Tucker Road.

Cyrus tapped on the partition. "Driver, please stop here. I want to celebrate."

He and Ronald watched the counterman create a pair of foot-longs, packed with salami, pepperoni, provolone, lettuce, tomato, and green peppers.

Back inside the limo, he ran a hand through his graying hair, as his thoughts centered on his dad. It was the smell of the sliced delicacies that rekindled old memories. Each Sunday during his early teen years, the senior Markum would demonstrate his mastery of the "Dagwood" sandwich and carefully prepare two for their usual father and son Sunday outings. Cyrus recalled the excitement he felt when his dad unfurled the wax paper and exposed the tasty prizes within.

A frown replaced the expression of happiness. Unfortunately, the relationship with his dad didn't last. Another woman enraptured the master sandwich maker's heart and he had little time to spare for his son and none whatsoever for his spouse. His parents separated. The relationship with his dad deteriorated, and eventually, he'd lost complete touch several years prior to his father's death.

His mom was the biggest loser. Heartbroken, she'd never remarried, hesitant to trust another with her heart. But she survived and learned to be independent, assertive, and resilient. Her son now carried on in her stead.

The overstuffed sandwich was everything he'd hoped for. With the sun at its apex and few clouds to interfere with the clear blue of the afternoon sky, Cyrus kicked off his sandals and tucked away his wire-rimmed glasses. He wriggled on the hammock, making himself comfortable. With the ends of the net fabric looped around the trunks of a pair of southern magnolias, he lay only ten feet from the water's edge.

Above him, a woodpecker hammered away, while a family of crows cawed and clacked as they hopped from branch to branch. A dozen waterfowl swam nearby, quacking and honking.

What a wonderful time in my life, he mused. *This is simply delightful.* A gentle breeze rustled leaves while two gray squirrels played tag beneath them.

Cyrus tried not to focus on the expected call from the CDC. Usually practicing meditation as his way of calming brain activity, now would be the perfect time to take an excursion into the center of his own universe and sooth his overtaxed nervous system. As his mind accepted its oneness with the universe, the sudden sound of Ronald's voice jolted him back to the physical plane.

Cyrus' body lurched forward, almost forcing him to lose his balance and fall to the ground. "Yes, yes. I'm awake. Are they on the phone?"

"No, Doctor. I thought you made like a glass of pink lemonade."

He fought back his exasperation. "Not right now. Please let me know when Director Walton calls. Meanwhile, I'd like a bit of privacy. I want to decompress for a bit and visit with my inner spirit. You do understand?"

"Of course, Doctor. I'll let you know immediately."

As his assistant walked toward the cottage, his crew-cut platinum blonde hair glistened in the sunlight. A wry smile crossed his lips.

Adapting to the quirks and nuances of his employer, Ronald never acted put off when rebuffed or chastised by his slightly eccentric boss. It had been twenty-six months since he'd embarked on this career and wasn't sorry for it in the least.

He'd earned a master's degree in electrical engineering at UCLA, but been unable to find work after graduation. His dad, an acquaintance of the wealthy doctor, informed his son of the possible job availability. He had no real interest, but his father, weary of his son doing nothing, convinced him to set up an interview. Cyrus and Ronald made an immediate connection.

His duties were simple enough. He kept the doctor's home neat and clean, cooked once in a while, and drove him around occasionally. With his boss gone most of the day, he had free run of the upscale three-bedroom residence.

Humming the melody from a Beatles song, he headed back inside.

Cyrus didn't hear him. He shifted to his right side, replicating the Buddha pose, the position the master used the last time he'd drawn breath on the earthly plane. He felt at ease in this posture. Planting his elbow in the coarse fabric of the hammock, he supported his head with his right hand. Relaxing his physical body, he concentrated on the concept of nothingness. Successful in his efforts, he dozed off after only a few minutes.

*   *   *

The call from the CDC came at six-nineteen that evening.

"Hello, Doctor Markum's line. This is Ronald, his assistant. How may I help you?"

He listened for a few seconds, then handed the phone to his boss who sat across the kitchen table. Ron wore a huge grin, his eyebrows raised in expectation.

Cyrus was psyched, ready for success. "Hello. This is Doctor Markum," he answered enthusiastically.

"Hello, Doctor, Mary Masters, from the CDC. Director Walton is presently indisposed and requested that I apprise you of the situation in Washington. The administration greeted your report with respect and optimism. The staff thanks you for the job you've done. Director Walton will be contacting you in the morning and provide further details and instructions. Have a good evening, sir."

Before Cyrus had the opportunity to say a word, he the sound of the disconnect. *That's it? There must be a mistake. Her message sounded as if she was reading from a paper.* He couldn't have been any more disappointed.

He handed the phone to his assistant. "That's rather odd, Ronald. I find that government administrators are a species that subsist beyond the realm of my comprehension. They dance to the beat of their own drum. Their movements seemed ill-timed, and out of rhythm with nature."

He exhaled and sat down on the couch. "They'll call back in the morning, I suppose."

Ronald, adept at humoring his boss, provided a nod of affirmation. "Yes, sir. I'm certain that tomorrow will be a better day."

CHAPTER NINE

The Hidden Aspects of Betrayal

The brash sound of the ringer broke through the silence. Cyrus opened one eye, then the other. Early morning shafts of light caused him to raise a hand and shield his face.

"What time is it?" He mumbled, his mind slowly focusing. He snatched his watch from the bedside table and glared at it. It read six-thirteen.

The annoying electronic racket stopped and replaced by the sound of his assistant's voice. "Yes. Please hold on. I'll get him."

Who'd be calling at such an hour? Cyrus wondered.

Ronald stumbled in, smacking into the corner of his boss' bed, but maintaining his balance. "Doctor Markum, there's a Los Angeles deputy sheriff on the line. He said there's been a break-in at the Crestfield laboratory."

Cyrus pulled aside the bedding. He jumped up and grabbed the robe from the back of the chair and slipped it on. "What do you mean, break-in? Why would thieves break-into the laboratory? We have twenty-four-hour security. How could that happen?"

"I don't know." Ronald held out the phone. "Here, please, take this. The sheriff's on the line."

The assistant sat down on the edge of the bed and slumped forward, supporting his face with both hands.

"Hello. This is Doctor Markum. Please, tell me what happened? Are the animals okay?"

He had to wait several seconds before receiving a reply.

"Yes. Hello, Doctor. This is Deputy Slade. I'm on-scene. We've had a break-in at the facility and the contents stolen. I understand that you're out of town right now, but you'll need to come in and file a report as soon as you get back."

"Yes, of course." Cyrus felt faint. "What exactly did they take?" He looked at Ronald. "Please, would you go and make coffee?"

His assistant jumped up. "Yes, of course, Doctor. It won't take me long."

Cyrus stared at the handset before putting it up to his mouth. "Hello?"

The receiver came alive with the sound of the deputy's voice once again. "Are you there, Doctor? I thought I lost you."

"Yes, Deputy, I'm still here."

"I'm sorry to tell you this, but your facility is completely cleaned out. The thieves have taken everything."

The blood drained from Cyrus' face "What? No, that's impossible. What about the animals, Deputy? What about the records and laboratory equipment?"

"I know it's bizarre. They left nothing. I haven't seen anything like it."

Cyrus whimpered. Tears ran down his cheeks.

"This is what we know so far," Deputy Slade continued, "the preliminary investigation reveals that at approximately six p.m., the perps pushed their way into the building as your attendant arrived. They wore masks. At least one of them carried a pistol. When the guard on duty opened the inside door, he took a blow to the head. The two were blindfolded and tied up with plastic ties and duct tape. The midnight relief guard saw the blood trail and found them in a hall closet."

"Oh, dear. How terrible. What about the workers? Are they okay?"

"The guard who suffered head trauma is pretty bad. He's unconscious and in serious condition. He received first-aid at the scene and taken to Good Samaritan Hospital. The attendant's lucky. He only suffered a few scrapes and bruises. He gave his account to a detective before EMT took him to the hospital."

"Oh, my God," Cyrus groaned. How could this happen?"

"I don't have an answer for you, Doc. Forensics will check the premises and see what they can find. I can tell you this, these people knew exactly what they were doing. The detectives will want to ask some questions. How soon can you get back to Los Angeles?"

"This makes absolutely no sense. I can't believe this is happening."

Cyrus pulled the phone from his ear. His shoulders sagged. He closed his eyes. After several seconds, he put the receiver back up to his face. "I'm sorry, Deputy.

We'll make reservations to get back to Los Angeles as soon as possible."

"That'll be fine, Doctor. Here's the number where you can reach me. It's three one..."

Cyrus interrupted. "Deputy, wait. Please hold on a moment. I'll get Ronald to jot down the number. I'm too upset."

He held his hand over the mouthpiece. "Ronald! Would you please get in here? Bring a pen and paper with you."

"What can I do for you, Doctor?" Ronald asked, running back into the bedroom.

Cyrus handed him the handset. "Please take down the number."

"Of course, Doctor."

Cyrus walked into the kitchen and stood in front of the window He gazed out at the lake. A pair of geese tussled, rippling the water around them. He turned away, and pulled out a chair from under the hardwood table and collapsed on it. The stark reality of the situation grabbed hold.

Cyrus threw his head back and rolled his shoulders. "No. I can't allow this tragedy to control me," he murmured. "I will overcome this."

He dropped to the floor and flexed his legs. He took up the Lotus position, knees pushing against the floor, head reaching for the sky. Concentrating on his Zazen breathing technique, he rocked his body and slowly relaxed.

* * *

Cyrus and Ronald stood in line behind the stanchion ropes at the Southwest Airlines ticket counter. The local time showed 8:44 a.m. Their flight wouldn't be departing Hartsfield-Jackson until 11:45. They had plenty of time, but with the line moving along at a snail's pace. Cyrus fumed at the supposed inefficiency of the airline employees.

"These people, Ron, they probably get paid a bonus for trying people's patience."

"That's funny, but it's moving. We're lucky we could get tickets. We purchased the last two available seats."

Cyrus would have preferred first-class seats, but knew he should be happy with the small things. He and Ron's seats were several rows apart, with neither on the aisle or next to a window. Slightly claustrophobic, the doctor hated to cram into the undersized space. He figured that if he pulled out a fifty-dollar bill, he'd find another passenger willing to switch seats.

Finally, their turn came at the ticket counter. Cyrus dropped his bag and looked at the nametag on the young female agent's lapel. "Hello, Kristen. We have reservations for Flight 3472. Have you had any cancellations? We would like to change our seats, if possible, or upgrade to first class."

The agent reacted politely. "Yes, of course, sir. I understand. Let me look."

The perky lady analyzed her screen. She tapped her fingers on the keyboard. "I'm so sorry. I apologize, but unfortunately, your flight is overbooked."

Cyrus tried to show no emotion. "Well, thank you for looking."

"You're welcome, sir." She reached out her hand. "May I see a form of ID, please?"

The airline clerk pressed on the keys of her computer. The printer spit out the tickets.

Cyrus still rankled internally, but he remained calm. "I'm grateful for your help, Kristen. Thank you."

The men followed the signs to the food court. The big overhead clock showed almost nine-fifteen. They still had plenty of time.

"Ronald, why don't you get us coffees?" The doctor pointed to one of the unoccupied tables in the cluster of a dozen or so. "We can sit right over there."

His assistant made a bee-line to the empty table and dropped his bag. The doctor joined him and laid his briefcase and overnight bag on the tiled floor. He plopped down in one of the plastic chairs.

Cyrus pulled a twenty-dollar bill from his wallet and handed it to Ronald. "Black, no sugar, and I'll take a banana muffin, blueberry if they're out."

"You got it, boss. Be right back."

Ron rejoined his boss within a few minutes. He didn't care much for the bitter brew. Cyrus preferred it that way but found his muffin a bit too crunchy for his taste. He stood up and threw what was left of it in the trash.

Cyrus' eyes searched around the promenade. "I need to use the restroom. Please, keep an eye on our belongings."

"Sure thing, Doc." Ron continued to chomp on his garlic bagel. "This is tasty. You should have gotten one of these. Would you like me to get you one?"

"No. I'm not hungry. I'll be back shortly."

Cyrus angled across the concourse and disappeared through the door displaying a male stick-figure.

While Cyrus high-stepped toward the restroom, the deceitful sixty seconds began. The attractive redhead made her move. She headed for Ronald, just as he took the last bite of his bagel, and wiped his lips. He perked right up when he noticed the knockout coming his way.

She smiled demurely. "Excuse me. Do you have the time?"

Dressed in a short red skirt, she'd also donned a push-up bra, which allowed her cleavage to jut from the top of her tight-fitting sweater. Naturally, when her eyeglass case fell to the floor, Ron rushed from his seat to assist the damsel in distress. Bending down, he retrieved the purple polka-dot container and handed it back to her. This act of gallantry allowed the hungry wolf his opportunity to strike. Picasso would have been jealous of the misdirection play, an example of fine art.

Ronald had no clue what was happening. He ogled the young lady's fine legs, pondering how good she might be in the sack.

She flapped her eyelids. "Thank you for your help. I have to catch my flight now."

The frustration showed on his face. "Where are you heading?"

"Vacation. I'm on my way to Bermuda for two weeks." She gave him a wink. "Wanna come along?"

"Wish I could. Work."

"Well, goodbye then. Nice to meet you."

He watched the swivel in her hips and the sexy shake in her backside as she walked away, and out of his life forever. He sat back down and sighed, thinking over what could have been.

A tap on his shoulder reminded him of his reality. "Are you ready?"

"Yes, Doctor, all done."

Ronald stooped to pick up their belongings. The briefcase, where is it? He fell to his knees and searched around beneath the table. *Oh, my God!* The briefcase was gone.

"Doctor, I can't find your case."

"You can't be serious. Where could it have gone?"

Ronald's body trembled. "I don't know."

Then, like a roundhouse kick to the groin, the realization hit home.

"I'm so sorry, Doctor. I can't believe how stupid I am. It must've been that girl. Oh crap. I can't believe I fell for that."

Cyrus' body dropped into a chair. He fought against the rage that threatened to take control of his inner self.

"When you were in the bathroom," Ron tried to explain, "this beautiful girl, she distracted me. She must have had a partner. She dropped her glass case. I picked it up for her. That had to be it."

The doctor groaned. "Oh, my God. Oh, my God."

Tears ran from Ronald's eyes. "You can fire me. I'd understand. I can't believe how foolish I am?"

The doctor composed himself. "Nonsense, you're not being fired. These people are professionals. They waited for the right moment. I could've carried the bag with me. It's not your fault."

CHAPTER TEN

The Pudding Thickens

The police sergeant handed Cyrus the sheet of paper. "The incident report number is on there." He pointed to the upper right corner. "It'll take a few days, but you can call the number on there and request a copy."

"Aren't you going to look for them?" Cyrus asked, visibly shaken.

The sergeant held back his laughter. "Who would I be trying to find? Do you have a description of who took the bag?"

"Good looking redhead, tight red skirt," Ron volunteered.

The police officer shrugged. "You don't know for a fact that she had anything to do with the theft. Right?"

Ron scoffed at the assessment. "Not exactly, but I'm sure that she's involved."

The police sergeant put his pad away and smirked. "When did you become a detective, son? You didn't see her take it. There's nothing we can do right now. Like I said, give it three business days. Then call the number on the report."

Ron and Cyrus exchanged looks of frustration.

With the Crestfield laboratory debacle and the theft of the briefcase, it couldn't have been any clearer that a sinister plot had taken root.

The doctor walked to the payphone and dialed the operator, then the number Ronald had copied down earlier this morning. "Hello. I'd like to make a credit card call." He read her the number of his Visa card.

It rang twice.

"Hello, squad room, Sergeant Farmer. What can I do for you?"

"Yes, hello. This is Doctor Markum. Is Deputy Sheriff Slade in?"

"Just one moment, I'll check for you."

The line went silent. Cyrus waited.

"Slade, here. Who's this?"

"Thank goodness I reached you, Deputy. It's Doctor Markum. You called me about the Crestfield robbery a few hours ago."

"Sure. That's right. I remember. What can I do for you?"

"I'm calling from at the Atlanta airport. My briefcase has been stolen. The papers inside it are invaluable. I'm sure this is connected to the theft at the laboratory."

"Uh huh. It might be related, or possibly be a coincidence. We'll need hard proof to corroborate your suspicion. The detective in charge will discuss it with you. He'll be in at noon."

"I understand, Deputy. I'm certain it's connected. Would you please send a car to my home and check the doors and windows? I'll be back in LA at about two o'clock, California time."

"Ok, Doc, I can do that. I have your home address. I'll talk to the desk sergeant and make it happen. When you get here, I'll be off shift. Ask for Detective Thornton. He's the lead in the Crestfield case."

"Thank you for your assistance, Deputy. I'll see you when I get back. Thank you."

Cyrus clicked off the phone. He glanced at his watch. The time showed eleven-fifteen. They still had thirty minutes to make their flight.

"Ronald, we better get moving."

"Yes, sir. Again, I'm so sorry. If you can me, I'll understand."

"Please, no more apologies. It's not your fault. You're not being fired. The responsibility is mine. These people are professionals. They're professionals and would've found another opportunity to actualize their plan. If the theft hadn't occurred when it did, it would have soon after. I don't place the blame on you."

"I still feel awful, Doctor. I wish I could turn back time."

"Right now, you just need to get on the flight and fly with me to Los Angeles."

The gate attendant checked their passes and they proceeded to walk through the aerobridge. Moving single file down the aisle of the plane, they found their seats. Cyrus squeezed into 17B. Ronald walked a half-dozen rows further and dropped down into 23E. Each stuffed their bag under their seat, then fastened their seat belt.

Cyrus hadn't the stomach to negotiate with anyone for a better seat and found himself stuck between a chubby blonde lady in a blue sweatsuit, and a guy with a lip ring and a colored tattoo of a parrot on his neck. He ignored both, as he racked his brain, trying to imagine who might be responsible for these catastrophes.

He paid little attention to the movie on the flight, though he noticed Robert De Niro playing the role of a fast-talking bounty hunter and Charles Grodin in tow. The doctor couldn't care less. He anxiously awaited the moment when the plane would engage its landing gear. He pictured himself at the door of his Bel Air home.

About two hours into the flight, he managed to fall asleep. Dreams of the chimpanzee Charlemagne, the Formula Seven serum and the precious lab reports filled his fitful slumber.

The doctor's dreams faded. He awakened.

A male flight attendant stood in the aisle, refreshment cart at the ready. "Would you care for a drink, sir?"

"No, that's okay."

The steward pushed his cart to the next row of seats. Cyrus' eyelids drooped once more. No Charlemagne this time; instead, his mother paid a visit. She shook her head, mouthing the word "no," and pointed at a large outdoor arena. Automobiles and pickup trucks jammed the parking lot. The huge sign over one of the entrances read, "Farmers Stadium."

He opened his eyes as the plane began its descent. The strange images remained imprinted in his mind. He couldn't venture a guess as to its meaning.

A female voice came over the intercom. "Ladies and gentlemen, we're making final preparations to land. Please put your trays and seat backs in the upright position and fasten your seatbelts."

*   *   *

The thirty-five-minute drive from LAX to his home on Nalin Drive seemed to take twice the usual time. Cyrus checked his watch repeatedly. He knew that demonstrating impatience wouldn't be constructive, but found himself beyond the point of caring. Finally, the Lincoln Town Car pulled up to the curb.

Ronald paid the driver and collected the luggage. Cyrus pulled the keys from his pocket and streaked for the door. He twisted the single-cylinder deadbolt lock, then the double-cylinder. Both opened with no sign of tampering. He punched in the alarm code on the white keypad next to the door. The high-pitched beeper cutoff. Good. Nothing unusual there.

Cyrus ran to his bedroom. Ron followed him and watched as the doctor grasped each side of the Andy Warhol Moonwalk print and lifted it carefully from the wall. The cream-colored wall safe looked untouched. He entered the combination and pulled open the heavy fireproof door.

The doctor hyperventilated. He felt as if he'd been held underwater and couldn't breathe. On the top shelf of the safe, the two stacks of one-hundred-dollar bills sat undisturbed. The empty space below the "Benjamins" had contained the last of his *Formula Seven* reports.

He emptied the safe. His head spun. His knees felt weak. He felt nauseated and dropped into the wooden rocking chair. They were gone.

Any trace of his hard work had gone missing and been replaced by suspicion.

Who can be responsible for these acts? If his suspicions were accurate, those culpable might never receive justice. More importantly, without his lab reports and calculations, he's lost. What can he do?

He pulled out his handkerchief and patted his lips. "Ronald, would you please call the number the deputy gave us and see if you can get in touch with Detective Thornton? We need to report this."

His aide picked up the cordless handset from the desk. He reached into his shirt pocket and pulled out the notepad. Thumbing through a few pages, he found the entry and dialed. He listened to it ring.

A gruff female voice came through the handset. "Hello, Los Angeles Sheriff's Department. How can I direct your call?"

"Detective Thornton, please."

"Who's calling."

"Doctor Markum. The detective is expecting our call, thank you."

Cyrus stumbled from the chair.

Ronald passed him the handset. "She's getting him."

The doctor tapped his foot on the carpet as he waited.

"Detective Thornton. What can I do for you?" The depth of the baritone voice surprised Cyrus.

"Detective Thornton, I want to report a robbery. Someone broke into my home."

"Uh-huh. I see from the notes that we had a patrol car do a drive-by a few hours ago. They saw nothing unusual or suspicious." The detective seemed apathetic.

"Well, your people missed it," Cyrus protested loudly. "Whoever did this must have bypassed the alarm system, cracked the combination to the safe, and handed out death sentences to thousands of innocent human beings."

The complainant's outburst annoyed the detective, though he'd been on the job for almost seventeen years and jaded by all he'd seen and heard.

He knew not to overreact. "Just calm down, Doctor. We'll send a patrol car over right away. Don't touch anything. Give me about twenty minutes. My partner and I will be there."

"Thank you, Detective. We'll wait outside and try not to disturb anything."

"Okay then, Doctor. Just sit tight. We'll see you shortly."

The high-pitched sound of a dial tone replaced Detective Thornton's deep voice. Cyrus slid the handset back into its base.

"Ronald, we need to wait outside. We must not contaminate the crime scene or disturb any possible evidence."

"Yes, I understand."

Ever so carefully, they maneuvered to the front entrance of the ranch-style home. Cyrus held his monogrammed handkerchief as a buffer between his fingers and the brass knob of the mahogany hardwood door. They stood outside on the concrete walkway, right next to the lovely arrangement of trees that straddled the entrance of the property. Even in his sullen mood, the doctor enjoyed the sight of the small grove of Canary Island date palms he'd imported two years earlier.

The elegance of his palm trees served as a distraction for only a moment in time. With his life's work torn from him, hate filled his heart.

Who'd resort to such tactics and what is the reason behind it? An unscrupulous pharmaceutical company looking to capitalize on the tremendous financial potential of Formula Seven, might they bear responsibility? That doesn't make sense. To orchestrate such an intricate plot is irrational, the theft too obvious. So, who?

The black-and-white police car slowed to a stop. Cyrus discontinued his cerebral aerobics. Employing his handkerchief, he carefully opened the black wrought iron gate and walked to the blacktop. The driver, a woman in her late twenties, stepped out. A bit heavy, she had a lick of brown hair sticking out from under her peaked cap.

He read her nametag. "Hello, Officer McGowan."

She tipped her cap. "Hello."

The other officer, a tall black man, wore three chevrons on each uniform sleeve.

He offered his hand. "I assume you're Doctor Markum," he stated correctly, adjusting his cap, and pushing down on his holster.

"Yes, that's me."

"I'm Sergeant Stafford." He pointed a forefinger. "That's my partner, Officer McGowan."

Cyrus guessed the sergeant age as mid-forties, and, by the look of his muscular physique, hit the weight room often. McGowan took the lead while his partner jotted down information on her notepad. After five minutes of back-and-forth questions and answers, the sergeant slid into the passenger seat.

He picked up the radio handset. "Eight-Adam-Ten to Control."

After a few seconds, the radio speaker squawked back. "This is Control, go ahead Eight-Adam-Ten."

"Control, we've finished taking a 961 on that 459, our location. We're waiting for William unit, over."

"Roger. William unit on the way, Eight-Adam-Ten, stand-by."

After about thirty seconds, the speaker crackled again. "William unit's ETA your 10-20 in five, over."

"That's a roger, Central. Eight-Adam-Ten, out."

Sergeant Stafford clipped the handset to the dashboard and slid out from his patrol car. "The detective unit will be here in a few minutes, Doctor Markum. I think we have all the information we need for right now. The detectives will go over the details with you. I'm sure they'll have follow-up questions."

"Okay. Thank you, Sergeant."

Cyrus watched Officer McGowan work her way around the outside perimeter of his yard, scribbling occasionally on a pad. He had questions of his own. *Does God actually exist? If there is an omnipotent being, how could he allow this to happen?*

He didn't have long to consider the answers. A blue four-door sedan pulled up. Out from the passenger door came a large man, the top of his balding head visible as he bent forward and set his feet. A detective's gold shield hung from his left jacket pocket.

"Doctor Markum? I'm Detective Thornton." He extended his hand. "We spoke earlier."

"Yes. Hello, Detective."

"Okay, excuse me a minute. I need to speak with the first officers on the scene."

He walked toward the two patrol officers, who waited outside their patrol car.

Thornton's partner had been busy on the two-way radio when they'd pulled up. He climbed out of his car and joined the doctor. "Hello. I'm Detective Rossetti. I have questions for you."

He flipped open a notepad. "Do you take any prescription medications?"

Cyrus recoiled. "Are you serious? Why are you asking me that? What does that have to do with the robberies?"

Rossetti cocked an eyebrow. "Just touching the bases." He ignored his subject's indignation. "Do you take any psychotropic drugs?"

Now, Cyrus became enraged. "Of course not! Why are you asking me these questions? Do you think I hallucinated this? You're an idiot. How did you ever become a detective? Where did you find your shield, in a box of Cracker Jacks?"

Now, Rossetti took his turn to act upset. "Hey, wiseguy! You wouldn't want me to write down that you refused to cooperate, now would you?"

Ronald stepped between the two men. "Stop treating him like that. We were together. I can verify all his statements. Look! We had a break-in at the laboratory, our home burglarized, and thieves stole his briefcase at the airport. He does not do any drugs or have a drinking problem."

Rosetti put his pad away. "Just rippling the waters, a bit. Don't take it personally. Okay?"

He left the two befuddled men and joined his partner. The doctor tried to listen as the detectives spoke with the patrol officers. He could make out about half of what the police discussed, but enough to comprehend.

Stafford and McGowan walked down the street together, then separated. "They're going to canvas the neighborhood," Thornton explained, walking toward Cyrus.

Thornton laid a hand on his shoulder. "Look, Doctor. Don't mind my partner. I don't think he ate lunch today. He gets a little cranky."

"I understand, but he definitely could use a semester in charm school."

Thornton chuckled. "Yeah, probably. We're gonna head into the house. You two wait out here."

*   *   *

After ten or fifteen minutes, the detectives came down the steps. They peeled off their latex gloves and booties.

Rosetti gave the doctor a sidelong glance. "Didn't mean to ruffle your feathers before."

Cyrus still smoldering, felt embarrassment from his earlier comments. "It's okay. Don't mind what I said. We're even."

"Doctor, do you think this could have been a random robbery?" Thornton asked, scratching the top of his head. "Upscale neighborhood, no one home, a crime of opportunity, maybe?"

Cyrus gritted his teeth. "Nothing random about any of these crimes."

The detective nodded. "Okay. I got it. Thanks."

Thornton motioned to his partner. "Rosetti and I are going to ring some doorbells. We'll see if any of the neighbors might have seen anything suspicious. Don't touch anything. We'll be back in twenty. Forensics should be here soon. They'll comb through the house."

"Right. We'll stay clear," Cyrus answered, paced about on the sidewalk. Ron let his back slide down the trunk of a palm and parked his butt at its base.

*   *   *

By the time the white van pulled in behind the detective's car, an hour had slipped by. The doors opened and two men and a woman, garbed in blue lab coats and lugging cases, climbed out. Detective Thornton spoke to one of the men.

Cyrus moved closer but could only make out Thornton's parting words. "O'Hara, the house is all yours. You and your team can perform your magic. Me and Rossetti are gonna go look around and scope out the houses next door."

O'Hara's lips formed a smile. "Affirmative, Detective. We'll see if we can pull an ace or two out of our sleeves."

Thornton threw a finger salute, and he and Rossetti headed around the side of the house.

After half an hour, the detectives returned.

"Detective Thornton, did you find anything?" Cyrus asked.

"Please! Give us time to gather our facts. Don't worry, we'll let you know when we have something."

He'd expected more. "Detective, you don't understand the importance of this discovery."

Thornton grimaced "We can't perform miracles. Okay?"

After waiting another forty-five minutes, the criminologists came down the steps from the house.

O'Hara threw Thornton a mock salute. "Give me a day. I'll call you."

The forensic team climbed inside their van.

Thornton handed Cyrus his business card. "Would you meet us at the station?"

"Of course. Can you give us a chance to clean up first?"

"Sure thing. You've got the address on the card. See you in about an hour, then?"

"Yes. That's fine."

Forty-five minutes passed. Ronald guided the sleek black Mercedes down Sunset Boulevard, on the way to the West Los Angeles Community Police Station. Cyrus sat in the back seat.

The young man liked the way this car handled, but he preferred the red Thunderbird convertible. When he went riding with the top down, he imagined himself a part of Hollywood royalty. The doctor didn't mind at all. He coveted his twenty-seven-year-old "adopted nephew's" loyalty and considered him his only family.

The time for fun and games had passed. Cyrus concentrated on the notes he'd brought along. Still modestly optimistic, he had serious doubts that these detectives could outsmart the people responsible for his problems.

* * *

Thornton led the two men into an interrogation room. "Please, sit down." He pointed to a pair of uncomfortable metal chairs. "I wish I had something for you. It's too early in either of the investigations. So far, the Crestfield robbery is a major zero. The thieves covered their tracks well. The attendant thinks there were three of them. They wore masks and gloves."

The detective cleared his throat. "The guard is in a coma and may end up a vegetable. I wish I had better news."

Cyrus groaned. "Unbelievable."

Thornton's eyes narrowed. He stared at Cyrus. "Do you have any enemies. Anyone you might think had it in for you? Maybe, someone with a grudge?"

"I think those that did this work for the government. I don't have proof, but that's what I think."

The detective sat back in his chair. "Let's talk reality. As far as the burglary on Nalin Drive, a neighbor saw two late model sedans parked outside your premises last night around nine. We got a partial, ran the plate, but no luck. We got only vague descriptions on the perps."

The doctor sighed. "I understand that these robberies are not the Lindbergh baby kidnapping to you, but the consequences can't be taken lightly. You have to assign more detectives to the case."

Thornton tried not to laugh. "I'll talk to my lieutenant."

"Let me," Cyrus demanded. "Maybe I can initiate more action."

The detective frowned. "Sorry. He's out right now. I'll let him know, though. Don't worry. We'll contact you when we have something. That's it for now. Thank you both for coming in."

* * *

Ronald guided the car back up Sunset. On this trip, Cyrus sat next to his assistant. "I've decided. I'm going to hire a private investigator."

"That sounds like a good idea, Doc. Do you know anybody?"

"Yes. My attorney, Miriam Lesgarten."

Ron looked puzzled. "I don't follow."

"Her younger brother. He's a former New York City narcotics detective. He has his own agency. They specialize in corporate espionage and that sort of thing. Miriam told me about him the last time I visited her office. I'll call her when we get home."

*   *   *

Evan Lesgarten carried a reputation for being a hard-nosed NYPD cop with a lot of juice. After a Bronx drug bust went south, Evan took a bullet in his vest and another in the shoulder. The wound gave internal affairs, already probing an earlier complaint, their opportunity. They laid out the options for the heavy-handed detective. Offered a choice to accept a half-pension and early retirement, or to run the gauntlet and face possible criminal charges, his decision was simple.

It had been three years since Evan moved west and enlisted his sister aid. Hooking him up with a private gumshoe, it didn't take long to get the lay of the land and hang up his own shingle.

Resourceful and ruthless, Evan cracked the Barnabus Clancy LTD case, which put him and his agency on the map. The white-collar crime's exposure proved to be close to forty million dollars. Evan tied up the details with a nice little bow and handed them over to his client, a member of the board of directors. The incriminating evidence traced the pilfered funds to offshore bank accounts and incriminated the company president, Stephenson Clancy.

Evan Lesgarten's smiling face graced the front page of the Los Angeles Times. From that point onward, his career shifted into overdrive. His customer base, as well as his bank account, swelled. He added a second and a third office in the Los Angeles area and a satellite location in San Francisco.

In the four days since Cyrus' plane landed at LAX, the police had gotten nowhere. The only other unidentified fingerprints found in the home belonged to a refrigerator repairman. He had a long arrest record as a juvenile, but he had an alibi, out coaching a youth basketball team at the time of the robbery. The Crestfield investigation yielded similarly distressing results. CDC Director Walton wouldn't take his calls. Neither would his assistant.

Evan remained cool as he folded up the twenty-five-thousand-dollar check and slid it into his top desk drawer. "Thank you, Doctor. As we've discussed, twenty-five thousand more will be due upon completion of the investigation, regardless of the result. A one hundred-thousand-dollar performance bonus will be payable, providing I recover your papers. Expenses, of course, are additional." Evan signed at the bottom of the contract.

He came around his desk and handed his client a pen. "Right here." Evan pointed to the proper line as he laid the agreement in front of his new client.

Cyrus added his signature. "Okay, it's agreed. I understand the parameters and will be only too glad to pay the bonus."

Evan emptied the contents of the manila envelope on his desk and perused Cyrus' notes. "I promise to contact you before the week is out. Rest assured, we'll find those responsible."

* * *

The call came in at nine on Friday morning.

"Hello, Doctor Markum, this is Evan."

"Ah, yes. How are you?"

"Terrific. I've gotten a break in your case. Today at noon, you'll be receiving a call from the people who committed the robberies. Don't contact the police. They insisted on that."

"Evan, you're incredible. But why would they be contacting me?"

"You'll have to discuss that with them. I'm merely the conduit. The rest is up to you."

"Fantastic! You've done a splendid job. I'll let you know the outcome. Goodbye, and thank you again."

"Okay, Doc. I'll be in touch."

Cyrus hung up and rushed into the kitchen. "The private detective called."

Ron jumped up from his chair. "What did he say?"

"It's complicated, but he's found the people. They'll be calling us at noon. I gather they'll be offering to return the reports, for a fee, of course."

* * *

Cyrus vaulted from the sofa when the electronic sound of the ringer interrupted the virtuoso violin sonata.

He twisted the knob on the radio. "Ronald, get ready."

His assistant awaited his cue in his bedroom and pressed the record and play buttons on the cassette recorder hooked to the extension. "Go ahead, Doc. We're good to go."

Cyrus was sweating. *Okay, I know I can do this.* "Hello, this is Doctor Markum. Who is this?"

"I'm Bob. You just listen, Markum. I want five-hundred-thousand dollars in cash, all in hundreds. I'll call back with the time and place. Once I see the money, you get the files you're looking for. Don't contact the authorities or tell anyone about this. If you do, I swear I'll destroy them. I want only you and your aide to show up. No funny business. Is that clear enough for you?"

"Yes, Bob, I understand. But, how can I be sure you have my files?"

"Walk to your front door. Your cover page is under it. You'll see I'm for real."

Cyrus rushed to the door. Sure enough, sticking halfway into his home, lay a sheet of paper with the words Formula Seven listed at the top.

"Okay, Bob. What's next?"

"Like I said, I want five-hundred-thousand, all in hundreds. Put the money in two gym bags. I'll call you at four this afternoon with instructions. Don't do anything stupid?"

"I won't. I'll be expecting your call."

He heard the click followed by a dial tone.

"Ronald, did you get that?"

"I'm pretty certain I did. Give me a few seconds. Let me rewind the tape and play it back."

It took only a few seconds to verify.

"Yes, we got it, Doc. It's loud and clear."

Cyrus dropped the phone on the kitchen table. His hands shook as he pulled open the refrigerator door and reached for the water pitcher. The call had taken its toll on his nerves. The one-gallon decanter came crashing to the floor.

Ron ran to his side. "Doctor Markum, are you okay?"

"Yes, I'm fine, but I made a mess. Would you please help me clean it up?"

* * *

A shade before nine on Friday night, the Mercedes entered the parking structure at the eastern end of Union Station. Cyrus and Ronald both felt anxiety running through them, unfamiliar with the Gateway Transit Plaza and worried about the exchange.

On orders from his boss, Ron had run to the post office and mailed two overnight packages, one to the law offices of Newhouse, Gladstone, and Company, the other addressed to Detective Thornton. A third cassette, wrapped securely in aluminum foil, he'd buried in the soil of the backyard vegetable garden, just beneath a sprouting tomato plant.

That major piece of evidence would help bring those responsible to justice. For the present, though, Cyrus only wanted to gain possession of his precious papers once again. Those documents meant more to him than any amount of money.

Ronald eased up on the gas pedal as he passed through Union Station's main entrance. Rolling past the first parking aisle, his right foot applied pressure to the brake. The car slowed down and came to a stop. Ron scrutinized the lot. About half the spaces looked filled. A few pedestrians walked about.

"Go ahead, keep driving," urged the doctor.

His assistant gave the engine a little gas. The car inched forward. "Just being careful."

The air conditioning pumped out frigid air, but perspiration dripped from the armpits of both men. Ron backed into a parking spot. He left the engine running, and flashed his high beams once, then again, and then a third time, as per the instructions. Across the aisle, a pair of headlights came alive. A dark sedan pulled out and drove toward them.

The car nosed in next to them, on the driver's side of the vehicle adjacent to Cyrus. The tinted window slid down. The doctor took his first look at the thief, a white male, a blue baseball cap on his head, clean-shaven, and probably in his mid-thirties.

"Bring out the money. Put the bags on the hood of your car," Bob ordered.

Cyrus and Ronald each grabbed one of the bags from the back seat. They carefully placed them on the hood of the car. Both occupants seated in the dark sedan climbed out.

Bob pointed at the bags. "John, go check 'em out."

As John moved to comply, Cyrus yelled out. "Where are my reports?"

Bob's associate didn't hesitate. He zipped open each of the bags and inspected the stacks of one-hundred-dollar bills, bound neatly with the bank's mustard-colored currency straps. "We got the money."

Bob flipped open the trunk of his car. "Don't worry, Markum. We have your merchandise. Come, take a look."

That comment struck Cyrus as odd, but he didn't think much of it, as he moved to secure his life's work. He'd never thought of his research papers as merchandise.

He gaped at the contents of the trunk. "What's this? Where are the reports?"

The truth slammed into the doctor like a Herculean hammer-shot to the solar plexus. Instead of his cherished documents, a group of paintings, tied together neatly with twine, occupied the space instead. An art aficionado of sorts, he recognized the top piece immediately. An original Andy Warhol pop art screen print of Mickey Mouse, stared at him.

His spirit was further dashed when the high-pitched shriek of sirens began echoing through the garage. Four police cars and a van pulled up and surrounded them. The rotating blue lights blinded the doctor.

A male voice thundered through a bullhorn. "Both of you, get down on the ground. Move, now, right fucking now. You hear me?"

The doctor and his assistant dropped to their knees. Several pairs of heavy hands helped push their torsos down to the concrete.

Cyrus groaned as they snapped the cuffs. "You're making a big mistake. We haven't done anything."

Bob dragged him up to his feet. "Shut your yap, thief. Save it."

John's foot connected with Cyrus' butt. "You just do what you're fucking told, mutt."

Cyrus' cry of pain went unnoticed.

Almost a dozen uniformed police officers pointed pistols or shotguns at the pair of "master criminals." Detective shields dangled from Bob and John's necks.

Reality can certainly be a bitch, especially when a nuclear worst-case scenario is exploding on you. Cyrus fought to control his temper as the cops led him and Ronald to separate patrol cars.

A police officer kicked his legs apart and rifled his pockets.

Bob pulled open the door of a squad car. "Get in and watch your head." He pushed his prisoner into the back seat. The door slammed shut behind him.

His aide received similar treatment. They each had their rights recited. After the ten-minute drive to the station, the prisoners removed their clothes and were thoroughly searched. This time a cavity check accompanied it. The cops held on to any personal belongings, including belts and shoelaces.

The fingerprinting process came next, then mug shots. Then, the fun could begin in earnest. An interrogation room awaited each of them.

The lead detective snarled at Cyrus. "What were you gonna do with the artwork?" He pushed his face closer. "Who else is involved in your ring? We want the name of your fence." His voice increased in volume. "Let's go, fuckwad! We need his name."

"I want to call my lawyer," Cyrus demanded.

The detective glared at him. "You're in big trouble, genius."

Ronald's interview went a bit differently.

"We know you two are guilty as hell," the detective claimed. "If you testify against your boss, we can give you immunity."

Ron, though terrified, bristled at the remarks. "We're innocent. We didn't do a damn thing."

The detective grinned. "Oh, come on. I've heard this shit a million times." He grabbed the suspect by the collar. "Confess and make it easy on yourself. Why are you protecting that guy? He doesn't give a shit about you."

The conversations in both interrogation rooms went around in circles. Finally, Cyrus got his call. He reached Miriam's answering service.

With hands still cuffed behind their backs, the prisoners were shuffled down the stairs to the basement. The excruciating stench hit them before the sight of their temporary home. Two uniformed jailors opened the gate. One removed each man's cuffs. The other pushed the pair inside their cage.

As the key turned in the lock, the doctor wrapped both hands around the metal bars. "You're not going to leave us in here, are you?"

The guard pulled the key from the lock. "You figure it out, smart guy."

The men in blue walked away, vanishing through a doorway at the end of the concrete hallway.

* * *

The lawyers looked annoyed, not happy about working so late. Byron Levinsky and Jack Cheatham, junior partners at Miriam's firm, sat with their clients in a small conference room. Two guards waited in the hallway.

Byron took the lead. "Miriam won't be involved with the case. Her brother might be called as a material witness and that would cause a conflict."

Ripples of rage raced through Cyrus. "But we didn't steal anything. The charges are bogus. It's entrapment."

Byron read aloud from the sheet of paper and shook his head in disgust. "Each of you will be charged with receiving stolen property, a felony under the California Penal Code number 496 and the federal charges under Statute 18 U.S.C. 2315."

Cyrus explained the chain of events after the meeting with the CDC. "It's obvious to me that it's the government. They orchestrated this and set up the exchange. I have recorded evidence of our innocence."

He pointed to Ronald. "Mr. Levinsky, Ronald recorded a cassette of the conversation between one of the conspirators and me. That will prove our innocence and show we're targets of an absurd shell game."

Mr. Cheatham frowned. "I'm sorry to inform you that California law prohibits the use of any such evidence. The tape is inadmissible. In fact, further charges would be levied against you should you produce it. We must come up with a counter strategy."

Cyrus slumped in his chair. "You can't be serious. We mailed a copy to Detective Thornton at the West Los Angeles Police Station."

Levinsky shrugged. "Unfortunately, that's the law. That tape's going to present another problem."

Cheatham stood up but didn't make eye contact with his clients. "The bail hearings will have to wait until the morning. That's when the judge will be on the bench."

Cyrus flinched. "You're saying we have to share space with the scum of Los Angeles until then? This just keeps getting better and better."

One of the guards opened the door. "Time for the prisoners to go back downstairs."

*   *   *

Knowing he and Ronald had right on their side didn't help them when the five gang-bangers, the new residents of the overcrowded holding cell, got a look at them. Once the steel door clanged shut behind them, the indoctrination commenced.

The smallest member of the group, a skinny guy with several neck and arm tattoos, schooled one of the holding cell neophytes on proper bench etiquette.

"Hey, stupid," he spat at Ron. "Who said you could sit down? Now you got to pay Ralphie the ass tax. You owe me a pack of smokes. Pay up."

Failing to grasp the seriousness of the situation, he ignored the warning and smirked at Ralphie instead.

That pissed off the tax collector. "What's wrong with you, white bread? You laugh at me 'cause I'm Chicano? You think you're better than me, *cabron*?"

The gravity of his predicament began to hit home. "No, of course not. I didn't mean any disrespect, Ron apologized." I thought you were kidding."

Cyrus attempted to intercede. "He didn't know any better. We're not familiar with jailhouse rules."

"Oh yeah. I'll show you one of them. Get off my fuckin sneaker, gringo," Ralphie screamed. He turned and gave his buddies a head nod.

The other four badasses, already on the move, surrounded Cyrus and Ronald.

Ralphie's forearm dagger tattoo was fully visible as he flexed his bicep. "Okay, Sweetpea, now you got fucking trouble. You gotta suck my dick." He reached down and unzipped his fly.

Ronald tried to back away. "Please, stop."

One of the crew spun him around. A fist connected to the dumbfounded assistant's stomach. Then a knee flew up and found his face. He doubled over and went down hard. Two of the gang prevented Cyrus from helping. Though lacking the expertise in matters of self-defense, he fought to pull his arms free. A dirty sneaker connected with his scrotum. As his body crumpled, his forehead smacked the concrete.

* * *

Cyrus' head throbbed. He felt a sharp pain in his testicles. He watched as ceiling tiles and fluorescent lights passed above him. His gurney passed under the flashing emergency room sign. He could see the blue of the police officer's uniform walking beside him. A silver cuff held his right wrist fastened to the side rail of the carrier.

He heard a voice, sounding much like his own, rising a bit above the squeal of the rubber wheels. "What's happening?"

The guard looked down and placed a hand on his shoulder. "Just relax. You're in Good Samaritan Hospital's emergency room. You had an accident."

"Accident? What accident? I was attacked."

The officer ignored his comment.

Cyrus recalled the pain in his head as he hit the ground. Then darkness surrounded him.

"What about the young man who came in with me, Officer? How is he? They attacked him too."

The guard reacted with mild surprise. "I told you, I don't know about any attack. Your friend left the cell on another gurney, ten minutes before you."

Cyrus fought off the overpowering urge to scream. He couldn't allow hopelessness and depression take over. He must not overreact.

The gurney rolled through the triage center. He glimpsed a male in a white outfit and a female in blue scrubs ministering to a patient lying on a table. The curtain quickly closed, but he'd gotten a glimpse of the patient's face. It was Ronald.

Ready to explode, he held back his anger. Instead, he made a promise to hold those with filthy hands responsible. He'd find a way to strike back. The sword of justice would find its mark and cut to the quick.

CHAPTER ELEVEN

Newton's Third Law

October 12, 1989

The conditions delineated by the lawyers from Newhouse and Gladstone sounded absurd to Cyrus.

"Doctor Markum, if you're both convicted, you could each receive twenty-year sentences," explained Mr. Levinsky. "We strongly suggest you take the deal the government's offered."

"But we're innocent," Cyrus harrumphed. "How could I live with myself?"

The federal district attorney offered a five-year suspended sentence and one hundred fifty hours of community service. The half-million dollars seized in the attempted acquisition of the illicit artwork would be forfeit. As part of the agreement, the state charge of illegal eavesdropping, under California Penal Code 632 PC, would be dismissed.

The most heinous stipulation in the arrangement would prohibit any pursuit of the Formula Seven vaccine. This egregious proviso was never memorialized in the twelve-page documentation but verbalized by the federal attorney. The slightest evidence of any breach would negate all aspects of the agreement and enforce the original jail sentences.

Even as a scientist, Cyrus had grown up believing in God and Jesus, but no more. He now understood that evil rambled throughout the world. The faceless entities who controlled our country had no regard for the citizenry. Incapable of dodging the droplets of glue suspended on the silk web of the spider's sticky web, he was ensnared. He realized he had no choice but to acquiesce.

"I want to throw up, but I know you're right, Byron. If there aren't any travel restrictions or provisional riders in the agreement, I'll accept the terms, as will my assistant."

Levinsky raised a hand. "I'm glad that you've seen it our way, Doctor. Our job is to keep you out of jail. I'm sure the government will have no objection to your request. They're looking to rid themselves of this case."

He scribbled something on a sheet of paper. "I'll call the state attorney."

Cyrus and Ronald had been offered Alford pleas, which were admissions of culpability, but with claims of innocence entered into the court record. With the preponderance of the evidence sufficient for a jury to reach a guilty verdict, this negotiated settlement would satisfy both parties. A lesser charge of misdemeanor grand theft, under California Penal Code 487 PC2, would be entered into the court record, and any other charges dropped in favor of the plea.

Without witnesses to confirm their story, they had no other remedy. Any party with any knowledge of the true facts refused to come forward. Evan Lesgarten, the private investigator, feigned ignorance. His sister claimed she knew nothing of the circumstances surrounding the arrests. Any Crestfield staff involved with the development of Formula Seven had found Federal jobs in other states. He and Ronald were on their own. Cyrus' faith in humanity, just like Formula Seven, no longer existed.

Standing before the judge on that Thursday morning was the worst moment of his life. On October the twelfth, 1989, the planets shifted. His motivation and philosophy of life refocused.

* * *

The community service proviso in the plea agreement stipulated that the two would-be art thieves belonged to the Union Rescue Mission for six weeks. As displeasing as this arrangement might be, Cyrus and Ron would have to live with it. On the positive side, the state agreed they'd forego any probationary obligation or limits on personal autonomy.

One of the largest and oldest centers of its kind in the country, the Union Rescue Mission's dormitory housed more than seven hundred cots. Their kitchen served more than three-hundred-fifty-thousand meals annually.

The dining room, fitted with several extended industrial tables, included several 19-inch wall-mounted color televisions. They played constantly from six a.m. until ten p.m., each TV tuned to the same channel.

On his first day at the mission, Cyrus saw his face. That long-haired preacher bounced around on every screen. More than five years since he saw him last, but the charismatic evangelist left an indelible impression.

Every morning, at seven-thirty, the show would begin. Each episode followed the same format. The preacher would speak to his congregation for ten minutes, interview one of the faithful, then the band would entertain for the last several minutes of the broadcast.

Cyrus' attitude had changed radically since that fateful morning at the Omni Hotel. He considered the eloquent preacher a holy-rolling carnival barker, busy hawking his product for financial gain. He doubted he cared at all for his flock. Like the Dodo bird, any pious beliefs were long gone.

The doctor's duties at the shelter tested his menial talents. Ronald made the best of it, but Cyrus grew increasingly disgusted with the mopping and sweeping. Each morning, when the televangelist's show came on the screens, the doctor's stomach churned. The knot in the pit of it grew a bit day-by-day. Sleep deprivation and spells of nausea became commonplace.

"There's no way I can complete another three weeks," he confided to Ronald, as they sat drinking coffee at home one morning. "I've lost eight pounds and I'm convinced that I've developed a duodenal ulcer."

His aide laid down his cup. "I've noticed that you haven't been yourself. What are you going to do?"

Cyrus flipped open his pocket calendar. "I've scheduled an appointment with a specialist for tomorrow afternoon. You'll drive me, of course."

"Certainly, Doctor."

*   *   *

Cyrus sat in the doctor's office.

The gastroenterologist scribbled on his pad. "The endoscopy disclosed that you have a peptic ulcer, but it's nothing serious. I'm prescribing a round of sucralfate."

He ripped off the page and handed it to Cyrus. "Take one pill, four times a day, on an empty stomach. I want to see you in six weeks."

"I have to take pills for six weeks, Dr. Abel?"

"Yes, and here's a booklet. It lists the food and drinks you should avoid."

The patient stiffened. "Drinks?"

"Yes. They're listed in the paperwork."

*   *   *

With their weekends free, Sunday morning found Cyrus and Ronald sitting in their kitchen.

The doctor dropped a handful of raisins and a spoonful of brown sugar into his oatmeal and stirred the mixture. "This situation is impossible, Ron. I'm limited to a morning eye opener and a late-in-the-day pick-me-up. You know I like the boost it gives me."

"It's going to be tough, Doc. I know how you like your caffeine." He continued thumbing through the newspaper. "I've read that black tea has almost as much as coffee."

"Really? That's interesting. Dr. Abel didn't say anything about tea. Remind me when we go out. We'll purchase a box from the market."

Ron jumped up and bounded to the opposite side of the table. "Doc, you've got to see this."

Ron spread out the full-page ad in the center of the Los Angeles Times entertainment section.

"Look who it is, Doctor."

The page staring up at them advertised a concert at the Los Angeles Memorial Sports Arena on November 25, the Saturday after Thanksgiving. Four Christian music acts would perform. Daniel Dundee and the Souls of Creation topped the bill.

A sound resembling a laugh escaped Cyrus' lips. Of even more interest to him, the half-page article on page two, with the bold headline shrieking: "Gang Violence Erupts in North East Los Angeles."

The story went on to explain that three Ninth Street *Asesinos* were dead, blown apart yesterday morning when a bomb planted under their car exploded. Two other gang members suffered serious injuries. The police suspected a rival gang. Detectives pursued various leads and expressed confidence that they would soon arrest those responsible. An accompanying picture showed the burned-out vehicle. Cyrus laughed hysterically.

Ronald thought his boss' reaction highly unusual. "Please don't mind me asking, but what's so funny?"

Unwilling to unveil the reason for his mirthful response, he easily deflected the question. "Oh, I just thought of something amusing. No big deal."

He would never let Ron find out that two of the dead and one of the injured were part of the gang who caused their jailhouse injuries.

Orchestrating vengeance couldn't have been easier. He'd visited Evan Lesgarten's office. The investigator, reluctant at first, agreed to help when Cyrus reminded him of his part in the Formula Seven conspiracy.

"I truly regret what happened," Evan confessed. "The Feds threatened to pull my license and swore that their forensic accountants would start ripping my books apart. They guaranteed if I didn't cooperate, my life would become a horror show. You know they are quite capable of seeing to that. What choice did I have? I did what they asked."

An expression of loathing came over the doctor's face. "I understand how those bastards can be, first hand. I'm not angry with you, Evan. I come to you for help and I'm willing to pay."

"Let me put a call into the law clerk that assists me occasionally. He'll get me access to the court docket. I'll look up the names of the gangbangers in lockup with you that night."

When the private investigator asked Cyrus for an explanation, he lied.

"A civil suit," he claimed, matter-of-factly. "We're thinking about suing for damages. Ronald had to pay for dental work and he required plastic surgery."

"Doctor Markum, I'm not buying that story. Personally, I don't care what you do. For the ten grand you're paying me, you don't have to tell me anything."

*   *   *

Pasco McGinty, son of the injured Crestfield security guard, wanted payback for h father who would need constant care for the rest of his life. A member of the Golden Dagger Motorcycle club, he served as chapter vice-president.

"I have good news for you," Cyrus informed him at their tête-à-tête at Riley's Bar. I've found the guys that robbed the lab and bashed in your dad's skull."

"Get the fuck out-a-here," Pasco replied. "Who are they?"

"Bad people, scumbags, but the cops aren't interested in solving the case. They're never going to figure it out. We should take care of this privately. These bastards can use a taste of street justice."

The biker easily took the bait. Cyrus paid an upfront fee of ten-thousand dollars. Yesterday evening, another twenty-grand found its way to the Dagger clubhouse. He considered it a bargain and felt no remorse, only self-satisfaction.

The time seemed right to disclose a few pleasant surprises to Ronald. "You know that I find you to be an intelligent fellow. You can do much more with your life than keep catering to my daily needs."

"Thanks, boss. But I enjoy doing whatever I can to help you. That's how I earn my pay. I'm happy to do it."

Cyrus placed a hand on his assistant's shoulder. "I understand that. I'm indebted to you. You're the only one who's stood by me through my travails. For what you've endured, I'm adding seven-hundred-and-fifty dollars to your weekly salary."

Ronald whistled. "Doctor, that's beyond generous. You already take care of me." He pointed to his perfectly capped upper front teeth. "Are you sure? You pay me well already."

Cyrus also paid virtually all of his expenses. The young man had managed to accumulate a nice chunk of change. More money's always nice, but, he didn't want his boss to think him greedy.

"Nonsense. I love you like a son. You've been my rock, always putting my needs before your own. You and I are going to visit my attorney tomorrow. He'll be drawing up a proper will. I'm making you my sole heir."

Screech! The grating of the chair legs against the wooden floor sounded almost deafening.

Ron grabbed the sides of his seat to maintain his balance. "Wow, is all I can say, Doctor. But please, I don't plan on you dying for a while. I love you and want you to stick around."

"Oh, I intend to. Just for your information, after selling off my share of the winery, my estate's grown to over one hundred and twenty million dollars. My portfolio contains mostly money markets and certificates of deposits. I've recently sold off most of the Pacific Rim mutual funds and high yield bonds. Our assets are liquid. We're free to pursue whatever business suits our fancy."

"Doc, I don't know what the heck you're talking about. Finances were never my strong suit."

Cyrus chuckled. "That's quite alright. I've got that covered." He turned on the hot water and rinsed his cup. "Let's finish up breakfast and take a drive to the Beverly Center. We have a date at Bloomingdale's."

Ronald looked shocked. "Bloomingdale's?"

Cyrus rubbed his hands together and stepped toward the table. "It's time to spend a little money. We want to look right."

"What are you planning, big boss man?"

The doctor puffed out his chest. "In due time, my friend. I have a strategy. Let's get ready. We're going to buy ourselves new wardrobes. We'll take the Mercedes."

* * *

The cost for their fashion makeovers came to slightly less than thirty-five thousand dollars. Giorgio Armani, Geoffrey Beene, Calvin Klein, and Kenneth Cole contributed to the stylish new attire and footwear collection.

"Put it on my Amex," Cyrus instructed, laying his card on the pile of accessories the salesman had stacked at the register.

"Are you sure about this," Ron asked, as a pair of expert tailors whipped out their tape measures and sewing chalk and began marking off inseams, trouser lengths, and jacket measurements.

"I need the delivery Tuesday morning," Cyrus informed the department manager.

"That won't be a problem, sir," he assured his high roller.

The experience exhilarated Ronald. He still did not know the full extent of what his boss had brewing. They sat enjoying their green curry chicken in the upscale Beverly Hills Indian restaurant when the tinder sparked inside Ronald and ignited. "Please, Doctor. You have to tell me what my part is. What's going on?"

Cyrus loved doling out surprises incrementally, but it seemed an appropriate time to release the cat from its carrier.

He wiped the corners of his mouth, then laid the napkin on the table. "As you know, Ron, we're visiting my lawyer tomorrow. Firstly, he'll be drafting a new will. Secondly, you'll be signing papers as one of the principals of our new corporation, Charlemagne Enterprises, Inc. You're the vice-president and a member of the board of directors. We're involving ourselves in the entertainment industry."

The newly named executive dropped his fork. "How did you come up with this? I don't know the first thing about it, and neither do you, no disrespect intended."

"I've taken care of that. Let me finish. Tomorrow afternoon, we'll be visiting our new suite of offices on Wilshire Boulevard, right off Hancock Park. I've hired a design firm and given them carte blanch to beautify the premises. It'll be ready for use on Wednesday."

Now he understood his boss' secrecy over the last couple of weeks and why he hadn't required him to drive. "Seriously, boss? Are you sure about this?"

"Don't you worry. We've purchased a management agency. They'll be moving their entire operation into our new facilities. I think you'll find the new arrangement enormously attractive. The firm has several important actors and recording artists under contract, including Daniel Dundee and the Souls of Creation."

Ronald lifted his water glass and took a swallow. "Doctor, do you mind if I offer an opinion?"

"Please, go right ahead. I'd like your input."

"Well, you seem obsessed with this reverend. What purpose will this serve?"

His boss regarded his assistant with a slight gleam in his eye and a taut smile on his lips. His stomach quivered slightly as his diaphragm expelled a short blast of manufactured laughter. "I told you not to worry, my inquisitive young fellow. I know precisely what I'm doing. Don't fret, all will be revealed in due time."

* * *

John Tremont and Devon Kimbrow owned the majority interests in Cambridge Entertainment Management, LLC. Diana Landis, a minority stockholder, had joined the Harvard business grads after serving a two-year apprenticeship in New York City with the William Morris Agency. Given the opportunity to excel as a major player in the management game, the Barnard graduate accepted the lucrative offer tendered by the former Hasty Pudding performers and abandoned the East Coast for the greener pastures of Hollywood.

That was three years ago. Since then, the young lady had matured into a live wire. A social climber with a brilliant mind, she possessed the insatiable need to achieve. Adept at maneuvering through the intangibles of any given situation, she'd grown into an enormous company asset. Her greatest achievement was coaxing Genevieve Francois, the French-Canadian mezzo-soprano and highly sought-after actress and spokesmodel, into taking a chance and adding her name and income flow to the company's growing client list.

Physically stunning and highly intelligent, she'd been awarded the title of "most beautiful" by her Camden, New Jersey, high school graduating class of 1980. In her four-inch heels, she stood a shade less than six feet. With long red hair and clear baby blues, her rosy cheeks accentuated her tiny upturned nose and full-bodied lips. Diana consumed little red meat or pork products and counted calories. Spending four evenings a week at the gym, she also jogged five miles each Saturday and Sunday morning. The aspiring show business aficionado was appealing in whatever attire she slipped on.

With her bosses taking less active roles in the agency, she served as the new figurehead at Cambridge Entertainment Management, termed CEM, for short. The two Harvard alumni, both planned to fully retire within the year.

"I'm sure you're going to like Diana," Cyrus assured his aide as they finished lunch. "She's extremely clever and quite an eyeful.

The company staff includes three more agents, a receptionist, two secretaries, and an executive aide."

"That's it?" Ron replied sarcastically.

"No, there's actually more. We have an intern from UCLA to round out the crew. Wait until you see the office space. We have fifty-four hundred square feet. You'll be thoroughly impressed."

With his check for five million dollars, Cyrus' new corporation, Charlemagne Enterprises now owned a sixty-three percent stake in CEM. Diana retained her 20-percent share, and the two senior partners retained the remainder, for the time being.

"You'll no longer be tending to my daily needs," announced the doctor. "You'll be trading in your mop, broom, and dishwashing detergent for a plush third-floor office and a breathtaking view of the park."

Ron laughed at the revelations. "This is happening so quickly. What about my replacement?"

"Don't worry. I've hired a new housekeeper. She'll be beginning her duties in Bel Air on Monday. Until then, I'll be fine. Oh, and by the way, did you see your letter from the Union Rescue Mission?"

"What letter?"

"I left it on your dresser."

Ron shook his head. "No, never saw it."

Cyrus bubbled with enthusiasm. "Then I guess you don't know we're finished scrubbing toilets. Our one hundred and fifty hours of community service have been satisfied. I guess the check I sent for ten-thousand dollars might have had something to do with it. It shortened our penance by two weeks, and better still, the money's tax deductible."

"Doctor, you never cease to amaze me."

"Only the beginning, my friend. You wait and see."

Ronald's road had been a bit bumpy of late, but at twenty-eight, he now embarked on an amazing new journey. The trauma and injuries he'd received in the holding cell had healed and the plastic surgery and first-class dental work fixed him up better than new.

November 25

The Los Angeles Sports Memorial Arena stood near the junction of Martin Luther King Jr. Boulevard and South Figueroa. Erected thirty years earlier, the venue accommodated more than fifteen thousand patrons.

Cyrus had insisted on doing the driving. His attitude had improved dramatically over the last few days. Ron attributed the positive personality adjustment to the release from indentured servitude and the excitement of their new business venture.

The backstage passes hanging from their necks afforded complete access to the concert facility. Diana, Ronald, and Cyrus stood at the bottom of the wooden staircase, ready to scale the eight steps that led to the stage. In their path stood a tall, well-muscled young man. He wore a black T-shirt with a white "Security" stencil printed front and back. He briefly inspected their authorization cards and waved them up. As they climbed the stairs, Ron laughed out loud and squeezed Diana's hand. Since stepping inside his office two weeks ago, the still-unfolding sequence of events had done wonders for his confidence.

Under the auspices and tutelage of Diana Landis, Ron was picking up the nuances and finer points of the entertainment management industry rather nicely.

Yesterday evening's excursion to the Troubadour on Santa Monica Boulevard did considerably more than demonstrate his new mentor's expertise in her Friday evening search for potential talent. Butterflies fluttered inside Ron's midsection, even before Diana pulled up in her black Saab 900 Turbo convertible. The fluttering wings picked up the intensity when the female dynamo made her feelings known.

"You know something, Ronnie. With my work schedule, I haven't thought much about dating, up until right now, that is."

Already enamored with this whirlwind of talent and sexuality, he wondered where the conversation was heading. "Uh-huh," he answered.

"You do know that women have a special gift. They call it intuition. I don't want to shock you, but I think fate brought us together. You and I have a special connection. Let's take it slow and see what happens. Okay?"

Ronald wanted to celebrate, but he concealed his excitement and remained calm. *How can this super-smart, gorgeous woman be interested in him?* "Funny that you say that, Diana," he replied. "I feel that you and I blend together very nicely."

Tonight, Cyrus, Diana, and Ronald enjoyed their "crow's nest" view of the Souls of Creation performance. They could be up close to the music and watch the reaction of the fans as the group played their latest hit single, "You Deliver Everything I Ever Need."

Tuning into the message of peace and love that Daniel and his bandmates delivered, the crowd celebrated by waving finite shafts of green lights. They created an array of tiny glowing circles that moved along the high ceiling, courtesy of the "Creation" flashlights. The concessionaires had taken a nifty profit, hawking the worship tubes and penlight batteries, as well as pushing tee shirts and CDs.

Ronald, stimulated by the Reverend Dundee's foot-stomping benediction-like extravaganza, found himself caught up in the contagion. His body moved in rhythm to the beat. Diana internalized her response. With a self-satisfied grin on her lips, she celebrated the band's success.

Cyrus couldn't have been any more pleased, but for a much different reason. In his mind's eye, he perceived a distinct vision of the future. His sociological scheme for a New World Order would take a little time to fully implement, but he had the patience and a foolproof blueprint. The anthropoidal nature of this antediluvian society needed reconstruction. He hadn't yet informed Ron, but he'd purchased a plane ticket to Germany.

CHAPTER TWELVE

GALILEAN INVARIANCE

San Francisco, California, June 1991

The official guest list originally included fourteen names. Serendipitously, one other soul would receive an invite and join in on the celebration.

Diana's parents and younger sister had flown in from New Jersey. Ronald's mom, dad, and maternal grandmother lived in Yuba City and would be making the two-hour drive. The Dundee family had already arrived by chartered jet from Denver.

Cyrus, who'd flown in from Germany and his stateside housekeeper, Naida, sat in first-class seats on the flight from LAX. The bride and groom occupied seats across the aisle. The travelers, in a festive mood, quieted down as the first officer's voice boomed over the intercom.

"This is Captain Warner welcoming you aboard Southwest Airlines Flight 323, nonstop to historic San Francisco, the birthplace of the hippie movement and the city that Janis Joplin, the Grateful Dead, and Jefferson Airplane called their home."

Diana laughed and tightened her grip on her fiancé's hand. He pulled her fingers up to his lips and kissed her knuckles.

"So, ladies and gentlemen, just sit back and relax," he encouraged his passengers. "Our flight time is one hour and twenty minutes. We should be rolling up to the gate by one forty-five."

The sound of a harmonica graced the ears of the passengers. His obvious talent showed as he worked the blues harp, blowing and bending the notes of "When the Saints Go Marching In."

Cyrus glanced over at Diana and Ronald. They both smiled, bemused by the bluesy serenade. The music cut off. One of the flight attendants began demonstrating emergency procedures as the plane slowly lumbered toward the runway.

The pilot's dulcet tones honey-dripped from the overhead speakers: "Ladies and gentlemen, we've gotten the go-ahead from the tower. Attendants, ready yourselves for take-off."

The engines thundered as the big bird picked up speed. The plane's momentum pushed the passengers into the rear seat cushions. Hurtling forward, the jet's wheels lifted and the Boeing 737 roared skyward.

Once the plane leveled out and the pilot disabled the seat belt sign, Cyrus motioned to the stewardess and ordered drinks for their party. He insisted on a toast. "To the future health and happiness of this wonderful couple."

As they passed over San Luis Obispo, the four lifted their glasses for another round, and Ron, the nascent tycoon asked for the floor. "To the continued success of CEM, the best management team in Hollywood. I'd also like to thank the doctor for everything that he's done for us. Without you, Cyrus, none of this would've been possible. Diana and I would never have met, nor would I have become so wealthy."

He paused and reflected for a second. "Or gotten arrested, and had my teeth knocked out and nose broken in jail," he added sardonically. "But my life is great, and I thank you."

"Here, here." Cyrus raised his glass. "It's my pleasure. You've been a great friend, a son to me, and loyal to a fault. You've made many sacrifices. You and Diana deserve all the happiness that's coming your way and..."

A slightly garbled voice came over the intercom system. "Ladies and gentlemen, we've been cleared to land. We should be at the gate a few minutes early. Thank you for traveling Southwest Airlines."

No harmonica serenade followed this time. The stewardess collected the cups and tiny bottles and motioned for the passengers to strap on their seatbelts and put away the tray tables.

Diana and Ron had a nice buzz going. Cyrus, trailing the couple as they deplaned, felt little pain himself. Naida, the least affected of the group, pointed to an overhead sign. Working their way through the terminal, they shadowed the arrows to "Ground Transportation and Baggage." The tall, long-haired driver, held up a sign for the Markum party.

The travelers slid onto the plush leather upholstery of the luxury stretch limo. Built to easily accommodate ten people, the gross display of capitalistic gluttony included a television set, a stereo system, and a crystal bar set. There would be little time to use any of the items. The ride to the Omni took less than thirty minutes.

* * *

Could it have been five and a half years since he'd last visited this Omni? So much had changed since the reading of Matthias' will.

Supported by the thick red banister, the doctor teetered down the hotel's marble staircase. Steadying himself, he stepped onto the lobby's marble floor. He stopped and turned, assuring himself the rest of his party followed along.

Diana and Ron walked hand-in-hand a few feet behind. Naida, with a somber expression on her face, trailed several feet behind them. Cyrus walked to the front desk and peered over the counter. The guest services clerk, a young lady in a chestnut brown vest, looked up. Seated next to her, a heavyset middle-aged man spoke animatedly on the phone.

"Welcome to the Omni Hotel, sir. I'm Alice," the short-haired brunette announced. "How may I be of assistance?"

"Hello, Alice. We're here for the tea party. The Mad Hatter invited us," Cyrus joked, still feeling the effects of the alcohol.

"I'm fine, sir, but the March Hare told me there might be a delay. The shipment from India is stuck in Boston."

"You're sharp. That's quite a witty return," he chuckled. "We have reservations. They should be listed under Cyrus Markum. We have a block of rooms."

He pointed at Diana and Ron. "These two lucky people are getting married tomorrow. Actually, the reservations should be under Charlemagne Enterprises. Would you see if any of the other guests have checked in yet?"

Alice smiled even more broadly. "Surely, sir, just give me a moment. Let me look that up, please."

She fiddled with her computer, studying the screen. "Yes, Doctor. I see your reservations right here. The presidential suite for the happy couple and two California suites, one for you and one for Ms. Perez."

Alice scrutinized the screen again. "I see that the Dundee family has checked in and so has the Landis party. We've already put through the transaction, but I'll need your credit card to run a hard copy."

Cyrus pulled out his wallet and handed over his corporate Platinum Amex. "Here you go, young lady."

Meanwhile, Naida stood spellbound, amazed by the grandeur and ambiance of the ostentatious surroundings. She leaned back against the counter. Now she knew for certain that the extravagances she'd seen displayed on *The Lifestyles of the Rich and Famous* did exist in the real world.

Ronald and Diana had no real interest in the garish surroundings. They'd settled into the soft cushions of a couch on the far side of the lobby. The lovebirds snuggled, cognizant only of each other. Cyrus found their public display amusing.

"Doctor Markum." Alice's voice interrupted his observations. "Please, sign the registration forms and credit card slip." She laid a pen on the counter.

He turned toward her and signed his name. "If we're finished, we'd like to go up to our rooms."

Two bellmen were already reacting, rolling a cart toward the front desk.

Laughing, Ron helped Diana climb out of the plush cushions.

Fior d'Italia Restaurant, 6:27 p.m.

With the minestrone soups cleared from the table, two waiters carried in trays holding the arugula salads. Cyrus was satisfied. This bistro couldn't have been a better choice for the Friday rehearsal dinner. Delicious food, fine wine, and mixed drinks helped to lighten the already festive mood. Only the Dundee twins, not yet twenty-one, abstained from imbibing. These two required no alcohol to free themselves from their inhibitions.

With the sounds of celebration ringing in his ears, the partially inebriated doctor left the private room and turned the corner on his way to the restroom. This Union Street restaurant occupied a soft spot in his heart. He thought of the meeting more than five years earlier when he'd dined here for the first time. His imagination conjured up an image of Matthias. He fought off the sadness bidding to encroach on his celebratory mood.

As he maneuvered through the dining area, those thoughts abruptly faded as the riveting gaze of one of the patrons caught him in mid-stride. The intensity and depth of her deep blue eyes seized hold. He halted. Unable to tear his eyes away, his face flushed.

A fuddled expression supplanted the smile on the lady's face. She peered across the table at her female dinner companion.

Embarrassed, Cyrus attempted to clear the air. "I'm sorry, ma'am. I don't mean to gape, but I feel a strong connection. Have we met before?"

She didn't miss a beat. "Weak pickup line, buddy, and believe me, I've heard plenty over the years."

His hand went up to his mouth. He needed to undo the damage done by his seemingly pretentious remark. "I don't doubt that. After all, you do happen to be quite striking. But it's the expression in your eyes. I'm certain there's a metaphysical connection. I must apologize for reacting so clumsily."

He placed both hands in front of his chest and folded them. "Please forgive my ineptness. I didn't mean to give you the improper impression. I know, it sounds odd, but I feel you're a special person."

Her purse snapped open. She offered him a business card. "No, your reaction is not unusual at all. Your instincts are sound. I happen to be a clairvoyant and psychic medium. That must be what you sensed."

She pointed to the card. "See. It's right there."

In the dimly-lit interior, Cyrus squinted to read the printing on the blue card. The top line, in bold black letters, showed her name: Lily Klein. On the line beneath it, in a slightly smaller font, her tag-line read: "Traveling Psychic."

"What a pretty name. May I call you Lily?"

She took a small swallow of wine. "Yes. It's actually Lilith, but I use Lily. It's biblical, you know?"

"Ah, yes, like Adam's first wife. Tell me, though, what's a traveling psychic?"

"That's simple. I've made a career catering to Hollywood's rich and famous. My specialty is providing personal readings while they ride around in their limos."

Cyrus clenched his fist and tapped his chest. "I knew you're unusual." He pointed to an empty chair. "Would you mind if I sat down for a moment or two? I feel the need to talk with you."

Though moderately flustered by his forwardness, she, too, believed in following her instincts.

She hesitated and looked across the table. "Mary, that's okay with you, isn't it?"

Her friend, an attractive woman of color, nodded. "Sure thing, I don't mind." She pointed to the chair. "Please, take a seat."

He pulled the chair out. "Good to meet you, Mary. I'm Cyrus."

They observed each other for a few seconds without comment.

Lily broke the stalemate. "Mary and I have known each other for over twenty-five years. I'm down from Los Angeles, wishing her bon voyage. She's flying to Africa tomorrow, going to visit her family for a few weeks..."

She suddenly fell silent and stared at the table top.

Cyrus noticed. "Are you okay?"

She drew in a breath. "I'd like to confess a deep secret. I don't usually tell people about it, especially strangers. But, I feel the need."

He leaned closer. "Of course. Go on, tell me."

"I know, this is going to freak you out, but I'm a kidnap victim. So is Mary. She'd just turned fourteen when human traffickers stole her from a village in Senegal."

Cyrus tried to stay focused. "Really?"

"Yes, really. One morning, my fiancé and I went out for a hike in the hills bordering Israel and Lebanon. We came to the top of a hill and three men with rifles attacked us. None of them said a word. One shot my boyfriend in the face. The other two grabbed me and threw me to the ground."

Lily picked up a napkin and dabbed at her eyes. "The animals held me down and took turns raping me. After they finished, they tied me up and blindfolded me. They dragged me down the hill and threw me into the back of a car. I can't ever forget the terrible smell, like stale sweat and motor oil."

"God, how awful," Cyrus empathized. "How old were you, then?"

"Twenty-eight." Lily shook her head. "You can imagine my terror."

The doctor's lips quivered. He covered his mouth. "No. I really can't."

The storyteller's eyes glazed over, but she didn't stop. "After bouncing around on bumpy roads for a few hours, we finally stopped. They pulled me from the car, cursed me out, and threw me to the ground. I started praying, thinking that's it. I'm dead."

She took a large gulp of wine, then balanced the stem of the glass on the table. "Instead, the bastards removed my blindfold and dragged me over to a rusty wash basin. They threw a bar of soap and a dirty towel down and ordered me to clean up. They forced me to put on a long-sleeved black dress and wrap a hijab around my head. Then, I was pushed back into the car and we drove. After a few miles of bouncing around on bumpy roads, the car stopped at a village. One of them pulled me out of the back and paraded me around in front of a group of men."

She picked up her half-filled glass of white wine. Lifting it up to her red lips, she swallowed the rest. Leaning across the table, she grabbed the tapered neck of the Pinot Grigio Alto Adige bottle and refilled it.

"My goodness, I can't believe I just told you all this. The words, they just came spilling out."

Cyrus offered a smile. Lily took another stout swig of liquid courage.

He laid a hand on her wrist. "I can't begin to imagine the hardships you endured. What terrible crimes. But, thank God, you're safe and free. Please, I'm extremely curious. What happened next? How did you get away?"

Slightly buzzed, Lily loosened up even more. She patted Cyrus on the shoulder. Her blue eyes sparkled. "Thank you. Thank you so much. I needed to hear that. It has been a long time since I've thought about any of this."

"No, I thank you. I'm flattered that you trust me with your secrets. Please go on."

She turned to Mary and frowned. "Okay. So, I became the property of Sheik Mohammed al-Sarat. I was one of nineteen women in his harem."

She pointed to her friend. "Mary arrived a few months after me. She made number twenty."

Cyrus shook his head. "How long until you escaped?"

"Well, the sheik's guards kept a close watch on us, but after almost a year, Mary and I received permission to visit the market with Ahmed, one of the servants. It was lucky for us that he held a grudge. A few weeks earlier, he'd been beaten by the sheik's men for showing a lack of respect."

She paused and poured more wine. "I convinced Ahmed to drive to the American embassy in Kuwait City. Mary and I told our stories and after a few days, granted asylum and eventually flown to Los Angeles. The driver had no luck. I don't know what happened to him. Mary and I stayed in America and now we're naturalized citizens. I've never gone back to Israel. The people in that part of the world are crazy."

Cyrus shook his head. "Wow, that's an amazing story. What about your family?"

"There's my sister and her family. They're here in the States. They live outside of New York City."

"Ah. That's good." He took hold of her hand. "Look, I have a great idea. Why don't you and Mary join us in our private room? We're having a pre-wedding celebration for my friends. Think about it. I need to visit the restroom. I'll return in a minute."

Lily, mystically gifted, felt a reciprocal bond with her new friend. "Hurry back. I find you interesting. I'd like to talk further."

Cyrus rushed past a nearby table, unaware that the two men seated at it, had eyes on him. Both wore conservative business suits and were decidedly skillful at remaining inconspicuous. Employing their FBI special surveillance group training, the inside team performed their job efficiently. Their two colleagues, equipped with 35mm cameras fitted with telephoto lenses, sat atop the building across the street from the restaurant.

They followed the movements and maintained a photographic record of Daniel Dundee and his contacts. Sonny Pastore Jr., the special agent in charge, handed the squad's their implicit instructions: surveil, document, and identify, with no personal contact. Weekly reports must be on his desk by Wednesday morning.

Why the interest in this "New Thought" evangelist? Officials inhabiting the upper reaches of the Washington administrative food chain had voiced concerns over the enthusiastic minister's dramatic elevation in the heaven-dispensing hierarchy. Without the need to justify their directives, they surveyed the action from afar. "Fidelity, Bravery, Integrity," those in the FBI carried out the mission. Sworn to protect and serve, the agents did exactly as instructed without question or objection.

Cyrus passed by the two operatives once again as he returned to the table. They sat quietly, sipping their espresso. He paid no notice, oblivious to their intended purpose.

"We've made up our minds," Lily chirped, a bit wonky on her feet. "Mary and I have decided that we'll take you up on your offer."

The doctor's face lit up. "That's terrific. I'll have the maître d' set two more places. I'll go take care of your checks."

Before either had the opportunity to object, Cyrus thrust a forefinger up to face level and wiggled it back and forth. "I insist. Please, don't argue with me. I want it to be my treat."

Neither of the ladies put up an argument. They waited for Cyrus to return while he found the maître d.' He paid their check and handed him an extra crisp, one-hundred-dollar bill and a pair of twenties for the server.

*   *   *

Once inside the private room, Cyrus called for attention. "I'd like everyone to meet Lily and Mary. They are my new best friends and will be joining us in celebration."

He took note of the bewildered expression on his former assistant's face. "Ladies, I'd like to introduce Ronald and his fiancée, Diana. They're tying the knot tomorrow. Aside from our business association, we're the best of friends."

Daniel stood. "Hello, ladies, I'm Daniel and this is my wife, Joanne."

He pointed to the twins. "Our kids, Iris and Cooper."

The children smiled.

Their dad kept up his repartee. "It's our pleasure to meet you, ladies."

He reached out his hand. Mary shook it politely.

When he touched Lily's, her eyes registered surprise. She felt his inner strength. "I sense your spiritual power and deep affection for mankind."

Dan stared into her eyes. "I believe that Christ's spirit is within each of us, though there are many still unaware of the true gift they possess. Every soul is connected to the same fabric and share a uniqueness with the universe. I make no promises. I only demonstrate my belief in God's word."

Lily's body tingled. "Your eyes reveal your truth. I sense that you've been to earth for several incarnations. We've met in a previous lifetime, many years before this current excursion on the physical plane."

Before the pastor could say another word, Cyrus stepped between them. "Would everyone please take their places and pick up their Champaign glasses? It's time to toast the bride and groom."

"We'll talk again a little later, Dan," Lily promised as Mary nudged her to her seat.

Cyrus lifted his glass. "I'd like to wish Diana and Ronald a continued idyllic relationship and successful marriage. They are two of the finest people I know. I'm thrilled that they have found each other. So, let us click our glasses, drink up and cheer for the bride and groom."

Ron's dad lifted his glass. "Here, here. I second that emotion."

*   *   *

Lily moved around the room, taking turns connecting with each of the celebrants. Cyrus, keeping tabs on his new-found friend, watched her interactions with interest. He had nary a doubt that this woman possessed unusual qualities. He tottered over to Lily and Diana. The two women, deeply involved in conversation, paid him no heed.

"Pardon me, ladies," he interjected, slurring his words a bit. "I have a wonderful idea. Since Mary is leaving for Africa, I think you should stay and join us for the wedding tomorrow."

"Oh, I can't," Lily objected. "I have nothing to wear. Besides, my flight is scheduled to leave in the morning."

He waved his left hand. "Nonsense! None of that will be a problem. I'll see to the arrangements. You've blended in so nicely. It would be a shame if you didn't attend."

"Yes, please," Diana added. "Why don't you stay? We'll have a wonderful time."

Lily thought it over briefly. "Well, I have no appointments scheduled. So-ooh, I guess you've convinced me. I'll stay."

Cyrus slapped a hand on the table. "Outstanding, then! It's settled."

Saturday, Noon

Reverend Richard studied the couple as they moved into position. The groom looked handsome in his tuxedo. The bride's outfit sparkled. She too appeared undeniably exquisite in her white strapless gown.

The reverend had no idea that concealed beneath Diana's painted-on smile dwelled slight levels of angst and uncertainty. The wife-to-be tussled with her equilibrium, battling to maintain control of her emotions. Adding to her quandary, at the rear of the altar, shafts of sunlight sliced through the trio of stain-glass windows partially obscured her vision.

The bouquet of white gardenias almost spilled from her hands as her left heel caught on the second of the three steps leading to the ceremonial platform. The groom, noticing his bride's predicament, gently grabbed hold of her right elbow. This tender move allowed Diana to regain her balance and preserve her grip on the floral arrangement.

Like that annoying television deodorant commercial, her antiperspirant was failing. Fortunately, she wore a sleeveless dress. There would be no telltale stain to advertise that this normally cool, calm, and collected lady happened to be anything but.

She and Ronald had fallen hard for each other. Their six-month trial living arrangement confirmed their compatibility quotient. There seemed to be no doubt that marriage would be the right move.

Her life had worked out precisely the way she'd envisioned. Two nights earlier, Diana had pulled out her teenage journal and amused herself and her fiancé as they relaxed in bed. On page fourteen, she'd listed her six objectives in life.

"Look at this, honey," she whispered as she snuggled closer. "I wrote this during the middle of my freshman year in high school."

Ronald laid down his Pat Conroy novel and kissed her on the cheek. "Go ahead. Read it to me."

Her face flushed. "Okay, but I'm embarrassed."

"No need, you're among friends."

She fluffed her pillows. "Well, topping the list, get a great education. Second, I wanted to move to California. Thirdly, I dreamt about getting rich and running my own company." She picked up a pen from her night-table and put a check mark next to each entry. "Check, check, and check."

"What's next?" Ron asked, trying to peek at her writing.

Diana wouldn't have it and pulled the book away. "Oh, no. This is my story. You can tell me what's on your wish list next."

Her fiancé's grimaced. "That's not fair. I don't have a list."

Diana laughed and poked him playfully. "That's not my fault. If you want to hear the rest, don't interrupt."

"You know I do. Go on. Tell me"

"Okay. Number four, that's falling in love and getting married." She wiggled and squeezed Ron's hand. "Next, own a gorgeous home." She waved her free hand. "We do."

She slammed the book shut. "That's it for now."

Ron reached for the journal. "Oh, no. There's one last entry. I saw it there. What is it?"

She pushed her fiancé playfully. "Guess."

He only shrugged in reply.

At fourteen years of age, all dreams seemed attainable. She'd already scaled every peak, save for the last. That number six entry in her "Dear Diary" was left as the only question mark. That decision no longer would be a solitary one. She and her groom had been discussing the issue. He wanted children but would acquiesce to whatever his partner wanted. For the time being, she'd keep an open mind.

* * *

Diana shook off her daydreaming as Reverend Richard asked Cyrus for the rings. Ronald slid the circle of 18-carat gold around her finger. Mere seconds from becoming an "honest woman," the bride-to-be laughed aloud, happy, yet sad. Two tiny canals of tears ran down her cheeks.

Reverend Richard's voice resounded. "I now have the pleasure to pronounce you husband and wife. You may kiss the bride."

Their lips met for the moment that would remain forever etched in both their memories.

The invited guests, and the two dozen or so members of the church congregation who'd volunteered to fill seats in the Berkeley prayer chapel applauded. Diana's mom and sister cried. Ron's mother wrapped her hands around her husband's arm and wept.

Tradition won out. The males in attendance concluded the nuptials by forming a line and kissing the joyful bride. Her mate stood next to her, receiving handshakes, and accepting prayers for marital bliss.

Omni Hotel, Seven P.M.

Lily's girlfriend, halfway to Africa, had no idea what she was missing. The reception couldn't have been any more elaborate. The "traveling psychic," kicking it back and enjoying herself, knew she'd followed the right path.

At Cyrus' behest, the Omni's staff spared no expense and transformed the mezzanine conference space into a majestic party room. Just after sunrise, the newlyweds would board a plane and travel to Europe for their honeymoon.

Halfway through their second set, the Billy Weidman Jazz Trio fed the guests a varied and appetizing repertoire. And, speaking of good taste, the celebrants had the enviable task of selecting from a quartet of superb dishes. A choice of beef Wellington coated with pate foie de gras or filet mignon, accented with twin broiled lobster tails, created a difficult enough choice. Add the Cajun blackened swordfish resting on a bed of grilled sea scallops, and lastly, a dish of roasted chicken breast stuffed with goat cheese and shiitake mushroom relaxing in an expressive Spanish red wine sauce, their decisions met with almost complete impossibilities.

The banquet, meticulously prepared by two celebrity chefs, courtesy of the Barnabus Consortium Group, set a delectable tone. Cyrus greased palms and called in favors to make it happen.

Daniel and his wife had finished their meals and sat at their table holding hands and talking. Laying his water glass down, he winked at his wife. "What about a stroll? It's so nice out and it will help with our digestion."

Joanne let go of his hand and rose from her seat. "Sounds good. Let's ask the kids if they're interested."

She pulled her husband toward them. "Excuse me. Do you guys want to take a walk?" Joanne asked.

The twins, deeply involved in conversation with Lily, had paid little attention to their food and had no interest in taking a foray onto the gray concrete of California Street.

"Have fun, you crazy kids," Iris joked, her radiant smile displaying the true sentiment of her words.

Joanne draped her right arm over her husband's shoulders. "Oh, you bet we will. Don't we always?"

Even with fame and fortune, Daniel and Joanne had their feet planted squarely on the ground. They were thankful for the happiness their happiness shared, and for their musical success.

In the past two years, through hard work and ingenious marketing by their management company, their church's popularity had grown enormously. None of this would have been possible without the expertise and financial support of Cyrus Markum.

Their music mixed the cement, but the syndicated evangelical television broadcasts allowed it to harden. The Ministry of Collective Harmony and Spiritual Balance had added more than two million to the rolls of "Mindful Benefactors." Their monthly contributions allowed for an abundance of virtuous work that included the "People for Peace" volunteer network who traveled from state to state to share the love of the MCHSB.

All through the growth and decision-making process, the Dundee's collective affection continued to germinate and produce colorful blossoms, not just in the spring, but the year round.

"Honey, I love you so," Dan declared as they walked down the mezzanine steps. He followed it up with a kiss on Joanne's lips.

"Darn, you beat me to it, sweetie. You know, I love the heck out of you," she proclaimed, brushing back her husband's long hair in a gesture of romantic reprisal. She laughed energetically, planted her lips on her husband's cheek.

CHAPTER THIRTEEN

The Growth of an Empire

Seated in the cushy armchair across from the hotel's front desk, the sports section of the *San Francisco Examiner* camouflaged the FBI agent's true intent. The hotel lobby served as a perfect locale to intrude on the Dundees' right to privacy.

His superiors had no interest in the sanctity of the first and fourth amendment rights of the MCHSB reverend. The bureaucrats determined priorities and what constituted issues of national security. That, of course, would always take precedence over constitutional law. What the Congressional Oversight Committee didn't know... etcetera, etcetera.

As the Dundees walked across the marble floor and out into the street, they had no suspicion that a special government project had them squarely in its sights. Observing from the darkened window of a panel truck parked directly across the street, an agent worked a high-performance camera. John Richter, the man behind the Zeiss telephoto lens, clicked away.

Although considered a rookie by the rest of the squad, his narrative was none too shabby. He'd seen combat with the 82nd Airborne Division during Operation Just Cause in Panama and awarded a bronze star for heroism. After his discharge, he took advantage of his GI benefits and earned a bachelor's degree in criminal justice at Georgetown University. John easily navigated his training at Quantico, but with less than a-year-and-a-half of experience under his belt, he still jockeyed to earn the respect and trust of the rest of the squad.

The young agent snapped shot after shot of Daniel Dundee and his wife as they breathed in the cool evening air outside the hotel entrance. Through the high-definition viewfinder, John noted the subjects' faces showed joy and their body language displayed no apparent signs of tension. John chuckled. "*If they only knew,*" he mumbled aloud, loading a fresh roll of film into his Nikon camera. Conscientious to the nth degree when it came to his work, he'd already gone through four rolls of film by the time the blonde with striking good looks and stately breastwork joined the Dundees.

He estimated her age as late forties or early fifties. She carried herself well. In his physical prime and in possession of a macho self-image, John libido kicked into high gear. *This ravishing beauty could most certainly teach him a thing or two.*

"Come on, snap out of it," he mumbled. "Be professional, concentrate." All thoughts of human sexuality and erotica must remain for another time.

John didn't think about why the administration in Washington had developed a case of nerves regarding his subject. He was aware that in the past twenty-two months, the Ministry of Collective Harmony and Spiritual Balance had received an appreciable spurt in membership. That increased public visibility ruffled numerous tail feathers.

The Feds, still reeling from the Jim and Tammy Faye Bakker debacle and embarrassed by the sordid details of Jimmy Swaggart's recently televised confession, had instructed the Bureau to cast a watchful eye on this budding religious icon.

No more surprises to be sprung on America by another so-called "man of God," if you please. We had too damn much religion going around already.

Accusations of CIA mind control manipulation instigating the "Jonestown massacre" still swirled within West Coast leftist conspiracy circles. Not a shred of concrete evidence supported such claims, but the rumor still endured, even after a decade. Any truth, unfortunately, had putrefied alongside the bodies of Jim Jones and his brainwashed flock of misguided followers.

To complicate the FBI's current investigation, a white-collar criminal recently arrived on the scene. Highly instrumental in fostering the church's popularity, Cyrus Markum's intertwining relationship with the religious zealot, created elevated levels of concern. No physical proof of wrongdoing existed, but bureaucrats without proper moral scruples of their own naturally assumed everybody must be as dishonest as themselves.

Those with money and power had no patience for this upstart preacher and his religious ramblings. An overabundance of self-righteous dogmatists already preached the gospel of Joshua Ben-Joseph. So, keep those investigative peepers popping, and assure that the rabble-rouser doesn't awaken an excess of the slumbering electorate.

Unlike the demographics and leftist leanings of the People's Temple, Daniel Dundee's devotees and ministry faithful came from every level of society. MCHSB excluded no one, integrating diverse ethnic and religious backgrounds. The latest income tax filings and government field reports verified the net worth of the Ministry of Collective Harmony and Spiritual Balance as close to six hundred million dollars. That in itself tripped alarm bells.

The dozen-and-a-half undercover operatives who'd entrenched themselves within the five current church locations reported no spurious activities. A policy of truthfulness appeared to be the prevailing influence. The church's theologian ideology revealed no political affiliations, only advertising the conveyance of true spiritualistic valuations.

But John Richter had no interest in the philosophical or socioeconomic leanings of any collection of spiritual enthusiasts. His assignment evaded any evaluations. He followed his orders explicitly. Brought up as a Roman Catholic, John served as an altar boy at the St. Andrew's church in Rye, New York. That experience left him dissatisfied and disillusioned.

He'd been religion free since then and accepted the Bureau as his one and only deity. Taking an analytical approach, he employed the highest level of objectivity when it came to personal feelings.

With the sunlight fading, John dug into his canvas bag and screwed the night vision filter into the inner threads of the telephoto lens. His interest piqued when a white male in his early fifties, balding and bespectacled, joined the trio of photographic subjects.

He recognized him immediately, Cyrus Markum, the doctor emeritus of deception, stood within his sights. He'd read over the available files at the Los Angeles FBI office and adeptly aware of this man's past brush with the law. Already ultra-rich, the greedy bastard got caught red-handed in an attempt to procure several pieces of stolen artwork. The bastard bought his way out of jail with his wealth and political influence. He claimed European residency, but with his frequent trip to the States, the odds favored his pursuit of nefarious activities.

The agent fought off resentment. He'd grown up with a wooden fork in his mouth, the youngest of three children. His dad, a New York City firefighter, warned him that too much wealth and power would corrupt and ultimately destroy. Money made the world go around, but how much of it did one need? This Markum character had an accounting firm writing his checks and managing his enormous financial resources.

John came from a family of working-class stiffs. He had no aspirations of getting rich and becoming an asshole. Balancing his own checkbook and making sure his car payment hit the mailbox before the twentieth of each month, he could handle on his own.

Unable to read between the lines and as yet unaware of the information purposefully omitted from the Markum file, he knew nothing of the Formula Seven conspiracy. No explanation of the deception and subsequent entrapment were outlined anywhere in the dossier. In John Richter's world of black and white, the doctor of dirty deeds must certainly be on the prowl.

* * *

Over the past two years, Germany had served as Cyrus' home. Living in the midst of the European Economic Community afforded him the opportunity to achieve the financial success he craved. Initially, he'd rented a cottage, and set up shop in Bamberg. Locating a small company in need of working capital, he invested ten million marks and took the reins as CEO of Bavarian Plugs and Things. Within three months, through a consortium of French intermediaries, he arranged an initial public offering for the wholesale auto parts distributor.

Cyrus used the umbrella of the public corporation to form four dummy American subsidiaries. The first in Colorado, the second in Tennessee, a third in North Carolina, and the last incorporated in California. Shielding himself with the ruse of straw ownership, he possessed no stock in any but retained control by drawing up personal employment contracts with all corporate officers and board members.

Four of Naida's cousins, two of her nephews, and a half-brother on her father's side sat on the board of directors of each of the companies. Peruvian emigres, sharing Spanish as their native tongues, none of her family members read English very well, but that consideration mattered little. Paid a monthly stipend, they voted whatever way Cyrus instructed. Naida's brother-in-law, a college graduate, served as president and CEO of the four companies.

The government had no reason to question the expansion or project undertakings. The corporations paid their taxes in a timely manner, and no trace of illegality or impropriety required a second look. No suspicions were raised with the purchase of the majority shares in a Denver cinder block company, a Nashville cement factory, and a controlling interest in an Illinois metal works foundry.

Cyrus' ingenious business plan allowed Reverend Dundee's ministry to expand and build MCHSB wonderlands. The shadow corporations supplied the building materials. Private contractors performed the construction work. The Aurora location already had turned a profit and the Chattanooga hotel and theme park was on the verge of breaking even.

Persuasive in his original "Collective Harmonic" sales pitch, Cyrus illustrated the immense possibilities and the overwhelming probability of success. Daniel, also a man of vision, convinced the board to embrace the plans for the vigorous expansion.

The Aurora facility, which included a sixteen-story hotel with one hundred and seventy-two rooms and a large daycare center, was surrounded by a forty-six-acre theme park. Charlemagne Enterprises contributed a good portion of the start-up money. The additional funds came courtesy of two California investment groups and a Wall Street venture capital firm. Expecting to cash in on the projected overflow, a major hotel chain purchased land adjacent to each of the proposed "Collective Harmonic" locations and were close to completing construction.

The Chattanooga locale utilized approximately the same acreage as the Aurora facility, but the Fayetteville property eclipsed both, doubling the size of both its predecessor's combined. The ribbon-cutting ceremony would take place next month, with the North Carolina governor, three state senators, and two U.S. congressmen slated to attend.

The lynchpin to the strategic blueprint continued to be Daniel Dundee's religious philosophy and prophetic mystique. The Souls of Creation continued to sell albums. The touring schedule had lessened only a smidgen, with Cooper maturing into a major writing talent, musical arranger, and lead vocalist. His mom and dad contributed on a limited basis, having performed in only ten concerts over the past year. Their son's musical transition proved seamless. The fan base, especially the younger women, accepted and embraced the new singer and the band's grittier musical direction.

The relaxed schedule gave Daniel the opportunity to concentrate on what mattered most, spreading the word of God and the MCHSB. In September of 1993, he, Joanne, and a small contingent of the ministry elders traveled to Europe for three weeks. The couple performed as an acoustic duo and the delegation visited London, Paris, Rome, Copenhagen, Oslo, and Berlin.

"Our experience was truly amazing," Daniel confessed to Robert Rhoads, a reporter from the Christian Weekly Bulletin, on their return to Colorado. "Our management agency suggested we take the full band across the pond next spring."

Robert nodded. "That should be interesting. What would be your goal?"

Dan reached for his wife's hand. "I think we can accomplish remarkable things. We've received an offer from a Berlin TV station to host an Easter show. The church believes it would be a tremendous opportunity, as do we."

Robert pulled his Sony micro-cassette recorder closer to his lips. "I have a two-part question for either you or your wife, Reverend."

Joanne and Daniel's eyes met. He rubbed her shoulder.

The reporter looked a bit embarrassed and tried to ignore the display of affection. "Okay. Here is question one: To what would you attribute the immense increase in the church's membership over the past few years?"

"And the second part?" Daniel asked.

The journalist hesitated, a bit reluctant to add the kicker. He gathered his nerve. "Okay, question two: With the increased ratings on your cable broadcasts, we hear that one of the major networks is interested in broadcasting a Dundee Family Christmas special. Is there any truth to that?"

Robert pushed the recorder closer to Daniel, but as Joanne began to answer, he positioned the device several inches from her face.

"The first question is an interesting one." She tapped her chin with her right forefinger and thumb, reflecting for several seconds. "We're thankful for our success and are blessed to be co-creating with the Holy Spirit. The Souls of Creation are an artistic extension, and their success has opened many people's hearts and minds to the church's message of love."

Her brown eyes sparkled. "Devotion to God is what matters to us. The acceptance by so many fosters greater acceptance and understanding."

"That's an interesting point," Robert replied thoughtfully, angling the recorder toward his own lips. "What about the second question?"

This time, Daniel seized the opportunity. "Joanne is right. We're fortunate for all that we've received. We thank God for the success of the MCHSB and music ministry."

Dan took a breath. His eyes gleamed mischievously. "This is strictly off the record, Robert. It's not a rumor that we've been negotiating with one of the big four for a prime-time national broadcast. It's a done deal. The contract is not for a single show, but for Joanne and me to host six-episodes. The Souls of Creation will provide the music. Popular gospel and Christian artists will be guests each week. We'll include some comedians and religion-appropriate sketches."

Robert looked dumbfounded. "Please, Reverend, this can't be off the record. You have to let me report this. This story is important. Our readers need to know."

Daniel laughed, his long brown hair glistening, caught by the rays of the overhead track lighting. "Of course, you can write about it. The deal is going to be announced at a press conference Monday morning."

Robert bumped his chin with the small recorder as he straightened his tie. "Oh boy, oh boy," he mumbled excitedly, stuffing his recorder into his jacket. "I have to get back to the office and type up my story. I'll see you at the church on Sunday. I can't tell you how much this interview means to me. Thank you, again."

The couple walked him to the door. Robert, still a cub reporter, like Jimmy Olsen from the Daily Planet, knew the opportunity to break this story would help his career tremendously. As he rushed toward his VW bug, he hummed a tune from the last Souls of Creation album. The Dundees smiled and waved goodbye.

CHAPTER FOURTEEN

Hocus Focus

January 15, 1995, Aurora, Colorado

A Night of Harmony and Balance with the Dundees ran for two seasons. It would've continued for at least another had the hosts been so inclined. The Sunday evening show received an average Nielsen rating of 7.2., usually placing second in its time slot behind *60 Minutes*. Money didn't figure in the decision. The principals had other considerations, wanting to get back to their roots.

The couple brainstormed, and the "Forty Dates and Nights of Godly Reign," materialized. The Dundees, ready to climb aboard the coaches once again, would share their music and personal philosophy directly to the people. They planned to embark on an ambitious three-month tour that would visit thirty-two cities in twelve states.

At the press conference, Daniel took the stage and read from the teleprompter. "On June twelfth, the first leg of our tour will kick off with twin concerts in Seattle, Washington. Additional dates will follow in Portland, Boise, Reno, and Las Vegas. After a few days of rest, we'll undertake the California loop. That will include eight dates in five cities, most notably three concerts in Los Angeles and two in San Francisco."

His wife joined him on the stage. "You all know Joanne. She'll explain the rest of the schedule."

"Thank you, Danny." His wife stepped toward the bank of microphones. "After a three-day hiatus in Berkeley, the tour will head west for shows in Arizona, New Mexico, and four concerts in

Texas. We're taking our bathing suits along and plan on spending three days on the beach outside Galveston."

People in the audience snickered, enjoying her offhanded approach.

Joanne raised her hand for quiet. "The musical caravan will then head to Baton Rouge for one night and to New Orleans for a trio of gigs. After a one-night stand in Little Rock, we'll swing west for three dates in Oklahoma. Finally, the last leg will include eight dates in Colorado, culminating in a day-long concert at Farmers Stadium in Fort Collins."

She paused and lifted the glass sitting on the podium and took a sip. "We'll be inviting a few special guests to the finale, including Reverend Albert Williams and the Voices of Unity Choir. That televised prayer vigil and musical worship assembly will take place on Sunday, September the twenty-fourth. Write that down."

*   *   *

The excitement of the planning, reminded the Dundees of the good old days when their music was fresh, inspiration filled the original band members, and their spiritual enthusiasm spilled into the music.

Their old bandmates, Max, and Bud had gone their own way years earlier. The two, bored with the Christian influenced music, decided to get back to their first love. They formed the Blues Diffusion, a Chicago style, old-school unit, chromatic harmonica player and all. They never gained national attention but did record two albums and toured as opening act for Little Clifford and the Climbers. But one night on tour, the driver of their luxury coach fell asleep and their vehicle slammed into a bridge abutment.

Bud's wife, Gretchen, suffered fatal injuries and the drumming wizard's left leg so badly mangled, that doctors had to amputate below the knee. Max required only a few stitches, but his scars were more of a psychological nature. Irreparably damaged, he moved back to his hometown of Saginaw and gave up on music, and ultimately on living. Extreme alcoholism and drug abuse became part of his way of life. Multiple attempts at rehab didn't help.

A complicated twist of fate triggered Max's death, but to those who loved and cared for the playful soul, the truth was obvious. Why would anyone be out strolling at night during a blizzard?

Three days after the storm, with the temperature moderating and the snow beginning to melt, two teenagers, busy sledding on the packed snow of Imerman Memorial Park, noticed a gloved hand protruding from nature's white wonderland and notified the police. The death certificate listed hyperthermia as the cause of death, but the emotional trauma, combined with the drugs and alcohol, did the major damage. His friends and loved ones, deeply saddened, had accepted the inevitable a while ago.

Born in 1944, their pal lived to be forty-eight. He never married and with no kids that he knew of, as he joked many times, the talented troubadour left behind a legacy of delightful music, cramming plenty of living into his time on earth. As a final request, he asked that his cherished Cherry Gibson Bass guitar lay with him in the coffin; just like old Maxie, always lovable, and a wee bit crazy.

His friends understood. Each smiled in fond remembrance, as they threw a shovelful of dirt on the casket. A small table, sitting beside the gravesite, supported several pictures of the newly departed. The centerpiece, an eight-by-ten blowup, taken from the liner notes of The Souls of Creation's first album. The photograph featured the man of considerable talent at his best, in the groove and tapping his long fingers on the strings of his bass. Huge horned-rim glasses, long black curly hair, and intensely joyful gray eyes helped showcase his bountiful persona. A soulful brother, he'd always offer a helping hand to a friend in need, but one had to stay alert. The comic wizard specialized in sarcasm and ridiculous wisecracks.

Daniel delivered a moving eulogy, reciting a loving prayer written for the occasion. There wasn't a dry eye on the lawn. Max's mom and dad said their goodbyes first.

As the mourners passed the casket for the final time, each let a red rose fall from their hand.

When Dan's turn came, he spoke to the everlasting spirit of his old friend. "Good buddy, it's a long way from Madison. Both our journeys continue on. Though you're no longer on earth, your odyssey endures on the spiritual plane. I love you, my brother. See you on the other side."

He thought of that green "Merlin" tee shirt Max wore on that spooky September night. He dropped a plastic toy figure of the medieval wizard, along with the fragrant red flower, into his good friend's grave.

"Go in peace, my brother," he whispered, holding back the pool of tears. "I love you."

* * *

The caravan of cars drove through the cemetery gate and out onto Washington Avenue. Joanne had made reservations at Max's favorite restaurant, Sophia's Diner. Less than a mile's drive, it wasn't the food they craved, but the chance to reminisce.

After settling in at the restaurant, Cooper, about ready to implode, begged to be first to speak.

His dad shrugged. "Go ahead. Otherwise, you look like you might have a stroke."

"Thanks, Pop."

Cooper poked his sister seated next to him. "You remember Iris, don't you? We had just turned eight and the band was on a break from the road. They rented that big house in the Georgia mountains..."

Iris broke in. "Oh, no. You're not going to tell that story?"

"Of course, I am, Sis."

She shook her head. "Oh, my God! I can't believe it."

Cooper poked her playfully. "Quiet down, girl. Don't mess me up."

Iris scowled. "Go ahead. Make a fool out of yourself. I don't care."

"No problem. Okay. So, it's like this, Dad and I are fishing in the stream out back. We're sitting there, staring at our floats. It's been, like half-an-hour. Neither of us has gotten a single bite."

Cooper paused. He loaded a forkful of tuna salad, swallowed, and wiped his mouth.

"Sorry." He cleared his throat. "We hear the screen door open and naturally, we turn to see who's coming out on the porch. I thought maybe it was mom with sweet tea, but boy, no way. It's Max and his girlfriend, both stark naked. I turn beet red. I see boobs and can't take my eyes away. Sara, his girl at the time, tries to cover herself up with her towel, but Max, he doesn't move a muscle…"

Daniel's uproarious laughter intervened. He started choking and fought to catch his breath. Cooper helped him raise his arms and patted him on his back.

"Are you all right, Dad? Do you want a glass of water?"

"No, no." He coughed, slowly catching his breath. "I'm okay. Go ahead, go on."

Cooper reflected for a second or two. "Oh yeah, I got it. So, at that point, Max's girlfriend slides into the hot tub. I'm confused as heck. I can't figure out why they aren't wearing bathing suits. I guess I spoke yelled when I asked my dad about it, and my voice must have distracted Max. He slips and lands balls first, on Sara's head. He's screaming in pain and splashing around. Dad and I go running over to see if we can do anything to help."

He looked over at his dad. Dan laughed again, but this time under control.

Cooper perked up. "So now Max pulls himself out from the hot tub. The screen door opens, and Mom and Iris come out with a first aid kit. Bud and Gretchen are trailing right behind them. Max is still naked and rolling around on the porch. He's yelling: 'My balls are twisted; my balls are twisted.' I try to get a look, but Dad drapes a towel over his bottom."

"What about me?" Iris fanned the air with a napkin. "I was traumatized."

Cooper laughed. "Yeah! I'm sure. Come on. Stop screwing up my story."

Iris stuck out her tongue. "Sorry. I apologize."

"So, anyway. Mom goes back inside and calls 911. It takes twenty minutes for the ambulance to show up. By the time they get there, Max tells them to go away and insists he's fine. The rest of us wouldn't take no for an answer and convince him to go to the hospital."

Bud rolled his wheelchair back. "C'mon man, please. Let me take it from here. I helped him get dressed and rode with him to the hospital."

Cooper couldn't argue the point. "Well, okay, I guess. Go ahead."

"Thanks, dude." Bud grabbed the edge of the table and pulled his wheelchair closer. "So, we get to the hospital, and Maxie fills out the admittance forms. He's gotten his mojo back at this point and looking for payback. In his head, he thinks he owes somebody for his pain. The nurse checking his vitals takes the brunt of it. The girl's about twenty-five and her cheeks turn bright red when he insists on showing her his *injury*. She drops her tray and runs out of the room. Within a minute or two, the attending physician comes into the triage area. He warns Max that he better leave the nurses alone or he'll call the cops. Our crazy friend agrees, but insists he's got a 'massive case of blue balls.' The doctor laughs, and things are cool after that."

Max's demented sense of humor didn't diminish with his passing. Bequeathing the lion's share of his $1.7-million estate to his parents, he'd added two interesting stipulations. Included in his will, a ten-thousand-dollar endowment to the Merchant Seaman's Widow and Orphans Fund. No one had a clue why he would've provided such a donation since he had no affiliation with the organization whatsoever. Odder still, the five-thousand-dollar contribution to the Libertarian Party of New York. The lanky bassist never voted in any election and didn't care much for New York. Perhaps, it was his way of saying goodbye.

*   *   *

Time rolls on. Three years had passed since that day. Iris graduated summa cum laude from Colorado State and joined the staff of Shining Star Productions. A rambunctious and irrepressible young woman, the aspiring filmmaker immersed herself in her craft. Determined, clever, and resourceful, she traveled on the fast track. Initially joining the Hollywood movie studio as a proverbial "girl Friday," her work ethic and talent gained almost immediate recognition. Within six months, the title on her business card read: production assistant. Less than a year later, she'd maneuvered herself into an associate directorship on one of the company's feature film projects.

The bosses took note of her expertise and applauded her creativity. Now, with the backing of the studio and the monetary resources provided by Charlemagne Enterprises, Iris planned the documentary of the "Forty Days and Forty Nights of Godly Reign" tour. HBO would be airing the ninety-minute biopic entitled, *The View from the Ark.*

She and her crew would be riding in their own fully-equipped coach and recording select snippets of the caravan: the first two dates in Seattle, one of the concerts in Las Vegas, then, they'd join up again in Colorado for the final leg. Three camera crews would chronicle more than sixty-five hours of content. Iris and the editor would create a seamless ambiance with the footage and shape the finished product. The climax would feature the backstage preparations and live broadcast of the finale from Farmer's Stadium.

That television broadcast, with an expected viewership of more than two hundred million people in North and South America, would also find its way to Asia, Africa, and Australia on tape delay. Potentially, the telecast could draw a larger audience than the most recent Christmas Mass from the Vatican. The Dundees made light of such a comparison, but all involved were blown away by the prospect.

Iris enlisted her Uncle Harry to provide aid and assistance with *"The Ark"* project. Daniel's old LSD dropping mate from the Berkeley days worked as the ministry's audio-video production head and all-around go-to guy. Harry normally supervised every phase of equipment set-up and personally handled the sound engineering. He'd add reverb and delays and known in the industry for his own brand of special electronically enhanced effects. The film's sound crew would have full access to Harry's ten-channel mixing console, patching XLR cables directly into the live feed.

The church faithful believed in the concept of divine providence and fundamental inspiration guided by the light of God. The expected crescendo and groundswell from the Fort Collins extravaganza would be the jumping-off point for added good works. With plans for their continued expansion, a European reawakening campaign would take-off the following spring, and coincide with the Berlin MCHSB's grand opening. Bulldozers were breaking forest and clearing land in London and Paris, and architects prepared blueprints for the church's proposed Amsterdam and Lisbon affiliates.

The MCHSB, continually refocusing and evolving, sustained its upward trend with an amazing growth spurt. The eight U.S.-based parks, which now included facilities in Miami, Phoenix, and Houston, entertained more than three-quarters of a million visitors over the first six months of the current fiscal year. Gross revenues of $268 million allowed a realization of almost thirty million in net profits.

The parks' monetary successes paled when compared to the contributions provided by "The Mindful Benefactors," which averaged close to forty million dollars a month. This nonprofit business of faith and trust had grown into a major corporation, with Reverend Daniel only partially responsible. The person with the keen eye and vision for the future, the grand schemer, and the master planner, Dr. Cyrus Markum.

What precisely did this entrepreneurial wizard envision as his definitive goal? Icons in the finance world speculated how a man of science could turn on a silver Roosevelt dime and transform into a business phenomenon? For most individuals, this accomplishment would've been improbable, if not an almost impossible task. For Cyrus, it remained only the foreseeable outcome to a promise made on a Thursday in October of nineteen and eighty-nine.

At a little before ten o'clock on the morning of the twelfth day of that month, a slight vortex brushed past the doctor's face. It was the air displaced by Judge Renfro's hardwood mallet as it came crashing down on its sounding block, cementing the Formula Seven creator's fate. Betrayed and disgraced, that moment would be etched in time, and live forever in infamy.

CHAPTER FIFTEEN

The Smorgasbord Effect

Frankfurt, Germany, January 17, 1995

Sitting up, Cyrus allowed several droplets of cream to drizzle into his coffee. Satisfied with the shade of caramel, he set both the cup, and the small pitcher of half-and-half on the wooden end table. He stirred the steaming brew and took a small sip. Reclining in his favorite living room chair, he called out to his assistant. "Heinrich, would you please call my driver? I need him to bring the car around."

"Yes, of course, sir." Heinrich, in the guest bedroom, switched off the vacuum and picked up the cordless phone from the end table. He hit the automatic dialer and waited. "Hello, Bruno? The doctor is ready."

The young man played with the lobe of his right ear while he listened to the driver's reply.

"*Danke; Ich werde es ihm sagen,*" he answered, then slipped the newest invention in 900 megahertz communications back into its cradle.

Heinrich joined his boss in the living room. "Your driver will be here within ten minutes, Doctor. He's on his way back from the gym."

Cyrus pictured the buffed-up fitness freak and raised his eyebrows. That particular aspect did come in handy now and again. Aside from a having a permit to carry a sidearm, Bruno was a man of diverse talents. He incorporated discretion and resourcefulness along with his other duties. A former officer in the National People's Army of East Germany, his old position collapsed along with the wall in 1990. He'd bounced around before joining the Markum employ last year.

"Heinrich. It's not a major issue, but would you please make it a practice to speak English inside the apartment? I'm still not up to snuff in grasping the nuances of the German language." Cyrus' remark was more a command than a request.

Heinrich remained unfazed by his employer's demand. "Surely, Doctor. A slip of the tongue, I'll try and be more careful in the future. I only said I'd let you know that Bruno would be here shortly."

Cyrus stirred his coffee. "Thank you. It's not my intention to reprimand you, Heinrich. English is my native tongue. It taxes my brain cells to translate. You can understand my difficulty?"

"Yes. I certainly do."

Cyrus' eye's narrowed. "Danke schon, my young friend. Have a good time tonight." He kept a straight face at Heinrich's double take.

"That's amusing, sir."

A mild chuckle escaped the doctor's lips.

Heinrich's employment began only two weeks earlier. So far, the job seemed simple enough. He'd taken charge of the housekeeping duties, was keeping track of his employer's appointment calendar, and attending to his personal needs. This new gig beat standing behind a counter or climbing ladders to retrieve halogen bulbs and cabin air filters at the Plugs and Things auto parts store.

He'd been a shop employee the previous four months. He'd caught Cyrus' eye when the company CEO and his corporate staff came around for an inspection. It wasn't coincidental that Heinrich's father was well entrenched in the fiscal and political landscape. That undoubtedly had a major impact, but a perfect storm carried Heinrich through the waves and onto the shores of Doctor Markum's personal island.

Cyrus, requiring a high caliber, but malleable individual to look after his daily needs, found this young fellow to be an almost perfect fit.

"In many respects, you remind me of my former aide," he'd informed his new employee over their first dinner together.

Heinrich reacted with surprise. "I hope that's a good thing, Doctor."

"Ah, yes. Quite good. Ronald's gone on to reap great rewards."

Heinrich believed his employment offer spontaneous. Actually, the current corporate grandmaster conducted his erudite research and sought only verification of his prospective assistant's demeanor.

Overjoyed with his new position, the new hire earned almost double his former salary, resided in swanky digs, and consumed a fine variety of food. He attended most of the corporate business meetings, bringing along a portable cassette recorder to authenticate all discussions.

Once Lorelei, his boss' cute secretary, transcribed the recordings, he'd make three copies and personally stash each in a separate location. He didn't question the procedure, only adhered to it. One copy would be filed away in Cyrus' office, and another placed in the floor safe at his home. The company solicitor would receive the third, and the original stored in a safe deposit box in the underground vault in the Deutsche Bank.

Heinrich chalked up the meticulous process to eccentric behavior on the part of his employer, but the reason didn't matter. He went along with the program, happy for the job opportunity.

"Yeah, baby, that's why the boss pays me the big bucks," he bragged to Karl, during their evening out.

His pal laughed, hoisting his stein of Helles pale lager. "Let's toast to your continued good fortune."

"Nothing can stop me now," Heinrich growled, sipping his beer, and letting the liquid swirl around on his tongue. "Tastes sweet."

Karl raised his drink. "Your life is as golden as our brew." He took a swallow and wiped his lips with the back of his hand. "Look at you. Selling auto parts two weeks ago, and now you're riding high. You, my friend, have come up in the world."

Heinrich lifted his stein. "I'll drink to that."

Karl jumped up, splashing suds on the wooden table. "So down the hatch, my fortunate pal. Let's thank the Big Dipper for your success."

Tapping their earthenware mugs together, the two young men chugged their brews. Each thumped the bottom of the empty stoneware on the heavy wooden table when they finished. Even before they had the chance to catch their breath, Inga, the waitress with the plunging neckline was back. Fluttering the lids of her shadow enhanced eyes, she appeared ready to satisfy their thirst, and almost any other desire either of them might have. Her golden lip ring, spiked burgundy hairdo, and colorful body tats broadcast wayward sensibilities and a possible propensity toward erotic creativity.

The eyebrows of both males had elevated, and hormone levels spiked after they walked through the rathskeller door, and Inga led them to their table. Now, she posed once again, aware that with that killer body, she was treating the boys to another thrill or two.

"Hey, big spenders," she jested, "care for another round?"

Karl was the first to answer. "You looking for a huge tip, sweetheart?"

Inga leaned forward, resting her elbows on the table. Cracking her gum, she leered seductively and provided a deep frontal view of her impressive cleavage. The boys could see all the way down to the tiny silver boots of the "Black Knight" tattoo on her right breast. Of even greater interest, the top of her areolas peeked out at them from above the lavender bra. The enchanting frau moved closer, her nose almost touching Karl's face. He could taste the Brauhaus princess' warm breath.

"Of course, I'm looking for a big one, honey," she replied breathlessly. "Isn't a stout tip every girl's dream?"

Like a North Sea herring, Karl was entangled in a midwater trawling net. This wasn't your common drift net trailing behind a commercial trawler, but one woven of black fishnet hose encasing the creamy flesh of Inga's well-proportioned thighs.

"You know you're interesting," the floundering would-be beau wisecracked. "Are you busy after work?"

The waitress snapped her gum. "I have nothing happening. I was planning on going home and going straight to bed. Does that sound exciting?"

Karl made his move. "Splendid! Why don't we get together? And maybe you have a friend?" He pointed to Heinrich, whose face lit up.

The waitress flashed a wicked grin. "You're so forward. I like that in a man. I'm on the early shift tonight. I get off at midnight.

My roommate, Greta is gorgeous. I'll call her on my break. She's a lot of fun and much freakier than me."

"We can go straight away to my place." Inga grabbed the empty steins. "I'll call my roommate. Be back around with two more beers."

So, just like that, true love, or a reasonable facsimile thereof, took root in the Diekendorf Brauhaus.

Before their date with Inga and her roommate, Heinrich and Karl had an important matter to discuss, a subject much closer to their heart than women or sex. Every European male's first love, football. Avid fans and followers of the Eintracht Frankfurt sports club, competing in the Bundesliga, their loyalty began before either had climbed up on the potty.

Heinrich had a special surprise. "Karl, my boss has tickets for all home games at Waldstadion. I can use them whenever he's out of town or busy. The seats are behind our team's bench, almost at the halfway line."

Karl leaned over and planted a huge wet kiss on Heinrich's forehead. "I love you, you son of a bitch. And I think we're getting lucky later tonight."

Heinrich picked up a napkin and wiped away Karl's slobber. "I hope her friend's as wild as Inga."

Karl hugged his friend. "No doubt, baby. I have no doubt, whatsoever."

* * *

While Heinrich and Karl discussed football and looked forward to their midnight rendezvous, the doctor traveled to a tryst of his own. He relaxed in the back seat while Bruno piloted the shiny black BMW 750i.

Cyrus had found himself in a bit of a funk, and craved companionship, and the remedial sensation of the human touch. His driver, aware of his employer's preferences, had screened the personal listings in the local newspapers and made recommendations. Cyrus had a date for dinner and drinks at the Geschmack von Mexiko near the Kaiserstrasse.

This type of arrangement didn't enthrall him but it suited a purpose. He hoped the dining experience would lead to something more tangible than frozen margaritas and a plate of steak fajitas.

Bruno pulled the car up to the main entrance of the cantina and came around to open the door for his boss. Cyrus patted him on the shoulder. "Wait for me in the lot. I'll call you if things go well."

"Got it. I'll be out back, Doctor. I brought a magazine with me."

Bruno watched his employer pull open one of the double glass doors of the restaurant and let it close behind him.

As the doctor entered the waiting area, a young man looked up. "Hello, Cyrus?"

"Yes, that's me. You must be Theobold." He offered his hand. "It's nice to meet you. Have you been here long?"

"Oh no, less than five minutes." He stood up. "Please, call me Theo."

Cyrus noted his tight grip, and hand devoid of calluses.

The hostess stood behind a dark wooden stand with menus stacked on top of it. The blackboard behind her advertised, in Spanish, the specials of the day. The spices of the seared steak and grilled chicken filled the restaurant.

"Two, please, young lady." Cyrus held up two fingers. "It smells delightful in here. Do you have a booth available?"

The young woman wiggled a forefinger. "Yes, of course, sir. Please, follow me."

She pulled two menus off the stack and led them through the half-filled dining area. The two men sat opposite each other.

A balding man, wearing a black vest and a thin pencil mustache approached. "Good evening, gentlemen. My name is Ernesto and I will be your server this evening. Would you like to order drinks first or would you prefer to hear our specials?"

Theo and Cyrus exchanged glances.

The doctor interpreted his new friend's expression and answered for both of them. "No, not yet. We would like to order drinks."

His dinner date answered first. "I'll have a strawberry mojito, please."

Ernesto made a note on his pad. "And you, sir?"

"A frozen margarita, please. Would you make that mango?"

Ernesto made a note. "Of course. I'll be right back with your drinks."

While they waited, Cyrus had the chance to size up the man across from him. Theo appeared fit, probably in his mid-thirties, and quite cute. He still possessed the major portion of his hair, and his green eyes contained clarity. He couldn't quite put his finger on it, but he sensed a bit of preoccupation in his style. As they talked, Theo seemed to lose focus every now and then. The doctor wasn't about to let that deter him from his goal.

Their discussions centered on current events, the weather, the hole in the ozone layer, and how good their drinks tasted. By the time the food arrived, each had polished off their third cocktail. Neither paid much attention to his meal. Instead, they worked on becoming better acquainted.

This young fellow interested Cyrus; witty and good-looking, he lived not far from the restaurant. He laughed when the animal doctor joked about needing to travel only eight steps to work each morning.

Theo's glassy eyes focused on his dinner partner. "Please don't think me forward, but I have a suggestion. Why don't we go back to my place? I need to check up on my four-legged overnight lodgers. When I'm finished, we can relax and watch a movie."

Ah! Precisely what the doctor ordered. "That sounds fine, Theo. I just need to use the restroom. I'll be right back."

Cyrus left for the lavatory. Locking the door behind him, he pulled out his cell.

He pressed the speed dial and heard it ring. "Hello, Bruno. I'm going to be taking a ride and won't need your services for a few hours. You can pick me up later. I'll call you with the address."

"Very good, sir, I'll be waiting for your call."

Bruno turned up the radio. He could always use the time off. His army training taught him to be a man prepared. He carried his gym equipment in the trunk.

* * *

As Cyrus climbed into Theo's BMW convertible, he noted the dark-green paint accented by brown pin-striping on the exterior side panels. Once inside, he ran his hand over the svelte beige leather interior. He chuckled at the sight of the two small plastic dogs hanging from the rear-view mirror. Theo stepped on the clutch and shifted into second gear.

The doctor inched closer. "I'm having a nice time."

"I am, too. I'm so happy we met."

Cyrus hadn't been with anyone for several months and missed the emotional and physical interplay. He wanted nothing long-term. Theo looked like he might work out nicely.

Soft classical music filled the car as they drove along.

Cyrus felt a slight wave of claustrophobia wash over him. "How far are we from your home, Theo?"

"Don't worry. I'm in Oberursel, maybe another ten minutes. May I ask a personal question?"

"That depends but go ahead."

Theo hesitated for several seconds. "Do you answer these personal ads often?"

"No, I don't. I've become more of a solitary human being and haven't had a date in many years. How about yourself?"

"No, my first time. I was in a long-term relationship, but we had a bad breakup. He hurt me deeply."

"Believe me, I know, first-hand what you're going through, Theo. Years ago, my partner ripped my soul apart. I loved and trusted him. It'll take time, but the hurt will fade."

Cyrus sighed, luxuriating in the memories of Matthias. *My God, that seemed a lifetime ago.* "Theo, I've found that living in the past is counterproductive. You must let it go."

His words were far from the truth. The crimes committed against him by the U.S. government were the motivation for his entire existence.

Rays of moonlight broke through the clouds, glistening off the light coating of snow that blanketed the sides of the road. After another two or three miles, Theo downshifted. Applying the brakes, he turned into the driveway of a neat white house. In the center of the front yard stood a gray wooden sign with bold black lettering. It exhibited cutouts of a dog, a cat, and a rabbit. Beneath the caricatures, the name read: Theo's Tierklinik.

Two wooden posts, surrounded by a light layer of snow, held the sign aloft. Cyrus heard the sound of dogs barking as Theo pressed the automatic opener. The garage door began its noisy ascent.

"You have a cute home, Theo."

"Why, thank you."

Theo shifted into neutral. "Ivan and I bought this home ten years ago. When we split up, neither of us knew how to handle the property. We both wanted to sell, but with the clinic in the basement, I thought it best to buy him out and continue paying the mortgage."

"Seems like you made the logical choice," Cyrus replied, a bit irritated with the topic of conversation.

The yammering of the dogs grew louder as the engine idled, then ceased humming altogether. Theo slammed his door and led the way into the kennel. A row of aluminum cages sat on each side of the center aisle. Only three guests occupied spaces at the clinic tonight: a German shepherd and two pint-sized long-haired Chihuahuas. The little ones made the most racket. When they walked past the big dog, he barked a few times, then laid back down and closed his eyes. His yappy neighbors had much more energy and kept up their high-pitched yelping.

Theo checked the water supplies and added dry food to their dishes. "All set here. Would you like to join me upstairs?"

Cyrus nodded. "Sure, lead the way."

Theo's home was spotless It smelled of fresh pine. The two men shared white wine on the living room couch, pretending to watch a movie. Christian Slater barely had time to begin his *Interview with the Vampire* by the time they retired to the bedroom.

*   *   *

Naked, Theo rolled away from Cyrus and sobbed. "I'm so sorry. This is the first time I've been with anyone other than Ivan. My nerves got the better of me. I know I was no good."

"Cut it out. You've got to get over him. You were fine."

"Really?" Theo blew his nose into a tissue.

Cyrus picked up a condom wrapper from the nightstand. "What's this? It's unopened. You said you would put it on."

"I didn't use it. I got too excited and just lubed up."

"You're an idiot. That really pisses me off."

Theo began balling again.

"I can't believe you did that?" Cyrus slapped him across the face with the back of his hand.

Theo jumped up and ran into the living room. Enraged, Cyrus chased after him. Theo collapsed on the couch.

"Please, stop it." Cyrus sat down next to him. "Stop it. No more."

Theo couldn't hold himself back. "It began with Ivan telling me he needed to work late. But, he lied. He was playing around and wanted to have an open relationship. I couldn't tolerate that. Could you?"

Theo poured himself a glass of wine and guzzled it.

Cyrus boosted himself up from the couch. "Look, Theo, you've got to let go of the past. It does no good to keep going over it. Just forget about it. Life goes on."

"I know. I know. I'm so sorry. I wish I could stop thinking about him."

Cyrus shook his head in disgust. "Will you cut it out. You're acting like a child."

Theo wiped his eyes. "I have a confession. I feel absolutely awful."

Placing his glass on the end table, he looked up, the sadness evident in his eyes. "I don't know how to say this." He lowered his head and wept hysterically.

Cyrus had enough of his complaining. " Now what?"

Theo blurted out his news. "I'm HIV positive. I'm infected with the virus."

"What? You're not serious?"

"Yes, I am. I'm dead serious.

Cyrus clenched his fists. "Then, why the fuck didn't you use a condom?" His face turned a deep shade of scarlet. "You're a fucking idiot."

Theo barely managed to spit his words out. "I didn't have the nerve to tell you before.

The doctor was horrified. *After all that transpired, how could this be happening to him? It seemed so ironic, so unfair.*

Theo croaked. "I hate myself. I don't care if I live or die."

Cyrus surveyed the room and found what he was looking for. He gripped the neck of the horsehead paperweight sitting on the cocktail table. He stepped to the edge of the couch, and employing every bit of his strength, brought the five-pound silver statuette crashing down, piercing the top of the veterinarian's skull.

A tributary of crimson squirted from the huge gash. Wet brain matter added flecks of gray to the splotches of red squirting on Cyrus as he pulled the paperweight free.

Theo's body pitched forward and collapsed on the coffee table. The half-inch-thick tempered glass didn't shatter but supported his weight. In the midst of his death rattle, he quivered several times and expelled his last breath. Theo's front shoulders slid over the frame of the table. His head ricocheted off the edge and landed on the carpet. A dark red stain spread beneath it, growing larger and larger as the vital fluid seeped from the gaping wound.

Cyrus let the paperweight fall from his hand. It bounced off the table and rolled on the carpet. A small spider vein slowly spread on the glass top. He wrinkled his nose. The metallic scent of fresh blood was unmistakable.

"Now, look what you made me do, you idiot." *What should he do now?*

He whirled away from the corpse. *I've got to clean myself.*

Cyrus ran into the bathroom. Staring into the mirror on the medicine cabinet, he went ballistic. "Look what you've done."

He took several deep breaths and let his shoulders sag. "Just relax. Stay in control."

Allowing the sink to fill with water, he picked up the bar of soap and washed his hands and face. He stared at the mirror again. Patches of red still stained his body.

Cyrus frowned. *This will never do.* He stepped back from the sink. An animalistic howl formed in his diaphragm and ejected through his lips. *How could it have come to this? He might become a victim of the virus he fought so hard to defeat.* His maniacal laughter slowly subsided. Tears began to streak his face.

Sliding open the glass shower door, he fiddled with the knobs. Spray shot out from the overhead-nozzle. Closing the glass door behind him, he stood motionless, mesmerized by the sounds of the water slapping against the gray and white tiles. As steam filled the stall, Cyrus refocused and soaped-up.

"It was an accident and not my fault," he screamed at the shower head. "Theo did it to himself."

He slid to the front of the stall and let his face take the full impact of the pulse setting. Rivulets of water squirted straight into his iris and pupils. Flinching, he looked away. He wiped at his burning eyes, then stood over the drain staring down as the tinted water turned clear.

"Aha!" Cyrus yelled. "Success! Washed it away. I feel so much better."

Closing the faucets, he stepped out and pressed the soles of his feet on the bath mat. Lifting a towel from the closet rack, he patted his body dry.

Sitting on the edge of the bed, Cyrus slipped on a pair of Theo's briefs. After buttoning up his dress shirt, he stood and slipped on his trousers. The penny loafers provided the final element. Hunting through the room, he and found a piece of mail.

Walking back into the living room, he stared at the body. "I'm going to wake up from this nightmare," he rationalized aloud.

Theo's body hung awkwardly from the coffee table. Blood still dripped from the wound. He gawped at the symmetry of the body. The right side of Theo's face rested on the carpet, his left arm outstretched. The other laid across the coffee table, palm up, hand supported by his buttocks. If Cyrus didn't know any better, and if Theo hadn't been dead, he could well imagine the veterinarian busy practicing his freestyle swimming technique.

Picking up his cell, he pressed the speed dial. "Hello, Bruno. I need you immediately. Please, no questions, just get here as fast as you can."

He read the address from the envelope. "I'm at 53 Berliner Strasse in Oberursel. Call me when you're on the street and I'll open the garage door."

* * *

Dressed in sweat clothes, the muscular driver opened his combination lock, wondering what kind of trouble his employer had found this time. Bruno didn't have time to change. He gathered his belongings from the locker.

He threw his street clothing and gym bag on the back seat. Flipping open the glove compartment, he fumbled with the packet of maps, finding the one he sought. He spread it out on the passenger seat.

"Let's see." Bruno traced the route with his finger. He'd need to get to A5 north, ride for thirteen kilometers, stay right at Interchange 17, and take the Oberursel/Bad Homburg exit. Then, he'd get on A661 and drive for another four kilometers, make a left and then a right. "Good!" He looked at his wristwatch. He should be there by ten-thirty.

*   *   *

Cyrus waited in the garage. He'd found scrubs and slipped booties over his shoes. Surgical gloves covered his hands. The Chihuahuas kept yapping their heads off inside the kennel next door. Ignoring their protests, he pressed the button on the electronic door opener. Scrubs and booties sat on a chair nearby. He held an extra pair of gloves.

The drone of the high-performance engine drowned out the sound of the barking dogs as the big black car pulled into the empty space next to Theo's Beemer. The car's locks popped open. The motor shut down. The garage door protested loudly as it rolled down its tracks. The car door swung open, and Bruno stepped out.

"Thank God you're here. It's terrible, just terrible." His boss was frantic.

Bruno rested a hand on the doctor's shoulder. "You know that there's nothing that can't be fixed. Show me. What happened?"

Cyrus handed him the latex gloves and pointed to the white scrubs and booties sitting on the chair. "You should put those on."

Bruno slipped on the gloves. He stepped into the scrub pants, but struggled with the matching top, the fabric ripping at the center of the chest. He left it on.

"Follow me." Cyrus led the way through the kennel and up the stairs. As he twisted the knob on the upstairs door, he spun around. "I don't know what came over me. The rat bastard deserved it, but I didn't mean to kill him. I shouldn't have hit him so hard."

From the tone of his boss' voice over his cell, he'd assumed something like this. Bruno guided the doctor away from trouble before, but it never involved a killing. "Okay, Doc. Show me the body."

A blanket covered Theo's remains. A pair of blood-soaked towels that Cyrus had thrown down haphazardly, covered his head.

"Bruno," he whined. "What can we do?"

The former soldier didn't answer immediately. He weighed workable solutions. His eyes lit up. "Okay, I got it. Listen to me closely."

"Yes, of course, whatever you say."

"Okay, Doc. We're going to get rid of the body. Get me more blankets and a couple of pairs of trousers."

The big man rolled Theo's body off the coffee table and let it fall on the carpeting. His meat-hook hands encircled the wrists and dragged the corpse to the middle of the room. He pushed the table out of the way.

Cyrus ran back into the room and dropped the blankets next to the body and threw the pants next to them.

Bruno grabbed the blankets "Help me spread them out."

His boss didn't move. Bruno remained calm. "Come on. You need to keep your wits about you. I can't do this by myself."

"Okay," Cyrus replied, straddling the blankets. Grabbing hold of the corners, he helped spread them out.

Bruno grabbed Theo's ankles. "Okay, now let's move him over and wrap him up."

They rolled the body on the blankets and folded them over the corpse.

He pointed at the rocking chair. "Okay, give me the pants, Doc."

Tying one pair around the victim's head, Bruno knotted the other around the ankles. He stood up and pointed to the doorway. "We'll drag him down the stairs and stick his body in the trunk of his car."

"I don't follow."

"Doctor, don't worry. I have it under control. We're going to get rid of his car with him in it. I know where we can dump it."

"What about my fingerprints, they're all over the place."

"Don't worry, I've got that covered. We're going to destroy the evidence. Just listen to me and we'll get out of here fast."

Cyrus didn't look very confident but said nothing.

"Do you have his keys, Doc?"

"No. I'll go get them. I know exactly where they are." He streaked into Theo's bedroom.

Bruno licked his lips in anticipation of the enormous bonus he'd be receiving for his trouble.

175

Cyrus rushed back into the room, jiggling the keys. "Here, I have them."

"Good, give them to me. Now, help me move him."

They each grabbed an end of the blankets and dragged the body over to the stairway. The big man led the way, supporting the feet, as Theo's body slowly slid down the staircase. Cyrus, assisted, holding onto his end of the blankets from above.

When they dragged the corpse through the kennel, the dogs howled.

"Doc, go open the door."

Cyrus ran ahead to comply. Hoisting the dead weight over his shoulder, Bruno lugged the body to Theo's car. He popped the trunk and crammed in his human cargo. The sound of the lid slamming shut echoed loudly in the small enclosure.

"Now comes the interesting part, Doc. We need to find combustibles. We're going to give the authorities plenty to sort out. Go back upstairs. Find the liquor cabinet and gather whatever alcohol's in there."

Cyrus hesitated. "What are we going to do with it?"

The man with the expert military training threw up his hands. "Don't you worry. We're gonna make the place go boom." His eyes searched the garage. "Ah, good. I see there's a barbeque."

Theo's liquor cabinet held bottles of vodka, bourbon, and several other high-octane alcoholic beverages, that would be perfect for the party. The propane tank attached to the barbecue grill and the spare sitting next to it would do nicely. The jerrycan filled with twenty liters of gasoline that sat next to the emergency generator provided the final ingredient.

Thanks to his training, Bruno had expertise with the more creative facets of incendiary improvisation, fuse detonation, and time variation. He rigged up the furnace.

Cyrus ran into the clinic and released the dogs. The German shepherd flew out of the open garage door. The little ones barked a bit, then followed.

*   *   *

The two men were driving for three minutes when the sound of the explosion echoed through the neighborhood. They both caught the night sky's sudden flash of brightness in their rearview mirrors. Thirty seconds later the sound of an even louder blast reverberated for miles. Cyrus, driving his own car, flinched and gripped the steering wheel tightly. Bruno, guiding the convertible, took pride in the result. The major gas line had gone kerflooey.

The doctor followed the lead car for almost forty minutes. When Bruno's right turn signal began flashing, the doctor responded, and hit the blinker on his steering column. The exit sign for Staudenweiher, a lake and recreation area, came into view. The time on the dashboard clock read, well past midnight. He gagged but fought off the sensation.

His cell rang. "Doctor, pull over in that parking lot on your right, just ahead. Wait for me. I'll be back in a few minutes."

"Yes, of course, Bruno."

Streetlights provided the lighting. Every parking space sat empty. The doctor pulled into one. Even though the AC pumped full bore, the perspiration dripped from Cyrus' face and underarms. He fumbled with the radio and found a classical music station. A string ensemble played a piece he recognized. He listened for a few seconds. Racking his brains, he searched for the title without any luck. The plastic bag sitting on the seat caught his attention. Inside it, sat his underwear and the towel he'd used, the evidence of the craziest night of his life.

The sharp tap on the glass startled him. He recoiled. When he saw Bruno's face, he breathed easier. Cyrus slid down the power window.

The big man laid his hand on the car door. "We're done here. Would you like me to drive?"

"Of course. I'll move over."

Cyrus wanted to curl up in the passenger seat and stop his mind from re-experiencing the events of the evening. His savior slid behind the wheel and pulled the door closed behind him.

CHAPTER SIXTEEN

Preparing For Primetime

May 7, 1995

Bruno peered into the rearview mirror and pressed down on the gas pedal. His employer had a date at the Waldstadion; Eintracht Frankfurt and the Nuremberg club would be kicking off at three. The doctor had little interest in the football match. He had a meeting with Baron Klaus von Klieber, the man who could unlock the castle gates.

Once his generous political contribution primed the pump, the opulent aristocrat, a friend of Heinrich's father, cleared his schedule and traveled north from his Vienna estate. Of course, Cyrus picked up the tab for the private air flight, limousine, and hotel accommodations.

Not a modicum of doubt existed that he would convince Klaus of the incontrovertible merits of his definitive elucidation. It had taken several years, but all his i's had been dotted and t's crossed with meticulous attention paid to the details. There could be no question left unanswered, nor any doubt shrouding the legitimacy of the theorem. The final interlocking piece of the socioeconomic jigsaw puzzle was about to snap snugly into place.

Cyrus' financial empire included a score of companies in Europe and a dozen in the United States. His Swiss accounting firm estimated his liquidity and tangible net worth at approximately three hundred million dollars, securing him the thirty-second spot on the list of Forbes' "richest people in the world." His hidden assets, controlled by his proxies in California, amounted to another sixty million, a mere pittance when compared to the holdings of Baron von Klieber. Ranked fourth on the "wealthiest on the planet" hit parade, only Bill Gates, Warren Buffett, and John Kluge outshined him. Economists estimated his net worth at almost six billion dollars.

Cyrus would never allow himself to be ensnared in a tangle of unpreparedness again. He'd excavated and absorbed every pertinent detail of this affluent entrepreneur and potential patron. The amazing story began with the breech birth in Munich in 1920 and climaxed with the acquisition of sixteen major conglomerates. The baron had been declared the single richest German alive today.

Once Cyrus completed the biography, he reread the hardcover edition yet again, this time highlighting any items of import that might call for closer inspection or additional scrutiny. A color photo of the fire-breathing dragon's head coat of arms leaped off the face of the book's dust jacket. Embossed with large, golden script just above the artwork, the title read: *Order of the Dragon.*

Manheim Allied Security Agency (MASA), amplified the fact-finding mission. The firm performed an in-depth investigative study of this fascinating man and his business organization. Their sterling reputation for utilizing any available resources in fulfilling a contract included utilizing their network of unconventional and underworld contacts. They unsheathed a treasure trove of material. But, several questions regarding early business dealings remained unanswered.

MASA's eighty-six-page dossier explicated valuable specifics. Cyrus hoped that possessing such knowledge would give him an edge and allow equal footing. The in-depth study and editorialized report began as any might for the time-period in Germany.

In 1934, at fourteen years of age, Klaus von Klieber swore an oath of allegiance to the Nazi party, joining the Hitler Youth Organization. Upon reaching his eighteenth birthday, he undertook the OCS curriculum. Upon completion, Klaus received a commission as a second lieutenant in the *Wehrmacht.* Graduating first in his class of forty-six and with his father's connections and family history dating back to the Teutonic Knights, Klaus received a nomination for supplemental training. Afterward, he joined the *Schutzstaffel*, the most prolific Nazi killing machine of the day.

Heinrich Himmler, a frequent visitor to the von Klieber family estate in Vienna, tapped Klaus to be his aide. The lieutenant joined the Nazi stalwart at SS headquarters in Berlin in February of 1940. After serving admirably for more than a year, the young battle hungry patriot received a promotion to Captain by his *Reichsfuhrer* and assigned to the *Leibstandarte* division of the *Waffen*-SS. In April 1941, he earned the Order of the Iron Cross Second Class for helping defeat the Sixth Australian Division in the Battle of Klidi Pass and securing Height 997.

In a bedside ceremony, Himmler personally delivered his young protégé's medal, pinning it to Klaus' hospital gown while he recovered from a slight bullet wound to his right thigh. For his classic leadership and courage under fire, a promotion to major accompanied the award, as well as a transfer to Munich.

The change of station couldn't have been more fortuitous for the young officer. In late June, Operation Barbarossa commenced with disastrous results. The invasion of the Soviet Union hit a stone wall as the Third Reich attempted to overrun Moscow. His former company paid the price, decimated by enemy fire, disease, exposure, lack of logistical support, and access to proper medical supplies.

Instead, the newly promoted major reported to the *Kunstschutz*, the unit responsible for inventorying and guarding appropriated art treasures. Works by the masters, seized from occupied countries and booty "legally" confiscated from former Jewish citizens, came under his watchful eye. Stored in the heart of the Motherland for safekeeping, Klaus remained the supervisor of the storage facility until the war's end.

In early January 1945, with Germany's defeat inevitable, Baron von Klieber took personal responsibility in safeguarding two ambulance loads of priceless artwork along with a truckload of gold bullion. The small convoy motored southward to his father's estate in Vienna and the contents of the vehicles stored inside a concealed underground chamber.

Unfortunately for the men involved in the theft, Klaus accused them of treason and lined up the six men involved before a hastily arranged firing squad.

As a boy in knee pants and stockings, his father had schooled him in the fine art of survival and essential need for material success. "Always confront a problem head-on," his father encouraged his young son. "Grab the bulls by the horns and twist for all you're worth. Then, just hold on and don't ever let go."

Those would be words to live by and the baron understood their full import.

His career as a Nazi officer concluded in the spring of 1945. During the battle for the Munich airport, the newly promoted lieutenant colonel received a severe wound and taken captive by the Americans.

He wore no SS uniform at the time, but one of a common infantry officer. His falsified papers carried a purposeful misspelling of his last name. A chemical peel, by a doctor he'd paid handsomely, eliminated the SS blood type tattoo from under his left arm. In the confusion of the surrender, his subterfuge worked to perfection.

Requiring crutches for mobility, Klaus couldn't provide the Allies with much help in the rebuilding of Europe. His release from the detainment camp came in late November 1945, when the guards stuffed him into a train car and sent him home to Vienna.

From that point onward, the pages in the MASA report itemized his accomplishments. In his early days, a seemingly endless supply of investment capital helped build a multifaceted financial empire, with the source never mentioned or questioned. Over the last fifty years, Klaus had risen to become one of the most influential and powerful people on earth.

Involving himself in cultural organizations and children's charities, he spent more time greasing the gears of the political machinery of several European countries, and eventually became an advisor-at-large to the German chancellor.

What the report did not highlight, was the baron's deep involvement with an ancient order founded in Bavaria in May 1776, by Adam Weishaupt. Outlawed in 1785 by Charles Theodore, the country's leader at the time, rumors of the organization's dissolution circulated, but in fact, a safety net of deceit shielded the sanctified few. In secret, the society continued to flourish, never faltering or abandoning faith in their sacred doctrines. Their organization wielded immense power, concealed beneath the surfaces of societies worldwide.

Cyrus discovered several undeniable facts. The von Klieber bloodline ran deep within the order. Like his father before him, Klaus occupied a straight-back chair at the roundtable of thirteen and held a deciding vote on the Trilateral Commission. He'd inherited the prestigious title of Minister of Jurisdictional Malfeasance and Summary Reprimand. Since 1954, Klaus has been the man holding the lightning bolt, dispensing the tribunal's vision of justice, and enforcing the edicts of their sacred circle.

Most of the general population had no inkling of the secret society's existence. Standing above the fray, they manipulated the control bar and central rod. Pulling the strings, they directed the actions and reactions of their flesh-and-blood marionettes. They've continued to flourish, accumulating enormous wealth and influence over the past two hundred years.

Along with the French Freemasons, the Bavarian Illuminati propagated the revolution in France during the late eighteenth century. Aiding the Duke of Orleans, the grand master of the Grand Orient Lodge of Freemasons, the society's council bankrolled his purchase of immense stores of grain, denying sustenance to the masses. With starvation fostering discontent, the revolt and sharpening of the guillotine's blade followed immediately thereafter.

Cyrus agreed unreservedly with the assumptions of the shadow conspiracy theorists. The Illuminati shared responsibility for fostering the dissolution of the sovereign rule of the Bourbon monarchy, paving the way for Maximilien Robespierre's horrific terror crusade. The blame for the execution of Louis XVI, the Dauphin of France, and his wife, Austrian-born Marie Antoinette, belonged to the Bavarians.

Scalawags might argue that violence was a steep price to pay for the birthing of liberty and democracy, but many thought otherwise. To him, it demonstrated the vulnerability of the human condition. But enough with the analysis of history. He planned on dispensing his own conceptual brand of freedom.

* * *

He and Bruno stood at the main entrance of the Waldstadion. The doctor glanced at his watch. The teams would kick off in thirty minutes. He had to admit, European sports fans loved their football. In the past, the seats had come in handy cementing a deal or two. He hoped these tickets would serve him well today.

Cyrus remained reserved as he watched the black stretch limo pull up. The driver, dressed in a black outfit with matching visored cap, quick timed it around the car and opened the rear door. First to disembark, a blond-haired young man, with dark Ray-ban sunglasses in place. His face wore a resolute expression. His head pivoted left, then swung right, as he checked the area around him. A second man exited from the passenger seat and position himself at the front end of the car. His right hand reached inside his jacket.

The blonde fellow removed his sunglasses. "Hello. You must be Cyrus Markum. I'm Marcus. I'm chief of Baron von Klieber's security detail."

He wasn't looking for a response. He swiveled around and spoke to a party, as yet unseen, still seated inside the car. "You can exit now, sir. All looks secure."

The black cane emerged first, its silver tip glinting in the sunlight. Black wingtips followed. The chauffeur extended a gloved hand and helped his passenger exit.

The photographs didn't do him justice. Stately and distinguished, the baron looked quite fit for a man of seventy-five, albeit his slight rightward list, courtesy of his old war wounds. His hair, white from age, but mostly intact, was parted neatly on the left side. Wearing a dark gray suit with his dragon's head family crest embroidered over the left breast pocket, a beige shirt and black bow tie completed the ensemble.

Familiar with his physicality, his host had been ill-prepared for the atmosphere and vibrations of power surrounding the man. Waves of nervous energy ran through Cyrus' belly as he analyzed the manner and demeanor of this graceful gentleman of title. He took a breath and moved in for the greeting.

"Hello, Baron. I'm Cyrus Markum. I'm so glad you decided to visit. What a pleasure to meet you." He offered his hand.

His guest didn't change expression, only acknowledging the gesture with a simple nod of the head. Both his white-gloved hands remained positioned on the head of his cane as turned to his bodyguard.

"I'm sorry, Doctor," Marcus reacted. "The baron doesn't subscribe to the handshake ritual. He's extremely aware of disease-carrying bacteria and refrains from physical contact."

Cyrus, a bit befuddled, refused to allow a minor impediment affect him. He'd go with it and demonstrate his flexibility. "Of course, as a scientist and molecular biologist, I do understand your aversion completely."

The baron allowed himself a smidgen of a smirk. "I'm glad you do."

His speech pattern carried a textbook German accent. The noble gentleman blotted the corners of his mouth with a beige handkerchief, then cleared his throat. "I understand that you no longer partake in scientific research. You might be better served by referring to your doctorate in the past tense. I'm correct in that assumption, am I not?"

Cyrus remained mute, realizing the question more of a rhetorical nature, and required no response.

"Have no doubt, Doctor Markum, I know your complete and unedited history, the unadulterated truth, so to speak."

Cyrus showed no outward sign of ambiguity. He'd expected due diligence on the part of his guest. "I have nothing to conceal. My scientific accreditations are still valid, but like yourself, I'm currently practicing the discipline of high finance. I take immense pride in the scope of my accomplishments."

"As well you should, Markum. It's evident that you're quite capable. Your reaction to adversity is extraordinary. You've managed to exploit the negativity that invades your space and embrace it, developing a special knack for turning your trials and tribulations into vindicating solutions of almost unprecedented magnitudes. Believe me, I know you quite well..."

The baron cleared his throat again, this time coughing up a globule of mucus and spitting into his handkerchief. Cyrus could see the initials KvK monogrammed on one of its corners. Refolding the cloth, the baron placed it inside his inner suit pocket. "Yes, my friend, be assured, I know you as well as you know yourself."

The doctor remained cool. "I'd have it no other way. You see, I believe that you and I are much alike. We're adept students of life, constantly surveying the chess board and contemplating the possibilities and tangible result of all available moves. We plan our effective strategies and are loath to concede defeat. Rarely, do we retreat from a challenge."

His guest tapped cane on the ground. "You're correct. We both eventually get what we set our sights on. Do we not? *Einfach nur fantastisch.*"

Cyrus furrowed his brow.

Sensing the use of the German language improper, the baron slipped back to English. "Excuse my discourtesy. I was only alluding to the fact that I find your metaphorical illuminations enlightening. Your skills in philosophical reasoning are extremely refreshing. You're as I imagined you to be, a man of intellect and vision. I am, of course, extremely curious as to the true purpose of our meeting. You've been so gracious. Thank you for inviting me to Frankfurt."

Cyrus inhaled deeply and pointed the way. "Please, let's take our seats. I'll explain it all inside."

Bruno led the way. The two principals walked side by side. The baron's men occupied the rear-guard position. That mythological decisive moment would soon materialize. Much still needed clarification. The doctor had prepared a comprehensive illustration. He planned to provide the necessary evidence to demonstrate that his proposal merited approval by Baron Klieber's elite organization. Its acceptance would obviate the sacrilegious subversion of God and religion and dislodge the impostors from beneath the circular glow of the spotlight. In his brown leather case, he carried the report of condemnation and retribution: *The Ultimate Messianic Revelation.*

CHAPTER SEVENTEEN

Consulting the Seraph

Frankfort, May 22

Cyrus laid in a recliner napping. The sound of the phone jostled him awake. The living room carried the Rhein-Main news program, with the sound turned off. A classical radio station provided background music. Jumping up, he switched off the radio and raised the cordless handset to his ear.

It was more than two weeks since he and the baron had their meeting at Waldstadion. This morning, Heinrich had relayed a message that the call he expected should be forthcoming this afternoon. *This might be it.*

"Hello. Good morning. This is Cyrus," he answered calmly.

"Hello, it's Lilith. I'm calling from Hollywood."

He glanced at his watch. It showed precisely noon. With the nine-hour time difference, it must be the middle of the night in California. He hadn't spoken to his psychic lady friend for five or six months. *Why would she be calling?*

His agency guided her burgeoning career. Lily's new show, *Lilith, Psychic at Large*, was a major hit on one of the cable networks.

Cyrus, with his back to the TV and paying no attention to the screen, would've been extremely interested in the lead news story. The show opened with a live feed from Staudenweiher Lake. A black, algae covered BMW sat on a flatbed. A corpse, discovered in the trunk, and covered by a body-bag, was being loaded into an ambulance. It would shortly be on the way to the medical examiner's office.

Archived footage of a smoldering ruin followed. The voice-over went on to explain how a huge explosion had obliterated what had once been a home and animal hospital in the town of Oberursel. Next, came the backstory: Theobold Brandt, a local veterinarian who'd been missing for the last four months, was the presumed victim. Ivan Voltz, a Frankfurt pharmacist, and the former boyfriend sat in jail. For this capital offense, no bail would be administered.

The media loved a sexy headline and had labeled the case, "A Poisonous Prescription for the Doggie Doctor." People around the world ate up real-life crimes of passion, especially when they involved "deviant" sexual behavior. The people of Germany proved no exception. They reserved a special place in their heart for tales of such heinous activities.

Cyrus saw none of this. He would've been happy to know the specifics.

Instead, he focused on his conversation. "Why hello, Lily. How have you been?"

"I'm doing well. Thank you for asking. How about yourself?"

"Good, good, nothing new on this end. To what do I owe the pleasure of your call, young lady?"

"We need to see each other. Your mother contacted me tonight and told me that she needs to speak with you. She says that it's very important. When will you be visiting the States?"

"Lily, please... tell me. What did she say?"

"She didn't say anything more to me. She wants to speak with you directly."

Using his free hand, he dug out the date book from his vest pocket and flipped it open. "Well, let's see. I'll be in Los Angeles in three weeks. I have several meetings scheduled for the week of June twelfth. It'll have to wait until then."

"If that is what must be, then so it shall be."

"Is everything going well, Lil? Are my people taking care of you?"

"Oh yes, Cyrus. Things couldn't be better. You've left your company in capable hands."

"That's reassuring. My employees have my complete confidence. Stay well, my dear. I'll see you soon. Bye, bye."

"Blessed be your day, Cyrus."

The doctor grinned, amused by Lily's goodbye. Blessed be the day, an odd way to end a conversation. He replaced the handset and strolled toward the kitchen.

Refilling his coffee cup, he pulled out a chair and sat down. His unfinished *New York Times* Sunday crossword puzzle lay on the table. He picked up a pencil and went back to contemplating the answer to thirty-four down. The sound of the key turning in the side door broke his train of thought.

Heinrich was back from the post office. "Doctor, there had several items for you. One required a signature."

"Excellent, I'll look at them later. By the way, are you familiar with an eight-letter word for the assistant referee in a soccer match? It starts with an L."

"That's an easy one, Doc. The word you're looking for is linesman."

Cyrus used his number two, black lead pencil and filled in the small boxes. "Ah, yes. That fits in quite nicely. Thank you."

Heinrich carefully laid the envelopes on the kitchen table and checked his watch. "It's almost one. Would you like me to prepare your lunch?"

"No, thanks. I ate earlier."

The young man walked from the kitchen and hung his jacket in the foyer closet.

When the phone rang a few minutes later, Cyrus beat Heinrich to it.

"Hello, good afternoon," he greeted the caller.

"Hello. Is this Doctor Markum?"

"Yes, it is."

"This is Marcus. We met at the football match."

"Ah, yes, I remember. How are you?"

"I'm good, thank you. Please, listen. Tomorrow morning at seven forty-five, a car will pick you up. The driver will be taking you to a meeting. It's a long trip and we're not stopping on the way."

Gratifying waves of energy ran through Cyrus' body and goose pimples raised up on his arms and neck. "That'll be fine. I'll be ready. And, thank you."

"You're quite welcome. Good day, Doctor."

The time had finally come. Tomorrow morning would be the official debarkation point. Getting any sleep tonight would be close to impossible.

* * *

With only two hours of nighttime sleep under his belt, Cyrus felt reenergized once he'd swallowed his second cup of dark coffee. Not knowing how long a ride to expect, he forced himself to use the bathroom. He paced around the living room. His watch read seven forty-three.

Three short beeps from a car's horn stopped him in mid-step. He grabbed his light blue jacket and closed the front door behind him. He found Marcus standing outside the black Mercedes.

"Please, get in, Doctor." Klaus' main hired gun opened the back door of the limo. "And slide over."

Cyrus's curiosity was aroused. Why hadn't Marcus told him that he would be coming along for the ride? No need for him to create waves. He complied with the instructions without comment.

Marcus slid next to him and pulled out a black handkerchief. He pointed to the doctor's spectacles. "Please remove your glasses and turn around. I need to tie this."

Warning circuits sounded. "A blindfold, why do I have to wear that?"

"Orders, sir, I'm just following them. The baron is cautious and does not want to reveal too much, too soon."

The explanation made sense. The society must employ safeguards. Trust is earned.

Cyrus turned away from Marcus. "Okay, I understand. Go ahead."

"You'll be wearing this for a while," the baron's emissary apologized, tightening the cloth. "We'll be on the road for close to four hours. Would you care for a snack or a drink?"

Enough coffee coursed through Cyrus' urinary system already. He didn't need any more liquid. Hopefully, he'd be able to tough it out. "No, thank you, Marcus. I'm fine."

The doctor listened to the sounds of the road as the car zipped along. With his eyes covered and nothing to occupy his thoughts, he found himself contemplating the possibility of developing full-blown AIDS due to his sexual encounter three months earlier with that idiot veterinarian. Blood tests had revealed no abnormalities. The possibility that the virus hadn't been transmitted seemed likely. He would ignore the possible ramifications the disease could present and concentrate on more pressing matters.

The baron and his cronies had ample time to review Cyrus' proposal. Today, provided all went well, he'd be receiving the Trilateral Commission's endorsement. In his pocket calendar, he'd entered the date for retribution. If things went as planned, on that special day, he, and the Illuminati faithful would catapult into a position of immense power.

The soothing motion of the rotating tires and the monotonous hum of the high-speed motor slowed his brain activity. After another ten minutes, the aspiring autocrat dreamed of his place in the New World Order.

* * *

Cyrus stirred slightly as the car decelerated. The sound of the gravel kicking up around the car nudged him awake. The clanging of church bells shocked his senses. In a reflex action, he grabbed hold of the leather seat cushions under him.

He felt a hand on his shoulder and heard Marcus' voice. "Don't mind the racket, Doctor. We're here. Please, don't take off your blindfold yet. When we get inside, I'll remove it. Wait a moment. I'll come around and guide you."

Cyrus relaxed but insecurity still gnawed at him. "Thank you."

He heard a door open, then slam shut. The door next to him opened. Strong fingers encircled his forearm. "Just watch your step. We'll be going down some stairs," Marcus warned, helping him step out from the car.

The doctor counted ten steps as he descended to a lower level. They walked twenty-five paces forward before halting momentarily. Then, down another stairway, this one only six steps. Each footfall reverberated loudly. Cyrus visualized the stone construction. The temperature dropped dramatically. He felt the dampness and noticed a musty odor. They paused again. The creak of an opening door added to the intrigue.

"Please stay still, Doctor. I'm going to remove your blindfold."

As Cyrus fit his glasses back onto the bridge of his nose, his eyes slowly adjusted to the dim lighting. The soothing sound of harpsichord music filtered through his ears. He found himself standing before several men seated at a large round table.

"Doctor, please sit." Marcus gestured toward an oak chair.

"I will in a moment, but first, I need to use the lavatory."

"I'm sorry, Doctor. I should have offered. Please, right this way."

As Cyrus followed behind Marcus, he noted the stone construction in the passageway. The Renaissance period, he estimated, judging by the masonry. The harpsichord music he recognized as "Moonlight Sonata," a creation of Ludwig van Beethoven. *These individuals have fine taste,* he thought, smiling in appreciation.

Marcus pointed. "Right through that doorway. I'll wait here for you."

Inside, a modern-day bathroom greeted him. An easily recognizable, original black-and-white painting hung on the wall that faced the entrance. The open Eye of Providence, centered perfectly within the small pyramid, stared back at him. The phrase *Novus ordo seclorum* sat underlined beneath it. These same words, he knew, were inscribed on the reverse side of the great seal of the United States, as well as beneath the unfinished pyramid on the one-dollar bill. The translation being: "New order of the ages." He chuckled at the hokey symbolism.

The modern-day facility contained a sink, toilet, and shower, no stones holding this bathroom in place. Ceramic tiles decorated the walls. Track lighting hung from the drop ceiling.

He stared into the mirror that ran from the top of the vanity to the edge of the ceiling. Winking at his reflection, he breathed deeply several times, reminding himself to stay on an even-keel and show no signs of uncertainty. With the sound of the earlier chiming bells, he knew with certainty that he stood in the depths of a church. There were several possibilities, but he'd take that matter up another time. He must concentrate on remaining in the moment.

Marcus escorted him back to the main chamber. Cyrus noted his chair's positioning afforded unobstructed visual access to the people seated at the fine oak table.

"Ah, Doctor Markum, we're so happy that you've joined us today."

He recognized the baron's voice. The silver-haired nobleman pushed himself up from his seat and rested his hands on the head of his cane. "I'm not going to make introductions now, but at the proper time, you'll be given the information you're seeking."

This statement irritated Cyrus, but he said nothing. He knew he must demonstrate proper decorum and show his willingness to comply. "I understand," he replied. "There will be plenty of time for that."

The Illuminati's charismatic patriarch raised a hand. "We have debated over the salient points of your innovative proposition. Though we all did not agree on the first ballot, we have conferred further and unanimously accept the options outlined in your *Ultimate Messianic Revelation*. If you don't mind, I'd like to present an observation first."

Cyrus wrestling with the smile that fought to form on his lips. "Of course, I'm quite interested to hear what you have to say."

The baron's face took on a serious tone. "As you are well aware, people of substance, those of us willing to take risks, run the societies of the world. We're cognizant of the crimes the American bureaucrats have perpetrated against you. By claiming Formula Seven was a national security issue, they protected them against prosecution. Two agencies orchestrated the stark subversion of authority and wasted and undermined your genius. Because of their wrongdoing, many have suffered and died needlessly.

We agree with your hypothesis and are ready to become enablers and facilitators. The financial aspects will, of course, need clarification and proper organization. How does that suit you?" The baron took his seat.

Cyrus rose and looked around the table. "Firstly, let me thank everyone. Your decision is a wise one. I'm gratified that you concur with my findings."

The former Nazi lieutenant colonel took the reins of the conversation once again. "We recognize that you're an astute student of life. You possess a prodigious understanding of our concept for the New World Order. The people that you see here today are the thirteen members of the ruling council. All that we discuss must remain concealed from the outside world. I know that you can appreciate that precept, correct?"

"There's no question. I'll abide by your pronouncements." Cyrus raised his right hand. "I want to be a part of your collective vision and invest in the creation of a better world and..."

Baron von Klieber waved his cane and cut off his guest. "Why is it up to you to impose punishment, Doctor Markum? Do you think you're God?" His words, shaded by sarcasm, cut Cyrus deeply.

He didn't overreact, only lowered his hand, and reflected on his answer.

"You know me better than that, Baron. I do not seek personal gain, only a day of reckoning. The structure of the worldwide governments must undergo alteration. Those in power use the gargantuan apparatus to further their own ends. They care nothing for the rights of their citizens. The twisted power brokers have branded me a black sheep. I have come here today seeking comfort with those of a similar outlook and philosophy."

The prospect threw up both hands. "I pledge undying allegiance to the Trilateral Commission and embrace all philosophies of the New World Order."

The baron rested his cane against the table and applauded softly. The other men stood up and joined in. After several seconds, they ceased their noisemaking and once again, took their seats.

Only their leader remained erect. He pointed his cane at the prospect. "Nicely put, very nicely put. No further blindfolds will be necessary. You've shown the Council your true colors. I'd like to extend an invitation. Stay with me in Vienna for a few days next week. I hope you can clear your schedule. We'll have the opportunity to get better acquainted. The High Council will now take up other matters."

He looked at his security chief. "Marcus will see you home. We thank you for your presence here today."

Cyrus bowed. "Thank you, gentlemen." His voice was calm and filled with confidence.

He understood that the Trilateral Commission's shroud of secrecy must remain in place. Though not fully accepted into their boy's club yet, he knew it would be only a matter of time until he'd earn his official patch.

Baron von Klieber observed the men seated around him. One by one, each nodded and lifted his right hand, pointing a forefinger upward.

The Baron waved a hand. "I'll be in contact with you tomorrow. Good day and have a comfortable trip home."

Cyrus, following Marcus as they retraced their route through the underground labyrinth. He felt reinvigorated and not at all concerned with his abrupt discharge. The meeting went as well as he could have anticipated. He'd reacted well to the baron's attempt to irritate him and to gauge his temperament. The Council's applause verified that he'd passed his initial test. The invitation to the Vienna estate further validated that fact.

As he stepped out onto the church grounds, he lifted a hand to shield his eyes from the brightness. A slight chill hung in the air, but the cloudless skies allowed the sun's rays to warm his face. He looked up at the architectural masterpiece that rose above him. He recognized it, St. Michael's Church. Cyrus knew its history. During the late sixteenth century, William Duke ordered its construction as a gift to the Jesuits.

A dedication to the Archangel Michael, the biblical leader of the armies of God, who led the continuing battle against Satan and his hoard of sycophants. According to Roman Catholic scripture, the Archangel also accompanied the spirits of the newly deceased to purgatory and bring them before God for their final judgment. Operating the scales of earthly deeds, Michael would weigh the good and evil stored within each of the souls. How ironic that the Archangel watched over those of the High Council.

The ceiling of the Sistine Chapel best portrayed the so-called scene of judgment day. In Michelangelo's magnificent fresco, the angels are pictured blowing their trumpets while Archangel Michael announces the names of the blessed, those granted entrance into heaven. To Michael's left, two lesser Holy disciples hoist a much larger book that contains an even longer list; the names are those of the sinners who will suffer banishment and eternal damnation. Cyrus laughed at the concept of heaven and hell, believing it a medieval fairy-tale and a waste of papyrus paper.

The Illuminati subscribed to the belief that God had endowed them to lead the populace of earth to a new beginning. Their members considered themselves inspirational horticulturists, endowed to cultivate the garden and inspire germination. If unsightly wildflowers or weeds created a problem, a squirt or two of organic herbicide would do the trick. Biding their time, the dogmatic gardeners wait until the formation of a single totalitarian world government, meticulously articulated as the inevitable and joyful conclusion of historical and religious progress, will germinate.

The genesis of this New World Order, administered by the sacrosanct few, would include Cyrus within its ranks. The ripening crops awaited harvest and the second coming, but no Messiah would accompany the *"Parousia."* This judgment day would be socioeconomic and politically driven, and without the biblical promised land as a reward.

Through Jesuit emissaries providing material and philosophical support, the Vatican secretly championed the Illuminati. Until deemed appropriate, the connection between the two entities would remain shrouded. Instead, the presence of conflicting viewpoints would keep the masses beguiled. The Holy hierarchy of the Catholic religion employed patience until the New World Order took control. Then, the church would gain dominion over the world and control the soul of man.

CHAPTER EIGHTEEN

Spirits and Demons

Los Angeles, California. Monday, Twelfth of June 1995

The aromatic scent greeted Cyrus as he opened the front door and wheeled his suitcase inside. Though almost nine at night, Naida had prepared his favorite meal: calf's liver, bacon, and onions, mashed sweet potatoes, and steamed broccoli. He'd eaten only a light lunch on the flight from Frankfurt, and absolutely famished, he wolfed down his portion and took a second helping.

Wiping his mouth with his monogrammed napkin, he sat back and rubbed his stomach contentedly. "I see you haven't lost your touch. The food is simply delicious. I thank you so much."

Naida beamed. "Thank you, Doctor. Would you care for a coffee? I've baked your favorite dessert."

He patted his stomach. "That would be fantastic. I still may have a bit of room. But first, I need to make a call. I'll take it in the living room."

"Of course. I'll bring it in."

He pushed his chair away from the dining room table and walked slowly into the adjoining room. Pulling up the speed dial on his cell, he scrolled down and pressed the call button.

"Hello, Lily? It's me. Happy Sunday evening. I've just arrived."

"Cyrus? I hope you had a nice flight. I need to see you?"

He thought over his itinerary. "I have a pair of meetings scheduled for midday tomorrow, but I'll be free in the evening. When are you available?"

"Tomorrow evening's perfect. My show is on sabbatical and won't pick up taping until Wednesday."

"Perfect! How would you like to come over for dinner? I'll order from that Indian place on Wilshire. Chicken tikka is your favorite if I recall correctly, and let's see, you have a deep affinity for the goat pasanda. Am I good or what?"

He could visualize Lily's smiling face on the other end of the line.

"Yes, you did, Cy. I'd much prefer to meet at your home. I can be over around sevenish. Is that good?"

"That's fine, Lil. Seven it is. I'll see you then, with a warm naan in hand."

"I'll be looking forward to it." She let his attempt at culinary humor pass. "Ciao."

"Bye. See you then."

7:00 p.m., Tuesday,

The tangy aroma of the exotic delicacies greeted Lily as Cyrus swung open the front door. The two hugged and exchanged pecks on both cheeks.

"Oh, that food smells wonderful. I might eat it all myself," she teased. "I'm starving. I burned off a bunch of calories on the StairMaster. It's too bad that I didn't have time to shower."

The corners of her host's mouth turned up. He gave her a quizzical look.

She patted him on his upper arm. "Oh, don't worry. I'm just kidding."

His tiny smile blossomed into a full grin. "You had me going. I almost believed you, Lil."

"Well, I apologize, but I owed you one for your feeble attempt at humor with the naan joke yesterday. I ignored it then, but I needed payback."

He chuckled. "I'm sorry if my comment about the naan seemed a bit short on dough."

Lily wrinkled her nose. "Oh, you are so bad."

"I know. Why don't we eat?" Cyrus pointed toward the dining room. "Naida has set the table for us."

Lily pulled off her red blazer and handed it to him. "Can you hang this up for me, please?"

"Sure." He took the jacket, and carefully laid it over the arm of the couch. The powerful scent of the curry, marinated goat, and spiced chicken, guided them to the table.

He could hear the housekeeper moving around in the kitchen. "Come and say hello to Lily."

Naida shuffled into the dining room. "Hello, Miss Lily." Her greeting sounded stilted and a bit forced.

"Why don't you join us?" Cyrus suggested. "There's plenty of food."

Naida, quite aware of Lily's gift, found her abilities frightening. Raised a strict Roman Catholic, the housekeeper didn't believe in any such things as ghosts or the existence of a spiritual plane. She subscribed to the standard issue Catholic teachings about purgatory, heaven, and hell.

"Doctor, I've made plans to visit my brother in Reseda. I'm staying overnight. I didn't think you'd mind."

He scooped a helping of rice onto his guest's plate. "Sure, that would be fine. I have no objection"

"I'll see you tomorrow, sir. Good night, Miss Lily. Good to see you."

It took only thirty seconds for Naida to walk back into the kitchen, gather up her belongings, and push open the side door. She left before either Cyrus or his dinner guest had a chance to say goodnight.

Exchanging whimsical glances, the doctor, and his dinner guest dove into their plates of North Indian cuisine.

Lily took a swallow of water and set the glass on the table. She looked over at her host. "Do you remember that evening when we first ran into each other?"

"Yes, of course, I love that Italian place in San Francisco. You and your friend, Mary, I couldn't ever forget that night."

"Yes, that's right. Well, I've been curious. Why hasn't our relationship ever led to anything more than friendship and a business association?"

He found her question odd. Though he'd never discussed his sexual preference with her, he thought she realized that he had no physical or chemical attraction toward women. In any case, to carry on a meaningful relationship with anyone, would be a self-indulgence he couldn't afford. Matthias had been the only one.

Never again would he allow another to toy with his heart. The potential pain and emotional betrayal didn't seem worth it.

Cyrus evaded her question. "I'm so busy. My business interests are my only love."

She dipped a piece of her naan in the green curry sauce and took a tiny bite. "I can understand that, just curious."

Lily took another bite but paused chewing. What remained of her oven-baked flatbread dropped from her hand and into the dish. Her eyes glazed over. She blinked several times. Evidently, a visitor from the other side sought her attention. Lily bit her lip and laid her elbows on the table. Her shoulders slumped forward. Her head fell into her hands.

Cyrus laid his fork down and wiped his lips with the napkin. "Are you okay?"

Lily lifted her head. "Yes, I'm fine. Your mother wants to communicate. She's here with us now."

Her glassy eyes stared straight ahead. "I'm receiving a message. Your mother wants you to know she's proud of you but concerned with this new venture you've undertaken. She doesn't trust the baron and the people you've befriended. Dark forces are in control of the Illuminati. Nothing good can come from this."

Cyrus bristled. "My mother knows nothing of my affairs. Tell her I don't want her interfering."

"I don't have to tell her. She hears you. She's aware of whatever you do."

The screech of his chair legs scraping against the wooden floor drowned out Lily's voice. "Well, she's wrong!" Cyrus screamed. "She has no idea of my plans. I know exactly what I'm doing."

Lily remained mute.

He laid both hands on the tabletop and stood up. "What's she saying? Tell me."

"Your mom knows you've suffered, but she doesn't want you to lose sight of what's right. Think about the promise you made in honor of Leonard's memory."

He grabbed the chair and slid it against the wall. "My mother doesn't understand. I'm creating a better world. I don't need her advice. I'm smarter. I'm smarter than everybody."

Lily's eyes narrowed. "Another soul wants to speak with you. It's a male who's been gone for a decade. His first name starts with an M, Matthew or Mitchell or..."

"Oh, my God," he interrupted, "I know who it is. It's Matthias."

"Yes, that's right. He wants you to know that he's sorry for hurting you, but knows you've forgiven him."

"Lily... I haven't talked about this to anyone, but Matthias was my one true love. I loved him with all my heart and soul. I don't know if "forgiveness" would be the precise word I'd use. I think "pardoned" would be a better term. Yes, that's it! I can never forget the ache and emptiness that filled me because of his infidelity. I'm rich because of him. He left me the bulk of his estate, and for that I'm thankful."

A reservoir of tears broke free and ran down Cyrus' face. He picked up a napkin and wiped his eyes. He took a deep breath and slowly exhaled.

Lily sat silently. She waited for her physical host or the spirit guest to continue the conversation. The supernatural visitor reacted first. The medium listened.

"Matthias has seen the awful things you've done. You're not the man he remembers or loved. Your heart has hardened. A river of evil now flows through your soul. The path you're following can only lead to your destruction."

Cyrus chuckled as he righted the chair and leaned his weight on the back of it. "These words are laughable, especially coming from one who's proven so untrustworthy. He has no credibility. As far as I'm concerned, his counsel is unwarranted, ill-advised, and foolhardy. I don't need his opinion, enough of this drivel."

He walked out of the room and into the kitchen. He pulled open the refrigerator door and took out a glass bottle of spring water and twisted off the cap. He took a small drink, and holding on to the bottle, walked back into the dining room.

"I know this is upsetting," Lily confessed, "but don't be angry with me. I'm only the messenger."

"I understand, my friend. I hold no animus toward you. Matthias' presence shocked me. His audacity angered me."

Her eyes glazed over again. "Cyrus, a small boy's coming through to me. It's your brother."

His frown altered into a half-smile. "Little Leonard? He's the candle that helped light my way. He died before he had the chance to live. I dedicated my earlier life of science to him."

"Well, he's here now and concerned with your well-being."

A fork began to vibrate and moved several inches across the table.

"Leonard wants you to be sure you know it's him. He wants you to remember the pillow forts."

Cyrus laid his bottle of water on the table. "Oh, my goodness. When we played inside the house as little kids, we'd dress up as cowboys, and fight the Indians. Leonard and I would pile up our pillows and pretend we were inside a fort. The arrows couldn't reach us. We always defeated the enemy."

"Leonard wants you to know he's upset by your actions. He's been watching you and aware that evil has swallowed you up. He's talked with Theo."

The doctor glared at her. "No, that's impossible."

"Who is Theo? What does he mean?"

"Nothing, he means nothing!" Cyrus shouted. "That's his message? That's crap. I had complete justification. You tell him that," he growled, slamming both palms on the table. The glass bottle fell over. It rolled off the table and shattered as it hit the floor. Frightened, Lily pushed her chair back.

The doctor froze. "Leonard knows I had no choice. Theo deserved it. Tell him that."

She wiped her forehead with a napkin. "I can't speak to him any longer. He's gone."

Cyrus glared at her. "What do you mean, gone? Where did he go? Call him back here. Go ahead, tell my brother that Theo did it to himself."

Lily stood up. "I'm sorry, but that's not the way this works. I don't have control over the spirits. They come to me on their own. When they're gone, they're gone for good."

The doctor railed, pissed at the sand kicked in his face by those in the spirit world. He felt no guilt, nor any need to seek forgiveness or permission. This whole thing seemed a waste of his time.

He wouldn't allow anyone or anything to deter him from his true purpose. The plans had already been made. In less than three weeks, he would travel to Wisconsin. There, he'd conclude the financial arrangements and convert his personal ambitions into tangible achievements.

CHAPTER NINETEEN

America the Beautiful

Thursday, June 29, 1995

Albert Clark lived just outside the village boundary of Whitefish Bay, a conservative bedroom community located in the northern section of Milwaukee County. His fifteen-room estate, built on eighteen sprawling acres, included a private lake and indoor and outdoor pools.

His lineage could be traced to the Founding Fathers and "Committee of Five," the men who drafted America's Declaration of Independence. Though alleged to be connected through an illegitimate pregnancy, Albert never allowed such rumors to interfere with his quest for success. He'd gained the prestigious title of Grand Master in the Order of Freemasons and the ranking American in the Illuminati's Council of Thirteen. Cyrus had received an invitation for a one-week foray into Albert Clark's realm.

Once the early afternoon flight touched down at General Mitchell Airport, Cyrus followed the signs to baggage claim and collected his suitcase.

As his chauffeur pulled away from the curb, he slid open the partition glass. "Excuse me. Would you take the scenic route? I'd love a look at the sailboats on Lake Michigan shoreline. I hear it's rather festive with Independence Day coming up."

"Whatever, you say, sir. I'll drive wherever you instruct. I'm in no hurry."

The doctor checked his watch as the limo turned off Lincoln Memorial Drive and onto North Lake. Cyrus enjoyed the view, then sat back as the car swerved away from the lake.

After a few more minutes the driver stopped at the entrance of a large estate. He punched the code on the electronic keypad. The spiked-black-gate slowly swung open. As the car rolled up the driveway, Cyrus admired the floral carpet of colorful tulips and Grecian windflowers that surrounded the massive house.

A black man with curly gray hair answered the door. "Welcome, sir. You must be Doctor Markum. I'm Randall, the chief accountant." He snickered. "Just a little joke, sir. I guess you can tell I'm the butler." He pointed to his black outfit.

Cyrus appreciated his dry sense of humor. "Thank you, Randall. I took butler courses years ago. I never graduated. The teacher felt I couldn't pick things up."

The driver dropped the bag inside the doorway. Randall grabbed hold of it. "I've become good at it. I've had plenty of practice, been with Mister Albee for twenty-five years. Please, right this way, sir."

The doctor inspected the hallway. A wide piece of maroon carpeting stretched its entire length. Checkerboard marble mosaic tiling surrounded it on both sides.

He examined the twenty-foot ceilings and marveled at the quality of the original oil paintings that decorated the walls beneath the crystal chandeliers. These images brashly sang the praises of America's War for Independence. The Battle of Bunker Hill and a rendering of the Boston Tea Party hung side by side. Adjacent portraits of John Hancock, Thomas Jefferson, John Adams, and several other of the Founding Fathers and Sons of Liberty attested to the homeowner's obvious patriotic inclination.

Three likenesses of America's first historical rock star, the bespectacled Benjamin Franklin, and a large oil painting of George Washington graced the opposite wall. On either side of the foyer stood three-foot-high white marble tables. Encircled by wood and protected by glass, an aged copy of the Declaration of Independence balanced on one. The Bill of Rights sat atop the other.

As the doctor stepped onto the carpeted walkway, a flash of blue caught his attention. Through a glass door beneath our second president, the calm waters of an indoor swimming pool looked quite out of place, amid the testimonial to the Minutemen's first fight for freedom. On his left, a wide marble staircase rose from the sturdy main-floor construction and led to the second floor. Built into the wall beneath it, a gold elevator door served as the finishing touch to this specimen of absolute capitalistic decadence.

Randall noticed Cyrus' reaction. "Usually affects most people that way the first time they visit."

The double-glass doors at the end of the hallway bolted open. Seated in a motorized wheelchair, a rotund, gray-haired gentleman came rolling out. Smiling slightly, the occupant waved and gave his vehicle a little extra oomph. "Hello. I'll be right there. Won't take me a minute."

The doctor recognized Albert Clark from his photographs. "No hurry. Take your time."

A pretty young woman in red stiletto heels accompanied him. She was trim and wore a beige bathrobe. The gold trim on the pocket and collar matched her shimmering blonde hair perfectly. Wearing a deep tan, fake eyelashes, and a bit too much mascara, she balanced a black walking stick on her right shoulder. Tucked under her arm, she carried a folded white towel.

Schoolgirl giggles escaped her lips. "A good day to you. You must be Doctor Markum. I'm Mrs. Clark. Call me Alba."

She didn't wait for an answer.

"We're pleased that you could stay with us."

She waved the cane playfully before handing it to her husband. Albert Clark slowly rose from the wheelchair, leaning heavily on the cane for support. As he stood, his body bobbled slightly. His wife gave him a slight nudge, helping him maintain his balance.

Cyrus didn't want to be judgmental, but he thought it odd that this young woman hitched herself to a man three times her age and four times her body mass. The young Mrs. Clark could easily be mistaken for Albert's granddaughter, had she not already broadcast their marital headline.

She clasped her husband's arm. "I'll leave you, gentlemen. I'm going to take a plunge while you conduct your business."

Mr. Clark balanced on his cane. "Okay, sweetie, we won't be too long. I'll have Olivia prepare lunch."

The life-sized Barbie Doll gave her husband a long kiss on the lips and twisted away, walking toward the pool's entrance.

Randall followed and pulled the door open for her and turned. "I'll take the bag to your room, sir."

Cyrus smiled politely. "Sure. Thank you."

Albert staggered toward him. "She's really special, wouldn't you say?"

"Yes, Mr. Clark. She's charming and, uh, extremely elegant."

His host harrumphed. "No need to be so delicate, and please, call me Albee. I know it must seem humorous, Alba and Albee. Contrary to what you might be thinking, she didn't marry me for my good looks or virility. I take good care of her. Alba doesn't need to worry about anything."

Cyrus respected his host's candor. Whatever anyone thought about the association mattered little. If having a trophy wife at this point in his life floated his boat, more power to him.

The doctor knew Albee's biography well. Retired from the business world for three years now, his two sons looked after the family enterprises and investments. Cockling Investment Associates handled their money, the bulk of the funds invested in high-interest Treasury Bonds. Five years earlier, Albee's first wife fought a losing battle with breast cancer.

His host's financial or marital issues didn't concern him right now. Instead, he refocused to the present. The elevator door skidded open. Albert maneuvered his unwieldy frame through it. Cyrus followed him into the small metal compartment and squeezed in next to him. The door rattled as it rolled along its track and snapped shut.

Albert adjusted the position of his large frame, allowing his guest room. "We'll go up to my study."

The elevator decorations didn't let Cyrus down. On opposite sides of the cabin hung matching color prints, identical drawings of the reverse side of the Great Seal. On the back wall, dangled a pictorial of the floating Eye of Providence, suspended above the twelve lower levels, awaiting its cue to float down and complete the union. The curled inscription above it read *Annuit Coeptis*. The Latin words loosely translated to: "Providence favors our undertakings." The doctor recalled a high school history teacher explaining that Charles Thomson, one of the Founding Fathers, suggested the motto in 1782, believing the words quite fitting for the fledgling nation.

To the left of the door, hung a color print of an early rendition of the frontal view of the Great Seal, America's national coat of arms. On it, the majestic bald eagle, wings spread apart, supported a patriotic shield. Gripping an olive branch in its right talon, the bird of prey clutched a bundle of thirteen arrows in its left. His beak held a scroll with the motto: *E Pluribus Unum*; the meaning: "Out of Many, One."

Albee pressed one of the black buttons on the control panel. The antique motor engaged. The car shuddered and started its ascent. After thirty seconds, the door slowly opened. Albee gestured with his staff. Cyrus stepped from the elevator. His host worked his way out, leaning heavily on his cane for security.

"I move a bit slowly," Albee grunted, "so after you, my friend. My study is down at the end of the hall, the last door on the right."

"Thank you for your courtesy, Mr. Clark."

"Please, I told you to call me Albee. I believe that irregularity is the progeny of formality. We wouldn't want that. Would we?"

Cyrus digested the double meaning of his host's axiom. As he traveled down the narrow hallway, he admired the display of pictorials of America's history. Several were in black and white, but most in color. A wooden frame enclosed the glass that protected each.

On the right wall, an archive of perhaps two dozen pictures articulated the hard-earned victory in the war against the Spaniards in 1898. Teddy Roosevelt, then a colonel with the "Rough Riders," figured prominently in the remembrances of the Spanish-American War. Caricatures of Uncle Sam, an interpretation of the Battle of San Juan Hill, a Remington print of the Bloody Ford of the San Juan, and the image of the sinking wreckage of the USS *Maine* provided validity to the collection.

The opposite wall saluted the bravery of the men who defended our country during the War of 1812. Commonly called the "Second War for Independence," when unresolved issues, left over from the American Revolution, finally found their solutions.

The burning of Washington by English troops featured conspicuously in the display, as did several representations battles on the raging sea. The paintings, in varying sizes, also celebrated the exploits of General Andrew Jackson. *The Battle of Horseshoe Bend*, his victory over the "Red Stick" Creek Indians, figured prominently. Several pictures depicted the events surrounding the Battle of New Orleans, where Sam Houston and the pirate and privateer, Jean Lafitte, played leading roles in that decisive victory.

"Albee, your devotion to America's history is astounding."

"I'm glad that you value my acquisitions. Wait until you see the rest of the place. Right now, let's go into the study. We can relax and get to know each other."

Their discussions would prove key. All this American mumbo-jumbo would become ancient history once Cyrus' Messianic snare ensnared their quarry. *In the meantime, one foot in front of the other*, he reminded himself, as he entered Albee's sanctuary, a dedication to those who served bravely during the Vietnam conflict. Glass-encased newspaper clippings and photographs covered almost every inch of the study. The Marines owned one wall, the Air Force another, a third, dedicated to the Navy, and the fourth, a rousing salute to those who served in the Army.

Albee waved his hand. "Look around." He limped over to the wall dedicated to Army personnel. "Come over here and take a gander."

His host stood next to a photo arrangement featuring an army captain. In the center picture, the officer sat behind the controls of a Cobra gunship, the picture was taken through the front window of the cockpit. Above it, were two more snapshots of the helicopter, but with the officer leaning up against it. Two reprints from *Stars and Stripes* hung beneath the others. In them, the subject stood saluting a full bird colonel, who was pinning a Distinguished Service Cross on the pilot's uniform. A white placard, pinned to the wall beneath the collection, read, "Angelo Pastore Jr., Long Binh, December 1967."

"That's my sister's older son," Albee pointed out, his chest swelling with pride. "He also earned a Silver Star during the Tet Offensive. He received a promotion to major during his second tour and served in the Mekong Delta with Special Forces. Sonny, that's what we call him, is the fire-breather and snake-eater of the family."

Albee shook his head and frowned. "He cracked his tibia in a parachuting accident in Zaire in '76. The Army gave him his walking papers. Sonny rehabbed like crazy and when cleared for duty, joined the St. Louis police force. A year later, the FBI accepted him. He's a true patriot and worked his way up the chain of command. Sonny's an assistant deputy director."

Cyrus wondered why Albee was giving him chapter and verse but listened politely. "You and your family have good reason to be proud."

"Yes, thank you, we certainly are. He's an extraordinary person. You'll get to meet him. He's joining us for the weekend. Sonny is the Trilateral Commission's team leader and responsible for preparation and performance."

"Ah, now I see. I'll be looking forward to meeting him."

Albee turned away from the wall. "You must be hungry. I've had our chef prepare bratwurst and beer battered cheese curds for lunch. They're Wisconsin specialties."

Cyrus flinched at the offer of the unhealthy sounding menu. "Is that how your wife stays so slim?"

"Oh no," he prattled, oblivious to his guest's sarcasm. "She usually has tomato salad, with fresh tuna."

"Do you think it's possible that I have the same, and a cup of coffee, please?"

"Ah, I see," Albee chuckled. "I'll inform Olivia."

He pointed at one of the two matching brown leather recliners. "Sit, Cyrus."

Shuffling over to the old oak roll-top desk pushed up against the wall, he flipped open the tambour and pressed the button on the intercom stowed inside. "Hello, Olivia?"

After a slight hesitation, a female voice warbled through the speaker. "I'm here, Mr. Albee."

"Would you please prepare another tuna salad for my guest? Oh yes, and please, a pot of fresh coffee. And, while you're at it, a tea for me. Thank you."

"Very good, sir. I'll be up with everything shortly."

Albee trudged over to the second lounger. His body dropped onto the cushioning. He pressed the electronic control on its right arm. The motorized footrest elevated. Pressing another of the buttons, the chair adjusted to a more upright position.

"Olivia's a magician. You'll see."

"That's terrific, but I'm not so concerned with my stomach. I'd prefer to concentrate on food for thought. I'm here to discuss our reciprocal interests."

"Don't be so hasty, my friend. We have plenty of time for that. First things first. Before we get serious, I'd like a better sense of you, more an understanding of your expectations. I have read the report, but trust and compliance are the key ingredients here. Our relationship needs to simmer on the stove for a bit."

Cyrus played with a button on the chair. "My intentions are well documented, but I understand your hesitancy. What would you like to know?"

"Oh, nothing specific. I want you and me to become more comfortable with one another. No question and answer games. Please act naturally and I'll do the same." Albee's eyebrows raised. "Let's allow Father Time to release the waters that fill the dam of uncertainty. The river will surge and carry the water downstream to satisfy Mother Nature's thirst."

The maxim tickled Cyrus' funny bone. Apparently, Mr. Clark possessed a degree of unconventionality. On occasion, people accused him of demonstrating the similar attribute. "Albee, I plan to help you relieve the water pressure and assist the tributary of information in its downward flow."

"I'm glad you understand my point." Albee looked pleased. "By sharing the life-giving waters, you and I can fill the lake of eternal trust."

Cyrus was aware of the sound of approaching footsteps and the squeaking of wheels.

Olivia pushed a metal cart through the doorway. "Mr. Albee, I've brought food and drink for you and your guest."

Cyrus liked the intonation of her voice, exposing the slight trace of a Caribbean accent. Olivia looked to be of mixed racial heritage, her skin a light pigment of olive. Her figure was nice and trim. She obviously didn't partake in the Wisconsin specialties enjoyed by her employer. She picked up the tray and placed it on the cocktail table sitting between the recliners.

Albee fiddled with the armchair controls. "Thank you, Olivia. The food smells delicious."

"Very good, Mr. Albee. Will there be anything else?"

"No, thank you. Olivia. This is my guest, Doctor Markum. He'll be lucky enough to enjoy your fabulous cooking the next few days."

She watched without comment as the houseguest toyed with his chair. After a few seconds, he'd maneuvered himself into a vertical position.

She smiled, displaying her almost perfect teeth. "Good to meet you, sir. I hope you'll enjoy your stay with us."

"The pleasure is mine, Olivia, and please, call me Cyrus."

"Yes, sir... err, I mean Cyrus."

Olivia lifted off the metal tray cover and placed it on the cart. "Enjoy your meals, gentlemen." She turned and vanished down the hall.

"Food is the fuel of life," Albee philosophized. "Let us feed our minds adequate tinder to stoke their combustible engines."

He probably didn't recognize it, but his host was a very amusing fellow. This had turned into a delightful day.

* * *

Saturday morning came a-calling. Albee and Cyrus felt encouraged with the results of the last two days. They'd discussed a glut of subjects and their relationship thrived. Olivia's recipes had found a new fan. A veritable whiz at her job, her caloric contributions powered the machinery inside the minds and bodies of both men.

Tempted by the overpowering aroma and delightful taste, her new customer found it especially easy to swallow hefty helpings offered by the island chef. Cyrus easily understood how his host had packed on so much weight. Loosening his own belt, a notch, he promised himself to eat less jerked chicken and to keep away from those deliciously spiced beef patties.

Cyrus liked the library. Another pictorial memorial, this room displayed the evidence of the courage and sacrifice made by the men who served in the War Between the States. Above the fireplace hung three large oil paintings of the generals who commanded the carnage. On horseback, Robert E. Lee protected the left flank, while dressed in his field blues, General Grant guarded the right. Centered between them, the two men sat at a small round table, negotiating the surrender at the Appomattox courthouse.

Albee and Cyrus were busy working on their honeyed chamomile tea, indifferent to the images of the men who signed the peace treaty that ended the conflict. As the clock struck noon, both turned toward the sound of the knock on the library door. Angelo "Sonny" Pastore Jr. swung the door open.

"Hello, Uncle Albee. You remember my associate, John."

The younger man, dressed in a business suit, walked in behind him. "Hello, Mister Clark. How have you been?"

"I'm good, thanks. It's nice to see you again. Doctor Markum, here, is the Council's benefactor."

Sonny gave a finger salute. John grinned.

Cyrus put down his cup and stared at Sonny's huge frame. "Hello." Albee's nephew must have swallowed all his vegetables growing up and squeezed every inch out of his growth potential. Standing a head taller than most people, he undoubtedly took pride in showing off his six-feet-six-inch, bulked-up frame. But, his dedication to duty, outstanding performance record, and unquestioned allegiance were what had earned him accolades and the huge promotion within the FBI. It had been more than a year since the agency named him assistant deputy director.

During Sonny's tenure with the FBI, only a handful of people had shown, what he considered, the proper initiative. John Richter, his latest apprentice, was possibly the most gifted of them all.

He'd had no qualms sharing privileged information with him. John pledged allegiance and blind obedience to his mentor. The FBI's top-secret Markum file had visited the shredder a few years earlier, but Sonny had taken full advantage of his clearance level and pored over the clandestine dossier prior to its destruction. Recently, he'd briefed John on what he remembered.

As the special agent-in-charge of what the FBI dubbed "Operation Lab and Grab," Sonny acknowledged his responsibility in Cyrus' abrupt fall from grace. Had the press been privy to the true details, there would've been hell to pay for those responsible. For the sake of harmonious interaction, it would be impractical to re-address the past travesty of justice in any form.

Sonny smirked, imagining a possible Uncle Albee adage created especially for this particular occasion, something like: "let a sleeping dog slumber with dreams of soup bones to occupy his thoughts." In this instance, Sonny would second such a proposal.

He followed whatever instructions Baron von Klieber provided. Over the last ten years, whenever a "family" matter of substantial magnitude arose, Sonny, an Illuminati stalwart, and stealth operative, code-named "Knight Wind," would initiate the action. With his commitment to the precepts of the worldwide order, he carried that sacrosanct title and lived by the credo: "no price too great for the all-seeing eye."

The Everlasting Order of the Dragon's Claw, the enforcement wing of their organization, was once again being called upon to exercise its marque of expertise. Sonny, the Sovereign Sword in the Americas had shaped John Richter career. His current protégée had developed into an effective special agent as well as an invaluable member of the Claw clan. In seventy-two days, September the twenty-fourth, they would fulfill their sacred obligation once again.

Sonny pulled a rolled-up paper from his carrying case and spread it across the table. Albee and Cyrus moved from their chairs to his side. The illustration detailed all access points, entrances, and exits, as well as seating charts, the stage and surrounding area, waste receptacles, and possible escape routes from Farmer's Stadium. Circles of black marker outlined a dozen areas.

Sonny patted John on the back. "My cohort and I have scouted the location thoroughly. In analyzing the tactical considerations, I've outlined the most coherent plan of action. Rosselli's crew, out of Phoenix, and Finn's Chicago group, will be working with us. I've arranged for John and me to be in Ft. Collins on September the twenty-fourth. The Dragon's Claw will be primed and ready."

He hunched over and outlined the critical areas on the diagram. "Right here, here, and here. For each of these vantage points, two-man teams will be necessary."

Sonny's expression darkened. The glint of malevolence flashed in his eyes. He tapped the top of the paper. "Right here! Hidden inside this shed is the sniper's perch. That's the high ground and centrally located. There is an unimpeded view of the stage."

He extended a forefinger and laid it on the map. "Through this window, our Knight will take his shot. We'll have two people, one at either end of the entryway providing security and denying access to civilians."

He tapped on the paper three times for emphasis and pointed at the stage area. "Down over here, that's the kill zone." His finger traced a semicircle around the backstage area. "We'll have three men as rear guards and creating the diversion."

Sonny stepped away from the table. "What about the transfer of funds, Uncle? The operating capital must be in place by the first of August. I'll need stipends for Rosselli and Finn's team, plus travel and expense money."

"The proper measures perpetuate in sequential order, nephew," Albee hypothesized. "The doctor and I have gone over the arrangements. The two-and-a-half-million will be wire transferred from the Netherlands to the Cayman Islands on July the twenty-eighth. The courier will make the pickup on Monday, the thirtieth and take the red-eye from Grand Cayman to Dulles. He should arrive in D.C. about eight in the morning on the thirty-first. As soon as the Wells Fargo branch on M and Nineteenth Street opens, he will enter the bank and rent a safety deposit box. The exchange will take place at noon, at the front entrance of the bank. Your contact will be wearing a Baltimore Orioles baseball cap, blue shorts, and white Converse sneakers. Here is the coin."

Albee handed Sonny a Peace silver dollar. "Have your envoy give him this. The exchange passcode is "garden gate." Once the verification is complete, Cyrus' courier will accompany our representative into the bank and retrieve the funds."

Sonny studied the reverse side of the collectible piece of America's history. A bald eagle stood perched on it. He flipped over the coin. The Goddess of Liberty gave him a sideward glance. The date beneath the young lady's profile picture read: 1927. His uncle relished the peculiar cloak and dagger rituals. Why this particular coin, was not his concern. He'd focus only on a successful outcome.

Sonny flipped the piece of silver into the air. "Here, catch that baby."

His acolyte reached for the piece of hard currency as it tumbled, seizing hold of the Peace dollar just before it hit the wooden floor. Squeezing Lady Liberty tightly, John looked up at his boss.

Sonny smirked. "Good reflexes, John. You never know when might come in handy."

CHAPTER TWENTY

Ultimate Solutions

Oklahoma City, September 9, 1995, 8:45 A.M.

The light on the front of the telephone flashed amber. A split-second later the electronic ringer joined in. Daniel, relaxing in bed at the Quails Spring Holiday Inn, turned down the volume on the remote and grabbed hold of the insistent noisemaker from the nightstand.

"Hello, good morning and happy Friday. Daniel speaking."

"Good morning to you, Reverend. This is Trent Richards."

Daniel found it odd that the chief strategist for Governor Wiley and first vice-chair of the Colorado Democratic Party would be on the line. "Hi, Trent. I'm surprised to hear from you."

Dan slipped back into his steady-Freddie persona. "Mr. Richards, to what do I owe this honor?"

"I didn't mean to throw you for a loop, Reverend, but as you probably know, Governor Wiley's first term will be up at the end of next year."

"No, I didn't know that. I don't follow politics, but okay. You're calling to update me about that, why?"

Trent snickered. "That's what we like about you, Rev, you're tactful but never beat around the bush. Well, here it is. The governor's not going to run for a second term. With Randolph Whitaker's retirement, he plans on campaigning for his vacated Senate seat."

"Governor Wiley's a good man. He'll get my vote. That's not why you're calling though. Right?"

"Isn't it obvious, Daniel?"

Only a speck of sunlight had broken through so far. "Mr. Richards, I get the impression that you're not looking for spiritual guidance."

"You're very perceptive," Trent jibed. "I'm calling for a very different reason. My committee would like to meet with you after you've completed your tour. We'd like to discuss your future."

Dan's curiosity was awakened. "Discuss my future? In what way?"

"Please, don't play coy. Have you ever considered running for public office? We think you would be a great fit for the Colorado governorship."

Daniel picked up the remote and switched off the TV. "No, I never have. Wow. That's a mind blower."

"Don't give me your answer now. It's a big decision. I'll call you on the twenty-sixth. That's a little more than two weeks from today. That should give you enough time to think about it. Discuss it with your family."

"Okay, thank you," the reverend mumbled, unable to think of an appropriate witticism. "I'll pray about it,"

He didn't need two weeks to think over Trent's suggestion. Intrigued by the idea of governing and enacting legislation, he wanted to aid all the people of Colorado. Tempering his idealism with realism would be the hardest part, but he had no doubt he could make it work.

Well aware that the crunching wheels of temptation had mangled many a well-intentioned soul, he wouldn't let that factor deter him. His determination and faith in God would bridge the chasm. He'd forever remain a man of morality and constructive action and remain untethered by the political machinery would not be a stumbling block.

2:00 P.M., Five Hours after Trent's Communique

Room 201 of the Holiday Inn would serve as the hot spot for Dan's family summit. Iris and her brother bounced on the edge of one of the queen beds. Their parents sat across from them.

"Okay, Dad. What's so important?" Cooper asked.

Iris followed her brother's train of thought. "Yeah, Dad, what's happening? I gotta get back to my crew. I'm working on new storyboards."

Dan raised a hand. "Don't worry. This won't take long."

Joanne looked concerned. "Honey, you've been acting really strange today. Is everything okay?"

Dan stood up. "I'm far better than okay. This might sound weird, but more than twenty years ago, when my grandfather lay on his deathbed in Brookdale Hospital, he told me he always wanted one of his grandkids to run for Congress. Crazy, huh? Well, I'm not talking about the House of Representatives or the Senate, but what would you think if I run for governor?"

Iris moaned. Joanne grabbed her husband's arm and pulled herself up from the bed.

Cooper rolled forward and bounded to his feet. "Wow! That's unreal. Can you imagine, Cooper Dundee, the son of the Colorado Governor? What a nice syncopated sound. Maybe I'll grab my guitar and write a song about it."

Iris laughed. She had her own take on the announcement. "I'll say yes, Dad, but only if I can shoot the documentary of your campaign and inauguration."

Joanne shook her head. "Politics is a dirty business. I don't want you to get caught up in its nastiness."

Daniel shrugged. "I know how filthy it can be. I've considered the parameters. I know I can rise above them. It's a tremendous opportunity for us and the church."

He laid both hands on his wife's shoulders and stared into her eyes. "You know me as well as I know myself, maybe even better. I believe that good will always triumph and this is the proper path for us to take. We'll concentrate on the positive aspects. I'd never stoop to dredge up any dirt on my opponent. I'll make sure my campaign runs on the up and up. Spiritual abundance will triumph."

Joanne's eyes filled with tears. "If that's what you want, I wouldn't stand in your way. I'll help you in whatever way I can. I love you and believe in everything you stand for... what we stand for."

Daniel kissed his wife.

"C'mon guys," Cooper teased. Why don't you get yourselves a private suite?"

The room filled with laughter.

CHAPTER TWENTY-ONE

Breath of the Dragon

Phoenix, Four Days to Go

Buster Rosselli grunted as he let his body fall into the cushions of the wingback chair. He plopped his feet on the ottoman. Using a small hand-mirror, he added a tad of wax to the tips of his scruffy mustache and twisted the ends. Under the brown lip hair, he'd concealed a souvenir from an old knife fight. "Looks good, right?" He said aloud.

His blue Samsonite suitcase sat on the floor, packed and ready to go. His flight wouldn't be leaving until the morning, but Buster, just like the Boy Scouts, always wanted to be prepared. That philosophy had kept him in good stead with the Mongelli crime family and helped boost him through the ranks. He'd taken over as Capo five months ago.

"*Brinng, brinng.*" The sound effect of the ringer came from the beak of the white cockatoo.

Buster cracked up. "Pretty good, Nico. Keep it up. I might make money if I sell you to the phone company."

He looked out his window, reflecting on the Vegas junket, his promotion party with the boys. "That was pretty sick. Right, Nico? Yeah. That's right. Sin City's always a trip."

The bird whistled approval, then broke into his rendition of the theme song from *Happy Days*.

"That's what I like about you, Nico. You've got a great fucking attitude."

A young woman swished into the room. Her red slippers scraped against the wooden floor. "What'd you say, Busto?

"Uh, sure, Nicole. "Just talking out loud. I'm saying, I'll miss you."

The bird started dancing on its perch. "Pretty baby, pretty baby."

Nicole, his goomara, knew nothing of his trip last April. Buster and two of his boys split town and spent three days and nights of drinking, gambling, and whoring in Vegas. Nicole had ugatz for brains, but that's not why he kept her around. The broad threw a fantastic lay.

He'd told her he attended a convention. His wife also thought the same thing. Buster laughed. *Dummies!*

Nicole, a cutie just out of her teens, wore a sheer red negligee. Her black bra and panties peeked through. "What'd you say, Busto?"

"I'm gonna miss you, big time. I hate sleeping alone."

The bird fluttered his wings. "Freaking asshole, big asshole."

His eyes narrowed as he gave the bird a dirty look.

Nicole gave Buster a smooch on his cheek. Her bright red lipstick left a memento. "Ooh, baby. I miss you already. How long are you gonna be gone?"

"Four days, max. I'll be back before you know it, just business."

"Wish I could go with you, sweetie. "I'll have to sleep with my teddy bear."

"Next time, honey. I'll take you to Vegas for a weekend. We'll go take in a couple of shows."

"I can't wait, baby. Pretty please, can we stay at Caesar's Palace?"

Buster, busy examining his teeth in the small mirror, laid it aside on the side table "Yeah, sure, anything you want."

"I gotta go pee." Nicole threw a kiss at the bird and whirled away.

Buster knew he'd better stop thinking about group hugs and concentrate on the job. He'd be flying out to Colorado in the morning. Mickey and Big Sal would be driving. They'd leave Phoenix tonight in one of the rental cars. Johnny Bats, Meemo, and Frankie Mims were traveling in another.

Slated to work with the Chicago squad, they'd be meeting up with them in Denver. The Windy City group made their money locking up Buster's kind. That crew was made up of law enforcement, but they'd worked together before and could do it again.

The Mongelli family business had him and his guys out on loan. All the members of his crew had the *higher* calling, The Bavarian Association pulled the puppeteer's strings on this caper. The Council of Thirteen had a lot more juice than his crime organization. The generosity of the Colonel and his cronies didn't hurt one bit.

Mickey, his second in command, had picked up the money last month in the nation's capital. Buster's basement floor safe held his hundred grand, plus the other hundred large he'd skimmed off, twenty big ones from each of his guys, not too bad a haul.

He'd personally delivered a gym bag filled with a quarter mill, in bundles of crisp hundreds, to the Campobello Social Club, Gino Mongelli's share. Geez, the bastard didn't have to do a freaking thing for it. If he played his cards right, maybe he'd become the man at the top of the food chain one day.

Chicago, Three Days to Zero Hour

Peter Finn, on his way to O'Hare, stretched out in the back seat of the Lincoln Town Car. He had a brief vacation from his day job as a police lieutenant with the Bureau of Organized Crime. He'd been working in law enforcement for ten years, the first four as an agent with the FBI, his apprenticeship coming under Sonny Pastore. The last six, he'd served with the Chicago PD.

Peter grew up in Illinois. His family lived outside Cicero. The job shift, arranged by the Bavarian Association, drew nary a glance from anyone in either chain of command.

Finn had adapted well to the department. He'd received two commendations for bravery and managed a swift promotion to sergeant. He'd been a Knight of the Everlasting Order of the Dragon's Claw for the last eight years. Being fed inside information had distinct advantages. Two years ago, he'd taken down the "Little Willie Williams" crew, the biggest heroin wholesalers this side of the Mississippi. The Chicago newspapers carried Finn's picture on their front pages. The television stations featured him on the six and eleven o'clock news shows.

With fourteen arrests in the raid, the press coverage gained national attention and his unit received a "Meritorious

Performance Award." Individually, Finn chalked up a department commendation and named "Police Officer of the Month." He did well on the exam for promotion, and with his obvious ability to drag in the bad guys, his name topped the list.

Finn sneered. The brass would shit if they had any idea of his dual identity and how he was buddying up with mobsters. To the outside world, nothing looked unusual, a hero cop going for a vacation.

Richard Walker, an ATF agent and second in command, relaxed next to his team leader. Finn valued the capabilities of the pocket rocket. What he lacked in size, he made up for with tenacity. He stood five feet nine and weighed in at 175 pounds. Finn, with the size and strength of a professional wrestler, had profound respect for his deputy. The pair worked together on two task forces and their close personal relationship raised no hackles or caused suspicion. These men did not look like your average faces in the crowd. "Cue Ball," the moniker Walker sported due to his shaved head and milky complexion, subscribed to the pursuit of the *higher* purpose.

These two knights were booked on a direct flight and would leave Chicago at noon. To avoid suspicion, the other four members of the Dragon's Claw squadron traveled out on later flights with a connection or two thrown in for good measure.

Cue Ball rubbed his hairless scalp with the fingers of both hands. "Hey, Finn. Are we doubling up again or do we have private rooms?"

Finn threw him a wink. "First class all the way, brother. We're sitting up front on the flight. We have luxury rooms booked at the Hyatt."

"Totally cool. Thanks."

"You don't have to thank me. You can thank Sonny when you see him. He's footing the bill."

"Sure, I will."

Finn noticed Cue Ball's stare. "You have another question?"

"No, Pete. It's just that your eye color matches your brown hair. I never noticed that before."

The lieutenant laughed. "Cue Ball, you are one weird dude. But, that's a nice piece of detective work. I'm wearing special contacts."

Somewhere Over Utah, Friday, Two Days Until Genesis

Diana and her husband luxuriated in the first-class section of the jumbo jet. She sat in the aisle seat, sipping her Amaretto and orange juice out of the half-empty glass. Their mentor and business partner sat across the aisle. Already working on his third bourbon and water, Cyrus kept up a steady stream of jabber, not at all like his normally reserved self.

In two days, the Souls of Creation would be winding up their highly successful tour with the televised finale. The doctor was delighted with the prospect, but his celebratory attitude was influenced by the fact that this twenty-second day of the ninth month also coincided with his fifty-eighth birthday.

Extending his arm, he gripped the edge of the overhead compartment and pulled himself up from his seat. He stepped across the aisle and held on to Diana's seatback, steadying himself.

"I have a joke for you two," he mumbled, not waiting for a response. "Did you hear the one about the two friends who meet up in a bar for a drink?"

Diana shook her head. Ronald shrugged.

He took a slug of bourbon. "So, this guy tells his friend that he saw a bad car accident on the way over. 'How bad?' His friend asks. The first guy says that he's not sure if anyone died, but he saw an ambulance driving from the scene. His friend shakes his head and says: 'That's hard to believe.' The first guy downs his drink and asks him why's that?"

Cyrus hooted. His reluctant audience couldn't quite understand the bulk of his slurred words, but didn't say anything, hoping for him to finish.

The doctor went sprinting for the punchline. "Because I'm an atheist. Get it?" He roared with laughter.

Ronald and Diana shared a moment of consternation. If the joke had any humor, they couldn't see it.

"Why aren't you laughing? You don't get it?" Cyrus was disappointed. "Okay. I'll explain it. You see, the guy doesn't believe in God. He's an atheist. That's why he says it's hard to believe. Now you get it?

Diana and Ronald both shook their heads.

His eyes narrowed. "Aw, crap. You two are no fun." His cheerful mood faded as the plane encountered turbulence. He grabbed the top of the seat for support. "And you know what? That guy was absolutely right. If God ever existed, he's been dead and gone for a long time."

Diana and Ron smiled weakly.

The doctor spun around and staggered across the aisle and flopped into his seat. He emptied the rest of his bourbon in one gulp. "Fuck it!" Cyrus mumbled, thumping his cup on the tray. He turned away from his friends and stared out of the window at the clouds.

The stewardess, ambling by a few minutes later, stopped and reached for his empty cup. "Would you care for another cocktail, sir?"

"Are you kidding me? Those drinks are weak as shit. Tell the pilot he should use more alcohol next time. He pouted and folding his arms.

"Yes, sir," she answered, slightly amused.

She dumped the piece of molded plastic into her black garbage bag, and walked toward the galley, hoping the old coot wouldn't cause her any real trouble.

As the plane glided through a large field of white cumulus clouds, Cyrus' eyelids sagged. He rested the side of his face against the small pane of acrylic and fell fast asleep before the stewardess could finish tying her bag.

Forty-five minutes passed before the intercom came alive. "Ladies and gentlemen, this is your captain. We're beginning our descent into Denver International Airport. The temperature is seventy-three degrees. The wind's coming in from the west at six miles per hour. That's perfect weather in my book. We should be rolling up to the gate at about three-thirty. Thank you again for flying American Airlines. We hope to see you again on your next trip. Don't forget, we're something special in the air."

Denver, Friday, Late Afternoon

Since Sonny and John had arrived at the Denver Field Office yesterday, the two agents had utilized their time and performed an authentication canvas, verifying all possible stadium access points and any areas of concern.

Prior to his promotion to assistant deputy director, Sonny supervised the Bureau's surveillance activities at the MCHSB facilities. His request to coordinate the squad at the Farmer's Stadium extravaganza did not appear misplaced, and he'd received tacit approval. Eight special agents, aside from John and himself, were assigned to the venue. He made sure to set up their strategic positioning in non-critical areas, keeping them at arms-length from the Dragon's Claw operatives.

In adherence to proper procedure, he'd be contacting Uncle Albee on Saturday morning and receive final confirmation of the mission. He expected no change in status, but cancellation was a possibility, no matter how infinitesimal the odds might be.

The protocol of the Dragon's Claw mirrored that of the FBI's almost precisely. The foot soldiers followed orders explicitly, never dictating policy. Sonny no longer took an active role in the culmination of final enforcement, but his organizational skills and hands-on experience gave him a distinct advantage as an on-scene coordinator.

When he and John visited ground zero Thursday evening, they'd dropped off their bag of goodies. Presently, they were on their way to a meeting with Peter Finn and Buster Rosselli at the Poudre Bike Path River Bridge in Legacy Park. The time, set for sixteen-thirty.

Sonny chose the location. The area was surrounded by fields, with clear lines of sight to all entry-ways. John would serve as roving security. No disruptions were expected, but precautionary measures prevented surprises. After the briefing, Finn and Rosselli would head back to Denver and spoon-feed the tactical details to the members of their teams.

Saturday morning, Seven O'clock

Remaining inconspicuous shouldn't have been too difficult a task but leave it to two of Buster's stooges to have their photos lead off the Saturday morning news broadcast. As Sonny swallowed his first sip of coffee, two mugshots rocketed on the screen. A female voice provided the voice-over:

"Good morning. This is Rebecca Nash. Here's what's happening. Sal Dejocamo and

Frankie Marinelli are under arrest and being held without bail at the District 4 police station. They face numerous charges, including assault, aggravated battery, kidnapping, and unlawful imprisonment, stemming from an early morning incident."

About to bite into an English muffin, Sonny clenched his teeth and chucked it at the television.

"Those fucking morons," he shrieked.

On screen, a long shot of the reporter replaced the photos.

"Bob James is at the scene. We're going there right now."

The live feed came in from an outdoor parking lot, a red building visible in the background. A young male reporter stood in front of the camera. He held a slender microphone.

"Thank you, Rebecca. At approximately two-thirty Saturday morning, the two suspects, Sal Dejocamo and Frankie Marinelli, reputed members of the Mongelli crime family out of Phoenix, were taken into custody outside DJ's Pole Dance on Federal Boulevard. The suspects allegedly forced one of the female employees, identified only as Cookie, into their car. The club's bouncer took several blows to the face when he tried to intervene. Though bleeding profusely, he managed to call the police. The police had a patrol car in the area and responded quickly. Officers reached the crime scene before the suspects had the opportunity to flee."

Sonny heaved his stoneware mug against the wall. The brown liquid splashed on the white stucco wall and splashed on the bed cover as he shrieked at the TV screen. "Those damn fucking idiots. How stupid can they be?" Hives began to blotch his face.

On screen, the reporter continued:

225

"The pair surrendered without a struggle. Their victim was shaken up, but uninjured. Both men have long arrest records. Back to you in the studio, Rebecca."

Sonny seethed. The arrests not only endangered the secrecy of the Order but created a personnel shortage. He kicked over the waste bucket as he stormed out of his hotel room.

The prospect always existed that a twist of fate could throw a monkey wrench into best-laid plans, but unleashing stupidity of this magnitude cannot be forgiven. A transgression of this magnitude went against all the Dragon's Claw clan held sacred. There would be retribution, but that would come in due time. Right now, the Knight Wind needed to calm himself, and apply his improvisational skills. He dropped a quarter into the outside pay phone and dialed Buster's hotel room.

* * *

The meeting at the diner did not go well for Buster, caught up to his neck in quicksand.

"Look, Sonny, I didn't figure these guys would do anything like this," he semi-apologized. "I can't babysit them. You know how these guys are. They're used to having things their own way."

Sonny's hands trembled. "That's no excuse. This is serious shit. The assholes ignored direct orders. You know this can't happen. The Council's gonna expect payback."

Buster crossed his heart, then kissed his thumb. "Don't worry. My guys ain't rats." He put a forefinger up to his lips. "Omerta. They won't say a word to the cops."

Sonny grabbed Buster's hand. "Yeah, yeah. I don't doubt that, but that's not the point. Because of them, we have problems." He let go of the mobster's fingers and stared into his coffee cup. "I gotta figure this thing out."

It didn't take him long. Within thirty seconds Sonny's head lifted. Daggers of hateful intent darted from his eyes. "Just make damn sure that you keep the rest of your crew under wraps, no more playing grab-ass. We got one more day. Can you handle this?"

"You got it, boss. There won't be any more slip-ups." Buster pulled out the golden horn medallion hanging around his neck and smacked it with his lips. "Definitely!"

"There better not be. Otherwise, it'll be your ass in a sling."

Sunday, Twenty Minutes Until Genesis

John Richter waited inside the storage shed. A block of wood propped up the small glass window in front of him. He'd taken the kneeling-support firing position. The rifle barrel rested on the wooden sill. Two strategically placed potted plants, overflowing with ivy, shielded the rifle barrel from potentially prying eyes. He stared through his scope, eye focused on the stage.

John hadn't been too thrilled when Sonny drafted him for the job. He knew, though, that he'd earn a pocket-load of brownie points and would move up in the Order if he accomplished this mission. Big Sal, currently incommunicado, had been the knight slated to pull the trigger. Too bad his dick took precedence over his strength of commitment.

John, dressed in a utility worker's outfit, had a slight case of nerves but felt confident. Just like shooting a duck from inside a blind, he'd almost convinced himself.

Sonny had revamped the personnel dispersal in the concession area behind the stage. He'd have only two men to create the diversion, rather than the original trio. He figured that work fine. A few extra M-80 firecrackers dropped into a pair of garbage cans would make plenty of extra noise.

He glanced at the action on the stage. The Voices of Unity rocked on. The audience swayed, clapped, and sang along with the choir:

"Love is beautiful,
our lives are sweet.
God is within us,
our soulful journey will never suffer defeat."

Backstage, Daniel went over his speech for the umpteenth time. He'd memorized his lines, but would hold on to his notes, just in case. His intentions to run for the office of governor in the '96 election would be the climax.

He'd slipped on his gray suit and added the black and red tie Joanne had picked out for him. She stood backstage, clapping, and singing along with the rest of the true believers.

Harry had quickly edited down the earlier Souls of Creation's performance and that tape played right now in people's living rooms. The Voices of Unity would be going live for their final number. Then, Daniel's sermon would pick up. The Reverend knew that people cared more for the music than religious rhetoric. Ten minutes, that's all he'd need.

The Countdown Continues

John Richter's wrist-watch read eight forty-five, fourteen minutes until showtime. He wouldn't let jittery nerves affect him. He blocked out any thoughts of right and wrong, and repeated aloud: "For the higher purpose, for the higher purpose, nothing can interfere with the higher purpose."

Just beneath the concrete stairway leading up to the storage shed, Peter Finn stood lookout. At the moment, he was enjoying the show. His head bobbled a tad in time to the music.

Sonny strolled leisurely around the open area behind the stage. He saluted a uniformed state patrol officer who tugged on the front of his "Smokey the Bear" hat in recognition of Sonny's laminated FBI identification badge that hung from his left jacket pocket. He passed by Buster. The two ignored each other.

He came around to the left side of the stage. Smiling, he visualized the six red M-80s filled with flash powder burning a hole in Buster Rosselli's pockets. Once the brash gangster and his counterpart, Cue Ball, lit the improvised thirty-second fuses and made the drop, all hell would break loose.

Sonny checked the time: eight forty-eight. The Voices of Unity choir had just finished their last number, and the singers, dressed in black robes, were filing down the steps.

Cooper strolled out from behind the curtain. He raised the microphone as he walked to center-stage. "Ladies and gentlemen, please welcome a man who needs no introduction, my dad, and soul stabilizer number one, our Reverend, Daniel Dundee."

The stadium erupted with raucous applause and cheers.

Dan drew the maroon curtain aside and trotted to the middle of the stage. He hugged his son, then took his place behind the podium. He slipped the microphone into the stand and turned and smiled at his special guests. They sat on a row of director's chairs. Joanne anchored the left side, Diana next to her, with Ronald on her right. The couple sat with their fingers intertwined. Trent Richards came next. Cyrus, fidgeting in his chair, completed the line-up of notables.

Nervously, Cyrus checked his watch. *Why was his head throbbing? At this point, he should have no doubts. The guillotine's angled blade would soon slice off the serpent's head and redemption and world dominion would soon be his.*

The sound of thunderous applause picked up again. The Reverend, smiling broadly, waved both hands. After twenty seconds, he motioned for quiet. The crowd slowly calmed.

Dan took a deep breath. "Hello to all of God's people."

The crowd went wild, screaming his name, yelling amen and all right.

Dan let them have their fill, then raised his hands for quiet. He pointed with both forefingers at the mass of humanity before him. "A huge welcome goes out to the children of God. As one people, we're here, living in the right now. Don't worry about yesterday or tomorrow. Today is a celebration of music, and a festival in appreciation of God's word."

The Reverend turned. He raised a hand and threw a slight wave to his special guests. He loosened his tie and threw it into the crowd. A small boy grabbed hold of it and shoved it in his mouth.

Dan raised his hands. "We share one spirit and one soul. God put us on this planet to love each other and share in his, and our abundance."

The people cheered. Dan gripped the edge of the podium. "We face challenges. That's the way of the world. We must stay united and work together for peace. No matter what goes on around us, it's up to each one of us to spread the message of joy and embrace the Word of God. Celebrate and share your love with everyone you meet. Building a better world starts right here and right now. Each one of us is not just a worshipper, but a teacher."

He stepped back and tapped the left side of his chest, right over his heart, three times, just like he'd rehearsed. He leaned forward and leaned closer to the microphone angling out from the top of the pedestal.

This was a big moment in his sermon. His voice grew louder. "Can I get an AMEN!"

The crowd went ballistic and screamed back, repeating the word.

John Richter continued staring through the rifle scope. He watched the preacher move out from behind the podium and walk to the front of the stage. Sweat beaded John's forehead, his shirt soaked. He had no time to worry about the small stuff. With a clear line of sight, he would allow nothing to interfere with his purpose. Breathing a small sigh of relief, he wiped his forehead with a handkerchief.

*　　*　　*

Buster Rosselli circled one of the garbage cans sitting in front of the rear concession area. Tempted by the smells of the burgers and hot dogs sizzling on the grill, he licked his lips. Only ten feet stood between him and a hotdog. He looked at his watch. Yeah, he could make it.

Buster stepped up to the counter. "Gimme a dog. Hurry up, will you."

He looked at the clock above the stand. The time read eight fifty-six.

The chubby woman behind the griddle slipped a grilled dog into a bun. She handed it to him wrapped in a brown paper napkin. "Onions?"

"Naw, I'm good."

He pulled out a five and threw it on the counter. "Keep it."

Squirting a dollop of mustard onto the beefy footlong, he bit off a huge chunk and swallowed without chewing. He headed toward the trash can.

The preacher's voice boomed through the stadium speakers. "So, people, give thanks as we all raise our hands in praise." He looked out at the throng. Turning back toward the row of guests, he nodded to Trent. The Democrat bigwig returned a wink.

Daniel ran both hands through his long hair. "People, I want to digress for a moment if I may. I have an important announcement."

The decisive moment had arrived. He turned and stared at his wife. "We have been offered a tremendous opportunity. I've prayed about it and reached a decision. The Democratic Party wants me to run for governor of our great state of Colorado."

The crowd hushed.

"After thoughtful consideration, I've decided to accept the offer."

The audience stomped their feet. People clapped their hands. Cheers filled the stadium.

Bam! *Kaboom!* The roar of multiple explosions drowned out the sound of the audience's approval and admiration. Almost in unison, the entire crowd hushed. Smoke rose from behind the stage. The noise of additional blasts confounded the crowd. People shrieked. Many ducked down or scrambled for cover. Others stood in place, their eyes opened wide, shocked by the sounds of the detonations.

Cyrus rose from his chair. His intricate planning was about to reach fruition. His eyes as big as saucers, he stared at the back of Daniel's head. The time for New World Order had arrived.

John's held his hand steady. He felt his heart thumping in his ears. Taking a deep breath, he exhaled half the oxygen and held the rest. Ever so slowly, the tip of his forefinger applied pressure to the trigger. The sharp report of his weapon was drowned out by the ruckus of the panicked crowd. The rifle stock thumped against his shoulder. Too hyped up to react to it, he let out the stale air and breathed in deeply through his nose. The acrid odor of the smoking gunpowder drifted into his nostrils. He ignored the sensation and stayed glued to the scope. His target fell. He'd made the perfect shot, a bullseye, right between the eyes.

EPILOGUE

Denver, January 14, 1997

With the wheelchair resting in the trunk of the limo, Albee maneuvered his cane as he walked. Sonny helped him push through the crowd and find their seats. Bruno, with his dark sunglasses in place, positioned himself a row behind the pair. He peered around them, measuring the crowd.

Albee wore a down-filled brown coat. A pair of thick sheepskin gloves covered his hands. The beige cowboy hat he sported atop his head, afforded a bit of protection from the light falling snow. Wrapped around his lower body, a brown quilt provided warmth. They sat in the aluminum bleachers at the base of the Colorado state capital building steps. At the eleven o'clock hour, frigid temperatures prevailed.

Albee tugged on his nephew's sleeve. "It never ceases to amaze me. One can never underestimate the twists and turns the river follows as the waters seek their basin."

Sonny turned up his coat collar. "Chilly."

His uncle smiled. "This mission worked out well for us."

The sudden burst of applause interrupted Albee. He and his nephew craned their necks, looking up to the top of the marble staircase. On the concourse above, several dozen people sat in neatly arranged rows of folding chairs. The hand clapping slowly died down.

Sonny used the break to answer. "Yes, Uncle Albee. It did for the most part."

They were speaking of the successful Dragon's Claw operation at Farmer's Stadium. Aside from the arrest of the two morons from Buster's crew, the operation went off successfully. Too bad that once the two Phoenix jailbirds made bail, they both fell off the face of the earth. The authorities thought they'd skipped out, left the country, maybe. The Knight Wind had the answer. He knew the real story.

The applause picked up again as the governor-elect walked out onto the promenade, now only moments away from taking his oath of office. Daniel Dundee waved to the crowd of well-wishers.

Their show of appreciation gained intensity. Dan lowered his hands, calling for quiet.

That pause permitted Albee to continue on his train of thought. "Too bad about that Doctor Markum fellow. The man possessed quite a mind, you know, but unpredictable and could turn into a monster at the drop of a statue."

Sonny shook his head. "That's nasty."

Albee chuckled. "What unmitigated gall, thinking he could scheme his way onto the Council. The rich fool bit off too large a chunk of tobacco and choked on it."

He turned and winked at Bruno. "Markum had no idea we had eyes on him. We knew the intimate details of his every transgression. His so-called quest for justice reached its inevitable conclusion."

Albee kissed Sonny on the cheek. "How ironic, nephew? The misguided fool financed his own execution. He even paid for the bullet. We couldn't have come up with a better publicity stunt for the man we wanted to put in office. The Dragon's barbed serpentine tail can do much more damage than its fiery breath."

The crowd noise started up again. Sonny looked up at the top of the stone steps. The chief justice of the Colorado State Court raised his hand.

Joanne stood next to her husband. Iris and Cooper were positioned on opposite sides of their mom and dad. Joanne held out a Bible. Daniel raised his right hand and laid his left on the top cover. He repeated the justice's words. He promised to fulfill his duties as governor for every citizen of Colorado. Governor Dundee and the chief justice shook hands. The new man of the people kissed his wife, then each of his children. He wore a huge grin. Joanne wiped away a tear of happiness from her husband's eye.

Daniel stepped to the podium for his inaugural speech. By then, Albee and his nephew were walking back to the rented limo, Bruno on their heels. A light coating of snow made walking a bit difficult for Albee. Sonny, holding his arm, gave needed support.

"The Vatican can't be too thrilled about this New Thought patsy getting elected," Sonny whispered.

Albee huffed. "Our organization has been at odds with the self-righteous Roman Catholics for centuries. We usually don't see things eye to eye. Why should this case be any different? I understand that Baron von Klieber has already informed the Pope that he and his cardinals better keep their beanies on a while longer. Their time will come."

His nephew laughed aloud as the limo driver assisted Albee into the back seat. Sonny checked the traffic and hopped around to the other side. He pulled open the door and allowed his large frame to crumple onto the back bench. Unfastening the buttons on his topcoat, he reached inside his jacket and removed his handkerchief. Bending forward, he grabbed hold of a glass from the bar and carefully wiped it. He removed the cap from the bottle of Johnny Walker Red and poured himself two fingers, adding a like amount of water to mute the peppery taste.

The driver took his seat. Albee knocked on the glass partition. It rolled down, just as the car pulled away from the curb.

Bruno swiveled around in the passenger seat. "Yes, sir."

"We have an interesting job coming up. Sonny will give you the details on the flight home."

Bruno nodded. "I'm happy to hear that, sir."

A cloud of dark gray smoke spluttered from the exhaust pipe as the car accelerated. Sonny took a sip from his glass as the limo turned off Lincoln and hopped on the Interstate. Denver International Airport and Albee's private jet awaited.

www.ingramcontent.com/pod-product-compliance
Lightning Source LLC
Chambersburg PA
CBHW032040240626
47154CB00003B/1004